ALSO BY DARCY COATES

The Haunting of Ashburn House
The Haunting of Blackwood House
The House Next Door
Craven Manor
The Haunting of Rookward House
The Carrow Haunt
Hunted
The Folcroft Ghosts
The Haunting of Gillespie House
Dead Lake
Parasite
Quarter to Midnight
Small Horrors

House of Shadows

House of Shadows
House of Secrets

The

HAUNTING

of

ASHBURN
HOUSE

DARCY COATES

Poisoned Pen
PRESS

Published by Poisoned Pen Press, an imprint of Sourcebooks
P.O. Box 4410, Naperville, Illinois 60567-4410
(630) 961-3900
sourcebooks.com

Originally self-published in 2016 by Black Owl Books.

Library of Congress Cataloging-in-Publication Data is on file with the publisher.

Printed and bound in the United States of America.
VP 10 9 8 7 6 5 4 3 2 1

Emily C. and Joanne.
Thank you.

CHAPTER 1
FLIGHT

HUGE RAINDROPS HIT ADRIENNE'S exposed arms and face as her mother carried her out of the porch's shelter and down the groaning wooden steps. Her ears were full of pounding feet and gasping breaths, and her mother's arms held so tightly it hurt.

She turned to see her mother's face. Pat's eyes were huge. Tracks of mascara ran down her blanched cheeks, and she flinched when lightning cracked across the sky, blindingly white behind the house's silhouette.

Ashburn rose huge and twisted above them. Its white paint was flaking off to expose grime-streaked grey wood underneath, and the black windows seemed like dead eyes watching over the lawn. The sun had not long set, and traces of deep, angry reds and pinks tinged the undersides of the storm clouds. Wild animals screamed in the woods around them, and insects flicked out of the long grass as Adrienne's mother ran through it, carrying her to the car parked off the side of the dirt driveway.

She fell into the passenger seat, and the door slammed shut. Her mother didn't buckle her in, and that frightened Adrienne. Her mother had never forgotten to buckle her in before. She twisted to glimpse the house through her window and caught sight of the front door gliding open.

Her mother jumped into the driver's seat, the ignition roared, and the bald tyres skidded against the dirt as they struggled to find purchase. As the house grew smaller in the rear-view mirror, Adrienne thought she saw a figure appear in the open doorway. The silhouette was incredibly tall and dressed in a long black gown. Adrienne and the woman watched each other through the mirror until the car rocked around a corner, taking the turn far too quickly, and the house was hidden from sight by a thick copse of trees.

Adrienne's mother didn't speak but sucked in thin, panicked breaths as the tears continued to bleed mascara down her cheeks and mix with the drops of blood sprayed across her neck.

CHAPTER 2
A STRANGER'S GIFT

Seventeen Years Later

EVERY TIME WOLFGANG WAILED, the taxi driver grinned and chuckled as if it was the funniest thing he'd heard all day. Adrienne tried to match his smile, but her heart wasn't in it. Wolfgang was normally an even-tempered and silent cat; he had to truly hate the drive to protest so often. He was even ignoring the treats she'd poked through the cat carrier's bars, and he *never* rejected treats.

"Sorry, buddy," she whispered when he mewled for what felt like the hundredth time. "Not long now."

The massive grey tabby turned his sea-green eyes towards her and projected abject misery in the way only cats are capable of.

"Got family in the area?" The taxi driver, a young, cheerful man who was a little too forceful with the accelerator, had tried to start a conversation several times during the drive, but Adrienne was terrible at small talk even on her best days, and that morning was shaping up to be a long way from her best.

"No—I mean—apparently, I used to, I think?" It was an awful way to answer his question, but Adrienne wasn't prepared to explain that she'd been bequeathed a house by a relative her mother had claimed didn't exist.

He seemed ready to follow up with a second question, but then Wolfgang wailed again, and the driver settled for chuckling and shaking his head. She was grateful; the previous week had been so hectic she felt as though she hadn't had a second to herself, and a cacophony of anxious thoughts cluttered her mind.

Ms Edith Ashburn has bequeathed you her property...

Adrienne had never expected to receive any inheritance. She'd daydreamed about it, of course—light fantasies of discovering her father was secretly a king or that she had accidentally befriended a lonely millionaire—but those dreams had become increasingly rare as she'd grown up and loan repayments, medical bills, and debt had become her reality.

What made the bequeathing even more unexpected was how adamantly her mother had insisted they had no surviving relatives. According to the harried solicitor, Edith Ashburn was Adrienne's mother's grandmother's sister's daughter. She thought that made Edith her great-aunt, but she felt as if she would need to see a flowchart to be certain.

The taxi driver took a corner too fast, and Adrienne had to grab the cat carrier to stop it from being jolted against the door. Wolfgang wailed, Adrienne mumbled an apology she knew wouldn't be accepted, and the taxi driver grinned and chuckled.

"Here's the village, looks like," he said, and Adrienne glanced up from the carrier to see a patchy collection of buildings spread out below them.

Ipson was a tiny country town. According to online sources, its population was somewhere between eight and nine hundred. It struck her as unexpectedly pretty—large green trees lined the streets, and the properties were relatively clean and well tended. A small school stood beside the town hall two blocks away from the main street, which was full of small shops. Even from that distance, Adrienne could see a shining bronze church steeple. Houses spread outwards from the city centre, patchily shifting from suburban near the core to hobby farms at the outskirts.

They dipped into the valley. For a few minutes, the road ran alongside a river—a brilliantly blue twisting watercourse with willows clustered about its shore—and then they were entering the town proper.

With one hand pressed to the cat carrier's roof to stabilise Wolfgang against the worst of the car's jolts, Adrienne peered through the windows to catch glimpses of the settlement that was going to be her home. Snapshots of village life raced past her: a greengrocer stacking avocados, two elderly women having a cup of tea outside a café, and a florist's shop so packed with flowers that they spilled out the door and onto the sidewalk. Then the taxi screeched to a halt at a pedestrian crossing, and Wolfgang mewled as Adrienne scrambled to keep him on the seat.

"He's quite the chatterbox, isn't he?" The taxi driver laughed.

"Wolf doesn't like cars. Too many trips to the vet." Adrienne's attention had been pulled to a group of four well-dressed ladies gathered outside what looked like a second-hand bookstore-slash-coffee shop. They were in their early twenties—about Adrienne's age—and chatting animatedly. A tiny voice in the back of her mind suggested they could be friend potential. There would only be a certain number of ladies her age in this tiny town, and she might be looking at the majority of them.

The tallest lady turned towards the car and raised her eyebrows. Her lips, painted deep red to contrast with her blonde, shoulder-length hair, stretched into a mischievous smile as she tilted her head towards her companions and spoke. They laughed, their manicured hands rising to cover pearly teeth and their eyes shining with secretive delight.

The taxi screeched forward before Adrienne had time to turn completely red. *They were talking about me. Why? They couldn't know who I am, surely?*

That might be a very real possibility. She sunk back into her seat. The town was likely too small to have a dedicated taxi service, so the clearly marked car would signal a new arrival like a beacon.

That led into a series of questions that Adrienne had no answers for. *How well did this town know Edith Ashburn? Was she a regular at the café, perhaps, or a key part of the social committee or the owner of a popular business? How many in this town know she died? Have they watched her empty house and wondered who would move in? Has the town been watching for the taxi that would bring Edith's replacement?*

The idea that they were waiting for her made a band of anxiety tighten over her chest. She clutched the cat carrier a little closer, and Wolfgang, apparently feeling as uncomfortable as his owner, hissed.

They zoomed past more shops, and now that Adrienne was looking at the residents rather than the buildings, she was painfully aware of how much attention she was drawing. Heads turned towards the car as it neared, and flashes of understanding lit up faces. Adrienne could picture them turning towards each other as the car passed and whispering, *This'll be her. She'll be in Edith's house.*

"How—uh—" Her mouth was dry, and she had to lick her lips before she could speak clearly. "How far is it now?"

The taxi driver tapped the satnav on his dashboard. "Looks like we're headed to the other side of town. Pretty place this, eh?"

"It sure is." The quaint shops, tidy houses, and large green trees were certainly attractive, but they also worked to increase the sensation that she was an invader asking to be let inside a pristine bubble. She didn't know the town's quirks, hadn't shared in any of its memories or experienced its history. She wasn't welcome there.

Knock it off. She squeezed her eyes closed and tried to dodge the feeling of dozens of eyes fixing on the bright-yellow car. *You've got a home, and that's a darn sight better than where you stood a fortnight ago. The only thing you have any right to feel is gratitude.*

The car screeched around a curve, and suddenly, they were

on the other side of town and leaving suburbia behind them. Bushes and trees crowded more thickly along the road's edges, and the stream reappeared to their left. Adrienne took a slow breath. The squeezing anxiety had lifted once she was out of the townspeople's eyesight, but a surreal sensation had replaced it. The houses were thinning and giving way to empty fields.

Adrienne leaned forward and squinted to see the satnav. "Um, sorry, but… did we pass the house by accident?"

"Not according to this thing." The driver jabbed the screen. "Says to keep going."

"Oh." Adrienne sat back. She'd assumed she'd been bequeathed one of the small suburban properties, but at the moment, they were leaving even the farmhouses behind.

The taxi slowed then turned into a patch of bushes. Adrienne, thinking the car had gone off the road, clutched Wolfgang closer then exhaled as she realised her driver had found a narrow, well-disguised dirt driveway.

"Jeez," the driver grumbled. He'd leaned over the wheel and was squinting to make out the path. Adrienne didn't blame him; it was badly overgrown. For the first time since picking her up outside her friend's apartment, the taxi had slowed to below twenty kilometres.

A sign loomed on her left-hand side, and Adrienne pressed herself to the window to read it. The wood looked at least fifty years old, and its post tilted dangerously. The paint had peeled until it was almost illegible, but the phrase was familiar enough to piece together: PRIVATE PROPERTY.

Another sign came up on their right-hand side, this one nailed to a tree with a huge, rusted metal spike: STAY OUT. And a third had almost fallen off its post: TRESPASSING IS FORBIDDEN.

"Looks like this was the town's social hub," the driver said, grinning so broadly that he almost distracted Adrienne from a fourth sign: TURN BACK NOW.

She managed a laugh, but it sounded hollow. Wolfgang began crying again, but unlike his previous mewls, this was a drawn-out wail. Adrienne bent to check on him. His ears were flat against his head, and his fur, already fluffy, had bristled out to fill the carrier. "Hang on a few more minutes," she pleaded. "We're nearly there."

The dirt driveway was leading them uphill, and the winding road created an uneasy, heavy coldness in the pit of her stomach. It took her a minute to realise why: the trees in the town had all been green and healthy and spreading, but the plants bordering the driveway were growing increasingly wild and dark as they drove. The bark had deepened from a pleasant tan to a cold grey, leaves faded from emerald to dark khaki, and thick shrubs were swapped for thin, spindly, sickly things that struggled to survive amongst the weeds. It was as though the town had sapped all of the goodness out of the driveway and given it everything bad or sick in return.

They topped a ridge, and the taxi crawled around a bend. The woods finally parted, and Adrienne gasped as Ashburn House loomed ahead of them.

In her mind's eye, she saw lightning crackle across the sky, tracing the building's silhouette. Her mother's breaths, thin and desperate, echoed in her ears, and the heavy raindrops stung as they hit her arms.

Then she blinked, and she was back in the taxi, staring up at the leaning three-story wooden house.

"Bit of a fixer-upper, huh?" The taxi driver turned to grin at her, but this time, Adrienne couldn't even manage a smile in response.

I thought it was a dream. It felt so surreal, so bizarre… and yet, this is the same house…

The driver pulled to a stop and cut the engine. "I'll get your luggage, okay?"

"Huh? Oh, right, sorry—"

Adrienne carefully eased the cat carrier and its precious contents out of the car. She carried Wolfgang away from the driveway and set him on a patch of grass under a tree. The huge tabby grumbled deep in his throat but kept still.

The driver had already dumped her two travel cases out of the boot by the time Adrienne returned to him, and he was dusting his hands. When he told her the fare, Adrienne almost choked. It was higher than she'd expected, and it hurt to pass over the majority of the bills left in her wallet.

This is a fresh start, she reminded herself as the driver gave her a wave and slid back into his seat. *Good things rarely come without a cost.*

The car did a three-point turn then accelerated towards the driveway, leaving Adrienne standing alone in the patchy yard.

As the screeching wheels and rumbling engine faded, nature's subtle symphony moved in to take its place. Birds chattered amongst the trees, and insects hissed and hummed in the long grass. Adrienne stared up at the dilapidated house, her mouth dry and pulse racing, as the memory of that night replayed in her mind like a stain she couldn't get rid of no matter how hard she scrubbed.

CHAPTER 3
INHERITANCE

ADRIENNE COULDN'T GUESS HOW long she spent staring at the house, frozen as though in a trance, before Wolfgang's angry yowl shook her out of her stupor.

The dream—*no, memory,* she corrected herself—shocked her. She must have been young; she became too heavy for her mother to carry at around six years old.

What were we doing here?

She opened her bag to search for the key the solicitor had sent. At the same time, her mind struggled to reconcile the memory with reality. Her mother had told her they had no living relatives. When she'd received the solicitor's letter, Adrienne had assumed her mother hadn't known about their great-aunt Edith. Clearly, she had not only known about her but also had met her.

Why was she crying?

That was one of the most unnerving parts of the memory. Her

mother had been a stoic, calm woman with little patience for emotions. Adrienne couldn't even remember seeing her cry after her husband, Adrienne's father, passed away.

She found herself staring at the jumble of pens, lip balm, notepads, and receipts in her bag, and it took her a minute to remember why she'd opened it. *The key, that's right.* She found the heavy metal tool in an envelope hidden under a pack of tissues and pulled it out.

Was that really blood sprayed over her chin?

Adrienne looked back at the house as prickles ran over her arms. It had only been six or seven drops, but she was struggling to find any reasonable explanation for the red liquid.

What exactly happened in this house?

Despite the large patch of empty ground surrounding it, the house had been built tall rather than wide. One side had a half-octagonal extension, creating bay windows on all three levels. The roof was sharply peaked and tiled with dark slate. A porch extended from one side of the bay window to the end of the building, with the front door set deep in the shadows.

Wolfgang cried again, and the noise pushed Adrienne into action. She puffed as she hefted the carrier and staggered up the porch's steps with it. The wooden boards groaned under her weight, and small trails of dust fell from the overhang as the boards flexed. Judging by the sun's low position, they only had a couple of hours until nightfall, and she wanted to settle him as early as she could.

As much as she wanted to know what had transpired between Edith and her mother all of those years ago, she had to accept that she would likely never know. Her only memory centred on the last moments of the encounter when her mother had raced her out of the house and down the front steps. Both of the other present parties were deceased. Unless Edith Ashburn had kept a diary, the mystery would be lost to the corrosive effects of time.

It might have been an argument. Adrienne lowered Wolfgang to the porch and tore open the envelope containing her key. *It wasn't like Mum to hold a grudge, so she must have really hated Edith to tell me we had no relatives.*

The key slid into its hole below the doorhandle. The metal, stiff and rusted, screeched as she turned it, then a second later a quiet click told her the door was unlocked.

Perhaps Edith felt bad about what happened, whatever it was. She must have cared at least a little to leave her house to me.

She pressed her fingers to the wood and pushed. The door swept inwards, its hinges grinding as it stirred up small eddies of dust in the failing sunlight. Adrienne squinted to see into the hallway. Although the house had plentiful windows, they were all dimmed by decades of built-up dirt and grease, and the hallway was shrouded in thick, lingering shadows.

Adrienne cleared her throat, tucked the key into her pocket, picked up Wolfgang's carrier, and stepped over the threshold.

The air felt different inside Ashburn. It was heavier and drier and permeated with a musty odour that Adrienne struggled to identify. *Habitation,* her mind whispered. *This is a house that hasn't seen a new soul in half a century. The walls are saturated with her; the floorboards are worn down from her feet; the very air continues to carry her presence after her death.*

Adrienne tilted forward to peer inside Wolfgang's carrier and grinned at him. "That's not morbid at all, huh?"

Her laughter bounced along the hallway, climbed the steep stairwell at its end, and echoed through the upper rooms. The farther it travelled, the hollower the sound became, and she quickly closed her mouth. For a second, the building was returned to its natural state of silence, then Wolfgang released a low, rumbling growl.

A small, discoloured light switch was set into the wall next to the door, and Adrienne flipped it. She hadn't expected it to do anything, but a light hanging from the hallway's ceiling buzzed into life. It gave off a muted yellow glow, scarcely better than the anaemic light streaming through the windows, but Adrienne smiled at the sight of it. Ashburn had electricity after all; she'd been worried after seeing how remote the building was.

The hallway was narrow and travelled the length of the house. A threadbare carpet ran down its centre, and an odd collection of side tables, lamps, and umbrella holders as well as a tall grandfather clock clustered along the sides. Discoloured wallpaper dotted with tiny grey flourishes and red roses clung to the walls.

Adrienne drew the door closed behind her. Its whine was raw and loud in her ears, and she made a mental note to find out if Edith had owned any oil.

She moved forward slowly, absorbing details of her new home as she did. The furniture looked antique but well used. The carpet was a rich wine colour but had tan patches where the fabric had been rubbed off its base. Every surface looked slightly grimy, but there was surprisingly little dust; Adrienne suspected Edith had wiped the surfaces regularly but never washed them.

The first door was to her right, and she nudged it open. Inside was a spacious, tastefully decorated sitting room. Thanks to the large bay windows set into its front, the room was lighter than the hallway, and despite the fireplace, coffee table, and set of clean chairs with plush seats, it gave the impression of being infrequently used.

She left the door open but moved on. The nearest entrance to her left led into the kitchen and dinner table. At the room's back were an oven, an aged stove, benches, and sink. The wall next to it had two identical display units filled with china plates and glasses, all with a matching pink-and-red-rose design. When she moved into the room, she saw that two pale lines had been rubbed into the wooden floor at the table's head, corresponding to where the chair would have been scraped each night as its occupant sat down and rose.

She wanted to explore further, but Wolfgang's weight was making her arms ache. She needed a room with a few nooks that an anxious cat could hide in but no exits that he could escape through. She returned to the hallway and tried the next door to the right, opposite the stairwell.

The door opened into a lounge room. Unlike the corner space, though, this was very clearly used. Both the chair and couch's cushions were indented, and ash still filled the fireplace's base. A bookcase overloaded with old volumes ran up one wall, and an eclectic mix of shelves and cupboards—along with a piano—sat against the rest of the walls.

This'll do for Wolf. She nudged the door closed behind them, lowered him to the round wine-red rug in the centre of the floor, and unlocked the carrier's door. He turned his baleful green eyes on her but refused to leave the safety of the cage.

"Sorry, buddy." She sighed and offered her hand for him to smell before scratching behind his ears. He gave a languid blink in response to the attention but refused to tilt his head the way he normally did. "I know you don't like this, but trust me, it beats being homeless."

A low, discontented grumble answered her.

Adrienne gave her cat a tight-lipped smile then rose and went to collect their cases. As little as Wolfgang realised it, she hadn't been joking. The last four years of Pat's life had been a stream of specialist appointments, stints in hospital, and experimental treatments for the autoimmune disease that had ultimately claimed her. When her mother's health deteriorated too far for her to be alone during the day, Adrienne had left her job to stay with her and picked up whatever freelance writing work she could find online. She was proud to say they'd managed okay right up until the final hospital stay.

Pat had always tried her hardest to give Adrienne a stable home. She'd worked two jobs when she'd been healthy enough, but the appointments and treatments hadn't been without cost. By the time she passed, her house had been mortgaged twice and their savings had been converted into debts.

The weeks following the funeral had been a whirlwind of stress and financial problems digging through the grief. Pat's house, car, and furniture were sold to pay her outstanding debts. Adrienne had temporarily moved into a friend's apartment, but it was clear it couldn't be a permanent solution; the two-room space was far too small for four people, an irritable cat, and the friend's aggressive dog.

Adrienne had spent her free time looking for a new place to live, but the search had been demoralising. Her freelance work would only support a cheap apartment, and none of the places she'd viewed were welcoming towards cats.

The friend had suggested she give Wolfgang away. She might as well have asked Adrienne to cut off her own arm; she loved her fluffy monster too much to surrender him to a stranger. The letter telling her she'd inherited Ashburn had been, in Adrienne's opinion, a bona fide miracle.

Adrienne picked both cases off the grass and carried them back to Ashburn. The sun was close to the treetops, and its red glow spread across the horizon. Long shadows followed her back into the musty hallway, and the angry bird chatter swelled as the fowl prepared to nest.

She'd tried to keep her absence brief, but by the time she backed through the lounge room doors and turned towards the cat carrier, Wolfgang had already disappeared. She shut the door so that he couldn't escape and peered into the shadows that gathered around the room's corners as she opened the heavier of the cases.

"Hey, buddy," she called as she set out his litter box, poured a bag of chalky wood pulp into it, and laid his bowls beside the door. "Are you hungry? Hmm?"

She rattled the food tin, but the grey beast remained scarce. Adrienne sighed, poured the food into one of the bowls, then picked up the second to fill with water. As she let herself out of the lounge room, the light caught across scratches in the opposite wall's paper. Adrienne frowned at them. *They almost look like words.*

She took a step closer and inhaled. Someone had carved through the wallpaper to expose the wood underneath. They were hard to see at an angle, but the words became clear when looked at head-on:

NO MIRRORS

Adrienne glanced along the hallway reflexively. It was cluttered with furniture but didn't include any mirrors. She hadn't found it unusual before, but the words felt disquieting, almost menacing. She shook her head and crossed to the kitchen.

The sink was a huge, old-fashioned installation, and the handle screamed when she turned it. Pipes rattled above her head, and Adrienne gazed at the ceiling and imagined she could see the wooden boards shudder. Icy-cold water spewed out of the tap, ricocheted off the bowl, and sprayed over her.

Adrienne shrieked a series of very unladylike phrases as she fought to turn the tap off. Then, drenched and grumbling, she carried the water back to the lounge room.

"You'd better be grateful for this," she said as she placed the bowl next to Wolfgang's food.

The room was silent, but she thought she saw a flicker of

motion behind the piano. She knelt and leaned forward to see behind it. Wolfgang huddled in the gap between the piano and bookcase, and his huge green eyes fixed on her.

"You okay down there, buddy? Not too dusty for you?"

He gave her a single reproachful blink then returned to staring at the opposite wall.

The sun was dipping behind the trees, and the cooling air collaborated with her wet shirt and jeans to make Adrienne shiver, so she opened the second case and sifted through the few possessions she'd brought to Ashburn.

Packing had been depressing. Most of what she'd owned had been given away when she moved into her friend's apartment, and even less was practical to fit inside a taxi and cart across the state. One of the cases had been dedicated to Wolfgang's needs; the second held Adrienne's world—three changes of clothes, a towel, toiletries, the book she was reading, clean sheets, and her laptop. Her throat tightened as she stared at them. Her entire twenty-two years of life had boiled down to these items.

"It's a fresh start," she said to Wolfgang and tried to smile. "And I don't need much, anyway. Just you for company, somewhere for us to stay, and enough money that we won't starve. And look, thanks to Great-Aunt Edith, we now have all three. We'll be fine."

The great grey cat blinked at her, and suddenly, Adrienne wished he would come out of hiding so that she could hug him.

"We'll be fine," she repeated, her voice sounding small and lonely in her own ears as she pulled the towel out and dabbed at her wet clothes.

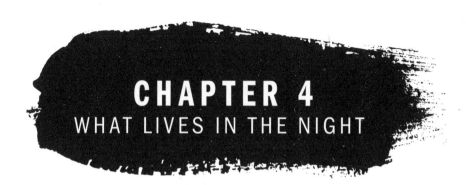

CHAPTER 4
WHAT LIVES IN THE NIGHT

ADRIENNE CHANGED INTO FRESH clothes and laid the wet shirt and jeans over the back of the fireside chair to dry. Wolfgang watched her go back and forth but refused to move from his cubbyhole even when she put his food bowl directly in front of it.

Despite the dry clothes, Adrienne found herself shivering and looked towards the blackened grate. She'd never lived in a house with a fireplace, but she'd been enamoured with the idea. A stack of dry wood sat in the bracket, a bucket of kindling sat nearby, and a folded newspaper and matchbox rested on the mantel.

Why not? She took the newspaper and checked the date. It was nearly three months old, which meant Edith would have bought it shortly before her death. Adrienne took a few of the pages, scrunched them into loose balls, placed them in the sooty grate, and set some of the kindling on top.

Once the newspaper caught, the flame easily spread to the twigs, and soon she was feeding it some of the larger logs. By the time the fire was large enough to be stable, she'd stopped shivering and was pleased to see that the flames lit the room better than the single light in the ceiling.

She gazed about the space, admiring how the golden glow reflected off the polished wooden chairs and bookshelves. The fire created long, dancing shadows that grew up the walls and tangled on the ceiling, and the crackles helped drown out the noise of the groaning trees and chattering birds outside the window.

A grandfather clock somewhere deep in the house chimed. She counted five long, metallic clangs and made a face. She hadn't realised how late it had grown. She'd skipped lunch, and when she paid attention to her body, she realised she was starving.

Her initial plan had been to spend her remaining money on groceries shortly after arriving at Ashburn, but that had been foiled thanks to the house's unexpectedly remote location. *Looks like we'll be scavenging tonight.*

She wasn't keen to explore the house with the sun so close to setting, but the longer she delayed, the worse it would become, so she left the lounge room, closed the door behind her, and crossed to the kitchen.

The room looked shockingly different when the sun was too low to come through the window. Even with the light on, the shadows built up in layers around the table, stove, and bench. She stopped at the head of the table, where long marks had been scraped into the wooden floor, and squinted at the wooden tabletop. There were scratches dug into the dark wood just above where a dinner plate might have sat.

Surely not…

Adrienne leaned closer and inhaled. As in the hallway, words had been cut into the shiny wooden top—possibly with a kitchen knife—and faced the head of the table so that whoever sat there couldn't fail to read them.

IS IT FRIDAY

LIGHT THE CANDLE

She chewed the inside of her cheek and tilted her head to one side. Little bits of dirt had become embedded in the scratches' indents, telling her the marks had been there for months if not years.

How bizarre. Was Edith all right? She must have been very old when she passed away. Maybe she had some form of dementia or Alzheimer's, and it made her do strange things.

Adrienne turned away from the table, but she couldn't scrub the image from her mind: Edith, well into her nineties by that point, wandering through Ashburn's narrow hallways in a confused daze, a steak knife clutched in one hand, cutting disturbed messages into the walls and tables…

No, don't think like that. She probably had someone staying with her. Or a friendly neighbour, at the very least, to keep an eye on her. Adrienne frowned and turned towards the fridge. *I hope.*

She opened the fridge door and gagged. The shelves were full of cardboard boxes, but their contents had long since rotted. She could still identify shrivelled carrots and a strangely dried-out cauliflower, but the other vegetables had turned into brown sludge. A bottle of rancid milk sat between a rectangle of mould-coated cheese and a punnet of what had once been strawberries.

The only edible items she could see were three unlabelled jam jars. *And jam on its own does not a dinner make.*

Adrienne wrinkled her nose and closed the door before the rotting odours could spread too far. *The house has been empty for nearly three months; of course the fresh food would have perished.*

She looked for a pantry and found it nestled in the room's corner. The doors creaked as they opened, and Adrienne felt her heart sink at the meagre range inside. While the fridge had been full of fresh produce, Edith clearly hadn't been a fan of long-life goods. She saw flour, baking powder, teabags, sugar, and salt on one shelf, a half-used bag of pasta—no sauce—on the second, and two tins of sardines on the third.

Okay. Could be worse. Adrienne sucked on her teeth, took one of the sardine tins, and began opening drawers as she looked for cutlery. *It's not a feast, but at least we won't starve. We'll just have to figure out how to get to town tomorrow.*

She opened the drawer below the china and inhaled at the sight of heavy and clearly expensive silver. *This set must be a family heirloom. She kept it in good condition; it's not even tarnished.*

The china plates displayed above the cutlery caught her eye, but she didn't take any down. It felt wrong to put something as mundane as tinned fish on the expensive rose-design dishes. She took a fork and closed the drawer.

An electric kettle sat on the bench beside the fridge, and behind it was an old-fashioned metal whistling kettle. She reached for the electric appliance first then hesitated, shrugged, and took up the metal pot instead. She made sure there weren't any spiders inside—just dust, she was relieved to see—then washed it out, half filled it with water, and fetched one of the teabags from the pantry.

Once again, Adrienne experienced reluctance to use any of the fine china in the display cabinets, but she couldn't find any other mugs, so eventually, she opened the glass doors and took one of the teacups. It felt incredibly fragile, and she held it carefully as she carried it, the kettle, the fish, and the fork back to the lounge room.

The fire had grown in her absence, and that wasn't the only change. Wolfgang's food bowl was empty, and the huge grey tabby sat on the rug in front of the fire, his paws tucked neatly under his body. He turned and blinked at Adrienne when she entered then returned to gazing at the flames.

"Should've known," she said, grinning, and set the precious teacup onto the small round table beside the chair. "I was starting to worry I'd traumatised you by carting you all the way up here, but you've already made yourself at home, huh?"

One ear twitched in her direction, but otherwise, she might as well have not existed.

A metal rod ran across the space above the fire. Adrienne found a pair of thick, blackened gloves sitting next to the wood and used one to hang her kettle on the rod so that the flames licked around its base. She then sat back in the wooden chair, took up her tin of sardines, and peeled back the lid.

It was one of the most surreal experiences of her life. She sat in a stranger's chair—one that had likely been inhabited by the same person every evening for fifty years before Adrienne came

25

along—and used a silver fork that was heavy and ornate enough to belong in Buckingham Palace to eat a tin of budget fish.

A soft, fluffy paw landed on her knee, and Adrienne looked down to meet Wolfgang's round green eyes. All indifference had melted away, and his expression was a perfect blend of plaintive and adoring.

"Oh, come on!" she cried in mock indignation. "You already ate!"

His mouth opened in a silent meow, and his fluffy tail twitched.

"You'll get fat." She pulled out a piece of the fish. "No, sorry, that's wrong. You'll get fat*ter*."

He scarfed down the morsel she offered him then licked around his mouth as he waited for more. She sighed and gave a fond smile as she shared the remainder of her fish with him. By the time they'd emptied the tin and Wolfgang settled down to lick the oil off its sides, the kettle was whistling.

She dropped the teabag into her cup, donned the gloves again, and pulled the steaming kettle off the fire. She poured the water with excruciating care, half-afraid that the heat alone would be enough to shatter the delicate floral beaker, and sighed in relief as she placed the pot on the mantel without any disasters.

For a minute, she considered getting the second tin of fish from the pantry—half of her dinner had ended up in the huge grey beast who had now returned to ignoring her—but she decided against it. She didn't know how long it would take her to get to town, or *how* she would get to town for that matter, and felt it would be wiser to ration out the food until she had a system worked out.

It took—what, twenty minutes to drive from the town's centre to here? That was at a slow speed, though. So maybe allow one or two hours to walk to town. Then the same amount of time to walk back. Uphill. While carrying shopping bags. She wrinkled her nose and blew steam off the top of the teacup. *Looks like I might meet my New Year's resolution to get fit after all.*

Edith Ashburn must have had a way to get to the shops. There hadn't been any vehicles parked at the front of the property, but she could explore around the back the following morning when the sun rose.

If Edith had owned a car, there was a good chance it had been given to someone else on her death or sold if she hadn't owned it outright. If that was the case, Adrienne would have to figure out a solution for herself. She could buy a bike, but good bikes were expensive, and she had less than twenty dollars in her purse and nothing in her bank account. That would improve a little when her freelance-article-writing accounts were paid, but two clients were overdue on their bills and hadn't replied to her emails in more than a week.

Wolfgang finished with the tin. He flopped onto his side and stretched so that his belly was facing the flames, and she thought she caught a faint rumble of contentment.

It must be nice to be a cat. No bills to pay. No difficult clients. No having to figure out how to say, "Send me my damn money!" in a pleasant way because if you're rude they won't hire you again and you can't afford to lose any work.

She leaned back in the chair and closed her eyes. The fire's heat felt amazing on her legs, and she took a second to realign her priorities. She had a house. It was old and smelt funny and was a long way from town, but holy heck, she had her own house. As long as the Wi-Fi worked well enough that she was able to submit her freelance articles on time, she could end up being very happy there. She thought she could grow fond of the town, too, and maybe even make some friends.

"And if no one wants to be my friend, I'll just get another cat," she said to Wolfgang. His front paws were making slow paddling motions and he kneaded the air. "I'll get a *dozen* cats and give them all cutesy names like Muffin or Flopsy and become the crazy cat lady who lives on the hill. How do you like the sound of that?"

There was no response, not that she'd expected one, but at least the grey beast looked content. Adrienne smiled and chewed at the corner of her thumb as she watched the last minutes of daylight fade. Without having to pay rent, her freelance work should be more than enough to support her. She would just have to get through the first few lean weeks as jobs were processed and accounts fell due, then she could start rebuilding her savings to give Wolfgang and her some security.

A growl startled her. Wolfgang no longer lay on his side but had rolled onto his front and half risen. His ears flattened, and the fur on his tail, already fluffy, puffed out.

"Wolf?" Adrienne placed her cup on the side table and leaned forward. The cat's eyes were saucer round and their pupils so large that almost none of the green irises remained visible. He faced the window closest to the fireplace, and his whiskers quivered as he exhaled a quiet hiss.

CHAPTER 5
PORTRAITS

SHE KEPT STILL, NOT breathing, and listened as hard as she could. The fire's crackles were a steady song to her left. The floors above her emitted faint groans as the wind caused the wood to shift. And outside was perfectly silent.

That gave her pause. The birds had created a cacophony barely half an hour before. And even if they'd all fallen asleep, she would have expected some of the insects to maintain their song.

Wolfgang transformed into a streak of grey as he turned and flew into the nook between the bookcase and the piano. Chills climbed Adrienne's arms as she watched her cat disappear. It wasn't like Wolfgang to take flight from a threat.

It's a new house. He's going to be skittish for a few days. She rose and took a step towards the window. Outside was nearly pitch black, and all she could see was her own pale face and the fire's glow reflected to her in the glass.

A pipe farther in the building rattled then fell still. The beams and supports above her head groaned more insistently as the wind buffeted them.

He probably saw a shadow and panicked. She moved nearer to the window, leaning so close to the smudged glass that she could feel its chill washing onto her cheek.

Outside was deathly quiet. She could make out the moon's glow, blurred and muted by the thin clouds that hung across it, and the trees' silhouettes against the sky. Scores of faintly glowing pinpricks were visible between the clouds, suggesting the heavens would be awash with stars on a clear night.

Her heart's thundering beats fought to be heard over the fire. She tried to block both noises out as she listened for a birdcall, a cricket, an owl—any proof that the world outside hadn't been muted. Even the trees seemed to be lying still despite the house's groaning against the wind.

She skipped her eyes across the yard, trying to pick out shapes in the near darkness. The window's light illuminated a rectangle of the long, weedy grass that stretched ahead of her but nothing else. She couldn't detect any motion, but she was also acutely aware that a person standing just outside of the block of illumination would be invisible. It was a sickening thought.

Cut it out. You're frightening yourself over nothing. Wolf got jittery, and now outside is quiet—that's all. The window is probably really well soundproofed or something—

All at once, as though an invisible cue had been given, the woods burst into life. Birds screamed and took flight, hundreds pouring out of the boughs and shooting skyward in a frenzy of whirring wings. Shrill insects began to buzz. Deep in the woods, some animal—a fox, she thought—shrieked. And behind her, Wolfgang began to yowl, the noise starting as a low rumble and growing in volume, pitch, and terror to become one of the worst sounds she'd ever heard.

Adrienne clamped her hands over her ears and dropped to her knees. Something terrible was happening, and although she couldn't see the cause, she could feel it growing closer, threatening to swallow and obliterate her very existence. An earthquake, or tsunami, or Armageddon—

The sound began to fade. Wolfgang ran out of breath, and his wail was reduced to a rumbling hiss. The screeches died out as the birds flew out of hearing range, and the insect trills began to fade. Adrienne slowly lowered her hands and opened her eyes. She was shaking, but nothing tangible had reached her. The house stood firm; no fires, giant waves, or asteroids swept through the yard. If judgement day had come, Ashburn House had withstood it remarkably well.

Wolfgang continued to grumble from his hiding hole, but the sound was less insistent than before, as if he were making a point rather than responding to any immediate distress. Adrienne stayed kneeling on the floor for several long moments, waiting, but the phenomenon didn't repeat itself. At last she stood, moving slowly, as though a wrong move could cause everything to unravel, and looked through the window.

The outside world was still once again but no longer perfectly quiet. She could hear the trees groaning as they moved in the wind, and a few metres from the window, a cricket chirruped.

"Okay." Adrienne rubbed her sweaty palms on her jeans and tried to breathe through the fear-induced band squeezing her chest. "Okay, that was crazy."

Wolfgang slunk out of his cubbyhole. He glowered as though Adrienne had been the cause of whatever had upset him and he wanted her to understand how badly she'd misbehaved, but he returned to the fire with the stubbornness of a cat who was too familiar with warmth and comfort to endure an existence without either. Adrienne waited until he took his seat—facing away from her as punishment—then returned to her own fireside chair. She sat, feeling a little shell shocked, and picked up her cup of tea with shaking hands. The liquid was lukewarm, but she still drank it. She needed the caffeine.

What on earth was that? I'd think earthquake, but nothing shook. What could distress both the birds outside and Wolfgang in here without me sensing it? Has some country declared war on us and detonated an EMP bomb? Is that even the sort of thing an EMP bomb can do?

The idea made her cold, and she suddenly wanted a clearer view outside the house. If, mercy forbid, something had happened to the little town, she wouldn't know, because the trees that surrounded her property blocked it from sight. But if she could get to one of the higher windows and see over the forest...

"Stay here, buddy," she said to the cat, who was very pointedly ignoring her. She grabbed her jacket out of the travel case, wrapped it around herself, and slipped out of the lounge room.

She'd left the hallway light on, but the bulb was so dirty that she felt as though she were suspended in twilight as she followed the hall towards the stairs at the back of the house. A little round table sat by the foot of the stairs. On it stood an old-fashioned oil lamp, a box of matches, and a metal jar, all neatly arranged on a doily. *It's a bit strange to have a lamp left out like that. Maybe Ashburn is prone to power failures.*

Adrienne passed the table and began climbing the stairs. The wood was old and groaned under her weight, and the noise seemed to travel up the narrow stairwell and flood the upper levels.

The darkness seeped out of the second floor and swallowed her as she left the hallway light's circle of influence. She turned the corner where the stairs hit the back wall and found her light reduced to almost nothing. She squinted to make out the edge of the steps, praying there weren't any missing floorboards or exposed nails and brushing her fingertips along the walls to help orient herself.

The stairs finally opened onto a landing, and Adrienne inhaled a little breath of relief. She was shaking again, partly from the unsteady climb and partly from lingering shock of the outside disturbance, and it took her a moment to realise there wasn't a light switch at the top of the stairs.

She stretched her hand out, running it up and down the floral wallpaper in long sweeps, but couldn't feel any kind of switch. An idea occurred to her, and she snorted.

No way. That'd be ridiculous. The switch must be at the other end of the hall or something.

She squinted down the passageway, struggling to discern the silhouettes that would be invisible save for faint moonlight coming through one of the room's windows. She thought she saw side tables, and large paintings on the walls, but she wasn't certain.

Still, the lamp at the base of the stairs niggled at her. It was so deliberately placed that she could easily imagine it being there to light the upper floors.

But rooms downstairs have electricity. Why would they install lights on the lower level but not the upper ones?

She looked back at the empty wallpaper then stepped towards the nearest door. It opened with a prolonged creak, and Adrienne passed her hand through the gap and felt the wall, running her fingers over the dry paper without encountering any plastic bumps.

"Oh, you've got to be kidding me." She gave the wall by the top of the stairs one final, incredulous look then began tramping back down the stairs.

The house was incredibly old. *Old enough to have been built before electricity was common. Perhaps the structure was too unsound to run wires through the higher walls. Or maybe Edith could only afford to do part of the house.*

Adrienne reached the hallway and faced the table. The lamp waited there, its glass slightly cloudy from smoke and built-up grease and with a nearly full box of matches beside it. She spent several minutes trying to figure out how to take the glass off to reach the wick, only to find the oil well empty. She picked up the metal container, felt liquid slosh around inside, and unscrewed the lid.

She had to guess how much to pour into the lamp. The last thing she wanted was for the delicate instrument to explode in her hand, but losing her source of light in a dark passageway would be far from ideal, too. She lit the wick, waited for the flame to grow steady, then replaced the glass.

The lamp's glow didn't extend far, but it made the stairwell much easier to navigate. When she reached the landing, she was able to make out the hallway's furniture.

Paintings, all contained within ornate gilt frames, coated both walls. Adrienne peered at them as she passed. They were all portraits. It took her a few paintings to realise the portraits were all of the same family: a man, two women, and a girl. Occasionally, they were painted as a group—or the man and the older woman sitting together—but most of the images were individual portraits.

The man had heavy-lidded, stern eyes and a thick brown moustache. The older woman—his wife, Adrienne thought— had darker hair and was often smiling. The second woman was a little younger with delicate features and lighter hair. The girl's hair was thick and long, like the first woman's, and she repeatedly appeared with the same serious, studious expression.

The tableau felt inherently wrong to Adrienne. There were more than fifty paintings, all of the same family, all crowding the same hallway, their eyes following her no matter how swiftly she walked. It quickened her pulse and set her teeth on edge.

Adrienne pressed her lips together, picked a door at random, and barrelled through it.

The curtains were drawn, blocking out the moon's light, and she had to raise her lamp to see the area clearly. A large four-poster bed was pressed against one wall, its wine-red drapes faded and tattered around the edges. Opposite stood a wardrobe, one door half-open, next to a bureau.

She'd taken three steps into the room before she noticed that the rug had been scuffed and one side of the mattress was indented from decades of use. Her insides turned cold.

This was Edith's room.

CHAPTER 6
SPREADING LIGHTS

ADRIENNE'S MOUTH DRIED. SHE started to back out of the space but stopped herself at the door. *No, don't be squeamish. You're not intruding. She left this house to you, and that includes her own room.*

It felt odd, though, to walk across the rug that had been worked down to threads by a single pair of feet and see the black dresses peeking out of the open wardrobe door. She sensed that she was a stranger to the window that must have seen the same face every morning for decades. Adrienne pulled the curtains back from the glass and inhaled.

She'd wanted to see over the treetops, and Edith's window gave her a spectacular view. Laid out before her was a carpet of trees, and the moonlight reflected off the canopy that gradually grew denser until the trees merged with a spread of lights.

For half a second, she thought the trees were burning and

Armageddon might have come after all, and but then she blinked and realised the glow came from hundreds of lit windows.

Ipson. I didn't expect it to be so close. Or so much lower than Ashburn. This must be a tall hill.

She squinted at the lights. The houses were too far away to appear as distinct shapes, but she couldn't see any smoke or signs of frantic motion. That was comforting; whatever had disturbed the birds wasn't an issue for the town.

She exhaled, and her breath formed a small puff of condensation on the glass. The outside chill was seeping through her thin clothes, but curiosity was stronger than her desire to return to the fire. She turned to face the room and gazed at its fittings.

What sort of person was Edith?

The indented mattress and scuffed carpet suggested she'd either been a woman of deeply ingrained habits or one who simply couldn't afford new purchases.

I wonder if that might have influenced why she left me the house. If she'd known about Mum's medical bills—if she'd suspected I would have money problems like she had—this might have been her way of helping me.

Adrienne felt warmed despite the cold air. She wished she could have met Edith—or met her properly, at least—and thanked her for the gift. She moved towards Edith's bed, lost in her thoughts, then stopped short as she realised what she was looking at.

Scratches had been left on the headboard, spelling out another message in the wood. The lines were layered and frantic—mimicking the downstairs writings—and placed just a few inches above the pillow so that someone lying in the bed could see them by tilting their head back a little. Adrienne raised her light and leaned close to read.

REMEMBER YOUR SECRETS

The lamp clinked as she folded her arms across her chest. Curiosity to know more, to understand the enigmatic woman who'd owned the home, battled with a desire to retreat to the relative safety and comfort of the downstairs lounge room.

The wardrobe door stood open a crack, showing a sliver of black silk, and Adrienne edged towards it. It looked like the type of wardrobe that would have a mirror in its door, but she already suspected this one would be different. She wasn't wrong.

The hinges complained as they turned, but the door opened smoothly. The inside of the wood was bare save for another scratchy message: NO MIRRORS.

"No mirrors," Adrienne agreed. Small holes in the wood at the top and base of the door told her that a mirror had once hung in the wardrobe but had been removed. *Why, Edith?*

Adrienne looked away from the door and towards the row of dark dresses. They surprised her, and she set the lamp onto the floor before pulling one of them out to get a clearer look at it. The gown could have come out of the props department in a Victorian-era film. Heavy black silk with lace detailing, a low hem, and a high neckline must have created a startling effect when worn. Adrienne blinked, and all of a sudden she was back in the car, her mother's frantic breaths echoing in her ears, as she watched Ashburn's door glide open. A tall figure, dressed in black, moved to stand in the opening, and Adrienne had an impression of a pale, long face and glittering black eyes before the memory faded and she found herself back in Edith's bedroom.

She sagged away from the wardrobe, breathing quickly. She was suddenly acutely aware of the gown's length. Adrienne wasn't short, but in order to keep the skirts from brushing the ground, she had to hold the dress so high that the lace gathered at the neck was at her eye level. She licked her lips as the new information coalesced with her existing knowledge of Edith and transformed the elderly woman in her mind's eye into a tall, gaunt, black-clothed wraith.

She couldn't help her height. The long, pale face from her memory burnt itself into the back of her eyes. *And she probably wore black in mourning. Doesn't stop her from being a good, kind person.*

The dress was hung back amongst its companions, and Adrienne reverently closed the wardrobe doors. Her fingers were trembling, and she balled them into fists to keep them still.

It was stupid to come up here on my first night. I should've stayed with Wolf and saved the exploring until morning.

A pipe in the walls behind her rattled, startling her, and she snatched up the lamp and hurried to the door. As she slipped through the gap, a dozen pairs of eyes arrested her. She stayed rooted to the spot for a second, scanning the row of portraits, then followed the hallway to the stairs and hurried down them.

She hadn't noticed it before, but the family in the portraits all wore Victorian-style clothes not unlike the ones she'd found in Edith's wardrobe.

Were they her family? Could she be the child in the paintings, perhaps?

The grandfather clock began chiming as she took the stair's corner. She tried to count the off-note clangs, but her mind was still buzzing with the new familiarity with Edith, and she lost count. It was either ten or eleven at night; either way, time for bed.

Wolfgang still lay on the rug in front of the fire but had rolled onto his back so that his four paws stuck up into the air and his belly was exposed. Except that one eye lazily drifted open at her entrance, he could have passed for roadkill. Adrienne laughed at the sight, and the unease created by the upstairs rooms melted away.

The fire was burning low, so she added two new logs and placed the kettle back over the flames to reheat. Then she pulled her sheets and pillow out of the travel case and looked about the room.

Other than the fireside chair, there were two lounge chairs. One had well-squished cushions, but the second seemed infrequently used. She chose the latter, draping one sheet over the cushions and arranging the second on top. She hadn't brought any proper blankets but had a thick shawl that would do until she could find out if Edith had a guest bedroom or similar.

"Want any more food, buddy?" she asked Wolfgang as she passed him on the way to the kettle. He followed her progress with the one open eye, but a low, rumbling purr told her he would be staying right where he was.

Adrienne reused the teabag from her earlier cup to make a

fresh brew then retrieved the book from the suitcase, turned the light off, and snuggled into her makeshift bed fully clothed.

She'd intended to read by firelight for an hour or two before sleeping, but the day had worn on her more than she'd expected, and she soon let the book sag so that she could watch the dancing flames and her fluffy pet. The fire's light caught in gaps between the floorboards, making them look like black lines scoring the floor.

"We're going to be okay here," she told him as she tried to ignore the eerie sensation that the long, pale face could be watching her from one of the corners where the shadows gathered thickest.

CHAPTER 7
GUESTS

A HUNDRED THOUSAND TINY scratches had cut into the wood, but it still wasn't enough. Her fingers kept scrabbling. Their nails had been chipped down to nothing, the skin scabbed and cracked; her bleached-white eyes stared sightlessly, and her breathing was a low, rhythmic grating as her fingers kept working. She wouldn't rest. Not when she was so close.

The scrabbling echoed in the tiny, cramped space, seeming to drown her.

So close.

More splinters broke off under her fingers, raining onto her white cheeks and black dress. She was so close to breaking through the wood and reaching the heavy, moist, dirt packed above her.

Adrienne started awake. A heavy weight pressed onto her chest, suffocating her, and she'd raised her hands with a panicked cry to fight it off. Then she felt it shift and realised what it was.

Sometime during the night, Wolfgang had migrated from the hearthside rug to sleep on top of her. The fire must have burnt down to the point where her body was the warmer haven.

He was heavy enough to be uncomfortable, though, and Adrienne carefully moved the cat off so that he lay beside her. He yawned, stretched, and settled down for a longer nap.

I had a dream. What was it? Something about not being able to breathe… being trapped… trying to claw my way out…

She looked down at her fingers. They were whole and her stubby nails intact. She blinked, trying to recall the dream, but the effort was like trying to chase water while it soaked into the ground.

Morning was well underway. Sunlight, muted by the grime, washed through the windows and painted patterns over the carpet and furniture. The room was still reasonably warm, but she could sense it was quickly growing colder as frosty outside air ate away at the lingering heat from the fire.

She slipped out of the makeshift bed, being careful not to disturb Wolfgang any more than she had to, and shimmied into a jacket.

First full day in our new house. What do we need to do? Getting food is a priority—but even before I figure out a way to the town, I need a shower.

She hadn't brushed her teeth the night before, and her mouth tasted like something had died in it. She grimaced and ran her hands through her hair, trying to keep the loose strands out of her face, and then poured out fresh food for Wolfgang. His apathy vanished at the sound of rattling kibble, and he had his face planted in the bowl before she'd finished pouring.

"Calm down; you're not going to starve." She scratched the top of his head, put the cat food onto a shelf, and took her towel and toiletries out of the suitcase before returning to the hallway.

The lamp waited on the little table at the base of the stairs, but she left it there. The morning sun was strong enough to light the narrow steps and the rooms above. She took the climb quickly and found herself back in the painting-lined hallway.

The portraits were clearer in the daylight, and even Adrienne, who lacked any kind of artistic ability, could tell the painter had considerable talent. The portraits were detailed and the subjects artfully posed, and many of the paintings were so realistic that she could feel eyes on her back as she moved along the hallway and peeked into rooms.

The first two doors she tried opened into storage areas full of cardboard boxes, shrouded furniture, and musty crates. The third was an office of sorts, and Adrienne entered it to get a closer look at the ornately carved desk below the window. The view looked over the wood-clothed hill that ran towards town. Thin fog wove among the trees and over Ipson's streets, lending them an otherworldly quality. The view was spectacular.

This would be a great place to write. She ran her fingertips along the dark-wood surface. *It would be okay, wouldn't it? I don't want to be disrespectful by using Edith's private room and favourite desk.*

She wiped a finger over the table. It was slightly dusty but not enough to assume it had been neglected. Despite that, the room had the feeling of a space infrequently used. The bookcase was too neatly stacked and the desk too clear for Adrienne to imagine the room had been touched except for cleaning within the last few years. *Maybe it belonged to Edith's husband.*

Adrienne backed away from the desk and tried not to scrunch her face up. For some reason, the idea of Edith being married felt wrong. She still knew almost nothing about her benefactor, but something told her Edith Ashburn had stayed single.

She left the office and passed the next door. She remembered its carved designs from the night before. She wasn't eager to examine the indent on Edith's bed or the rows of ornate black dresses again.

To her delight, the door past Edith's opened into a spacious and relatively clean bathroom. Unlike the rest of the house, which was predominately decorated in old-fashioned rose patterns, the bathroom was clean white with subtle sea-green accents. It looked modern, too, as though it had been installed within the past decade. A bathtub was set into the back wall with a shower-head poised above it and a spacious sink at its side.

Adrienne turned on the shower's water. Pipes rattled through the house, grinding and clanging for what felt like an eternity before the liquid spat out of the showerhead. While she waited for the hot water to flow through, Adrienne brushed her teeth and stared at the empty space above the sink where a mirror would normally sit. She wasn't surprised to see her reflection replaced by the now-familiar phrase, NO MIRRORS.

Looks like she's removed every mirror in the house. That's a pain; I didn't bring any with me. I'll probably look like a fright when I turn up in town today. No makeup, sweaty from the climb, probably twigs sticking out of my matted hair... it'll give them something to talk about.

She gave a wry grin then undressed and showered. The water was beautifully hot, but the room didn't have a fan, and condensation glistened on every surface by the time she turned the taps off. She searched for some way to aerate the room, but the only option was the large frosted window behind the shower. She never would have dared open it in the city, but kilometres from town and with no neighbours, she felt remote enough to unlock the clasp and crack one of the panes open.

Icy outside air rushed through the opening. Adrienne spluttered and raced to dry and dress herself before she froze. She was still pulling her jeans on when the sound of a motor disturbed her. She hesitated, one leg in its pant and the other one raised awkwardly in the air, and listened. *I didn't think I was close enough to the main road to hear any traffic.*

The motor grew in volume, and soon the crunch of small rocks being ground under tyres confirmed her suspicion. Someone had come to visit.

She pulled the jeans on the rest of the way, stuck her feet into the sneakers, and crossed to the bathroom window. A tidy sedan was rolling to a halt near the edge of the path. The driver had turned the vehicle around so that it faced the exit, as though preparing for a quick escape, and that unnerved Adrienne.

A lot of possibilities ran through her mind, none of them pleasant. She pictured one of Edith's friends or relatives becoming enraged that the house had been left to a stranger rather than them. Or someone who thought she didn't deserve the property and had come to vandalise it in retaliation. Or thieves, knowing she would be alone and sensing easy prey…

She pulled the jacket on while she raced along the hallway and flew downstairs. The front door had frosted-glass panes at its sides, and she pressed close to one of them to catch a glimpse of her visitors.

Four figures, huddled closely together, were crossing the yard. Two of them had their arms full with indistinguishable bundles. As they neared, Adrienne drew a breath. She thought she recognised them; they were the four fashionable ladies she'd seen outside the café. The tall one with shoulder-length blonde hair led her companions in a beeline towards Ashburn House's porch.

Adrienne drew back. Her heart was pounding, but she didn't know why. She doubted those glamorous women had come to vandalise, thieve, or intimidate her, which was good, but it left their actual motives an unknown factor. They'd been laughing at her taxi when she passed them the day before, and that didn't sit well with her. Had they come to gawk, perhaps?

Don't be paranoid. Maybe they're here to welcome you to town or invite you to join their book club or something. They could be friendly.

Her brain seized on that phrase and refused to let it go. *Friends. They could be your friends.*

Voices reached her as the group climbed the porch stairs. One, quiet and anxious, said, "I don't think I want to do this."

"Oh, come on, we're already here! If you didn't want to, you should've said so back in town."

"Shh, both of you. She might hear." The third voice used a theatre whisper that carried through the door. "Sarah, you can stay in the car if you want. But this might be our only chance to see Ashburn."

There was quiet for a moment then a muted, "Okay."

So they've come to gawk at the house after all. A bitter taste filled Adrienne's mouth, and she drew away from the door. *I could stay quiet. Make them think I've gone out. They'd have to leave eventually.*

The voice in the back of her head kept chanting: *friends, friends, they could be friends.* She was a little disgusted at her desperation but then remembered how small the town was. If she wanted companionship, the gawkers might be her only option.

One of the ladies gave three brisk raps with the knocker. The sound boomed through the hallway and made the wood shiver.

Adrienne kept still, frozen in indecision. *Let them in or turn them away? Risk humiliation or face isolation?*

"Hello?" The woman one who'd told Sarah she could stay in the car spoke loudly enough that it would be heard throughout the building. "Sorry for dropping by uninvited, but we wanted to welcome you to Ipson."

Adrienne crossed her arms over her chest and kept quiet. Her heart thumped against her ribs like a trapped bird as her mind continued to play tug of war over whether or not to answer.

A beat of silence passed, then the voice continued, bright and loud. "We brought some scones and jam and cream. Marion made the jam from raspberries she grew herself. It's really good."

That made the decision a cinch. She was hungry and had nothing in her cupboard except a tin of sardines and cat food. If letting a group of shallow, gossiping voyeurs into her house was the price she had to pay for scones, well, she could live with that.

She backed up the hallway silently then walked toward the door, making her footfalls slightly louder than normal so that the ladies wouldn't suspect she'd been lurking a few feet away from them. Swallowing her nervousness was painful and not entirely effective, but she hoped she'd managed to fix a natural smile onto her face as she turned the knob and opened the door.

CHAPTER 8
MASKS

THE BLONDE-HAIRED LEADER STOOD closest, her arms full of a cloth-covered basket and a bright smile stretching her red lips. Her three companions—a shorter, stockier lady with bobbed black hair, a tall, serious-looking woman with a long face, and a pale-skinned woman with a straight fringe—all lingered a step behind.

"It's so nice to meet you!" The leader extended the basket as though the peace offering would save her from rejection—which, Adrienne supposed, wasn't too far from the truth. "It's been too long since we've had anyone new in town. I'm Jayne."

"Adrienne." She impulsively extended her hand to shake Jayne's, but the other woman's were occupied with holding the basket, so she squeezed her fingers into a fist and dropped it back at her side with a nervous laugh. "Um, would you like to come in?"

She felt completely out of her element as she stepped to one side and allowed the glamorous women to enter. The only visitors they'd had at her mother's home had been close friends, and she had no idea what was expected of her when she was welcoming strangers. The anxiety wasn't helped when she thought about how unkempt she must look with her crumpled second-day clothes and damp hair.

She turned to lead them into her lounge room then stopped. The blankets and pillows were still strewn over the couch, and she didn't know how Wolfgang would react to strangers. So instead, she opened the door to the sitting room—the cleaner, fancier space that overlooked the front garden—and ushered them inside.

Sunlight streamed through the windows, bringing the floral-print lounges and dark wood fittings into sharp relief. Her guests made vaguely appreciative noises as they looked around the space, and Jayne placed the basket on the coffee table that sat between the lounge chairs.

"I didn't bring any plates, I'm afraid." Her teeth looked startlingly white in the sunlight, and golden highlights caught in her hair. Adrienne felt a twinge of jealousy. No amount of expensive salon products could make her hair that perfectly glossy.

"No problem, it's fine." She waved at the chairs. "Um, have a seat. I'll make some tea and get some plates too. Just a minute."

She managed to repress the urge to run as she left the room. Her breath came out in a rush as she closed the door and pressed her back to the wood. *This was a terrible decision. They're going to judge the heck out of you! You look a mess thanks to Edith's no-mirrors policy, and you don't even know if there's a teapot in this house. You'll be the town's hottest joke by evening.*

A voice floated through the closed door. It sounded faintly surprised. "I didn't think she'd be so young."

Adrienne pushed away from the wood and hurried into the kitchen to fill the electric kettle and put it on to boil. She opened every cupboard and drawer in the room, searching for a set of modern mugs, but eventually had to resign herself to serving their tea in the overly ornate fine china. Edith owned a teapot, at least. Adrienne found a tray and stacked the plates, teacups, saucers, and sugar onto it, but she didn't have any milk. *They'll have to make do with black.*

The kettle finished boiling. She dropped two teabags into the pot, filled it with hot water, and lifted it slowly, aware that she held a small fortune in china in her shaking hands. She tried to take deep breaths as she followed the hallway back to the sitting room.

The quiet murmur was audible from the hallway but fell silent when she bumped the door open with her hip. The ladies had arranged themselves around the lounge chairs, leaving the high-backed armchair for her, and all smiled as she entered. She felt as if she were stepping into some kind of Stepford social club.

Adrienne directed all of her focus on not dropping anything as she placed the tray next to the scone basket and began arranging the teacups. "Sugar?" she asked and was answered by a chorus of "Yes, please" and "No, thank you." She tried to remember who had answered what as she began pouring.

"There's no milk—sorry," she said with a tight smile.

The leader, Jayne, dismissed it with a wave of her manicured hand. "Black is fine. Thank you. Oh, I haven't introduced my friends yet, have I?" She indicated to the shorter black-bob woman who sat next to her. "This is Beth. She works at the Cosmic Coffee Café. And"—she gave a nod towards the tall, thin-faced woman opposite—"Sarah, who works at the library. She's been running a lot of fundraisers lately to help them purchase new books." She nodded towards the pale, brown-fringed woman. "And Marion is studying to be a vet."

Jayne, Beth, Sarah, Marion. Adrienne tried to cement the names into her memory and not spill the tea at the same time. It was a mammoth task.

Jayne leaned forward, her hands folded neatly in her lap. "It was Adrienne, wasn't it?"

"Yeah. Or, uh, Addy. Most people call me Addy."

She held a teacup out for Jayne, and that was when their carefully orchestrated interaction fell apart. She wasn't sure if it was her fault—she let go too early, perhaps, or her shaking hands making the cup difficult to grip—or whether Jayne herself fumbled the saucer, but the cup fell between their hands and crashed onto the coffee table.

Tea and broken china exploded. Jayne jolted out of her chair and swore then turned an intense shade of red as she snatched the cloth off the basket and began dabbing at the spilt tea. "I'm sorry—I'm so, so sorry—"

"No, no, it's fine." Adrienne tried to help clear the mess by picking up shards of the broken saucer and teacup and piling them onto the tray.

"Oh crap, no, I broke it. I'm so sorry, I'll pay for it—"

Adrienne looked into Jayne's pink face and saw embarrassed, shocked tears glittering in her eyes. And just like that, the perfectly cultured illusions sloughed away, and Adrienne was able to see the humans hiding underneath the women.

None of them were perfect after all. Jayne's lipstick was a shade too dark for what would have suited her and her skirt a little too tight so that the fabric bunched up. Beth's hair looked as if it took at least an hour to straighten and style that morning, but the bob was a little messy and incomplete despite the effort she'd put into it. Marion's laugh was anxious and tight. Sarah's smile looked awkward when it stretched her long face. The flawless, superior exterior they'd presented on the porch was just that—an exterior.

They weren't all that different from her—teenagers who had found themselves classified as adults by virtue of too many birthdays and who were trying to fumble and bluff their way through the world without anyone realising how thoroughly underqualified they were.

And they'd been trying really, really, really hard to make her like them.

The relief was intense. She wanted to laugh and cry at the same time, but Jayne was still spewing apologies punctuated with panicked swear words, so she took the towel out of the other woman's hands as gently as she could. "It's fine! It was my fault. Please don't worry. Edith had a million of these things anyway."

Jayne was blinking the embarrassed tears back, but her face was still beet red. "Really, I'm so sorry. I can pay for it or get you a replacement—"

"No, don't be ridiculous. I'll grab you a new cup. Just gimme a minute. No, don't try to pick them up; they'll cut you. Let me."

Jayne obediently sat back and gave her a cracked smile. "Thanks, Addy."

Friends, the voice in the back of her head sang as she scraped the broken china and soaked cloth onto the tray and carried it from the room. *They could be friends.*

CHAPTER 9
RUMOURS AND TEA

WHEN ADRIENNE ENTERED THE sitting room with a new cup and saucer, Jayne had regained her poise save for a pink tinge that lingered on her ears. She thanked Adrienne as she took the fresh cup of tea and then nodded towards a plate on the coffee table. "We made up some scones for you. I hope that's okay."

"Thanks." Adrienne took one and passed the plate to Beth on her other side. "You said Marion made the jam?"

Marion, the fringe-haired vet student, nodded. "Yep, first batch of the season."

"Wow, it's delicious." Adrienne spoke around a mouthful of the warm scone. She wasn't exaggerating; the jam was sugary and tart and tasted amazing.

Marion's whole face lit up with pride. "Ha, thanks! It's my nan's recipe."

The atmosphere was miles away from what it had been when

they'd first sat down. The disaster with the teacup had broken the awkward formality of first introductions; she was no longer afraid of them, and they were no longer afraid of her. Adrienne found herself relaxing as she took another bite. "I really appreciate this, actually. Edith didn't leave much food in the house, and I haven't had a chance to go to town."

"Did you know her well?" The question came from Beth, who was leaning forward in her chair.

"Not at all." Adrienne wasn't sure how much to share with her companions and settled on the simplest version of events. "I didn't even know I had a great-aunt until she passed. I wish I'd been able to meet her while she was alive."

The four ladies exchanged a glance but didn't comment. Adrienne looked between them as curiosity bloomed inside of her. "Why? Did you know her?"

"We didn't really *know* her." Jayne spoke slowly and glanced at Beth, who gave her a small nod. "But we knew *of* her. The whole town did. I… I don't want to be rude, but…"

"No, no, go on." Adrienne set her scone on the edge of her plate and leaned forward.

Jayne gave an apologetic smile. "She was a bit eccentric."

"*A bit.*" Beth snorted but sobered when Jayne shot her a glare. "Sorry."

"Well, see, she wouldn't let anyone into the house." Jayne raised one shoulder in a shrug. "You probably saw the warning signs in the driveway. The last time anyone set foot in this building was when John McManus was brought in to repair her bathroom a decade ago. He says it took him two days, and Miss Ashburn stood in the doorway and watched him the whole time. Not speaking, not moving, just… watching."

Tiny chills ran down Adrienne's arms.

"That's, uh, part of the reason we came today." Jayne gave another apologetic smile. "Wow, you're going to think we're so unbelievably rude. We really did want to meet you, too—and I'm not just saying that—"

"But you wanted to see the house." Adrienne allowed herself a smile as she released her breath. They had come to gawk after all, but she couldn't blame them. If a notorious house in her town had fallen empty, she'd have been curious to explore it too.

"Hell yeah," Beth said, her eyes blazing. "I wanted to see if there were really skulls decorating the hallways."

"Beth, *please*," Jayne hissed.

Adrienne snorted in laughter and had to cover her mouth so that she wouldn't spit crumbs over the table. "Sorry, none that I've seen. Yet."

Beth shrugged. "Oh well. I always thought that was one of the stupider stories."

"There are a lot of rumours about Ashburn," Marion said. "The kids in town love telling each other ghost stories about it. Heck, even we did when we were younger. It was like this holy grail of mystery. Edith came into town every day, but she never spoke to anyone except to do her shopping, and she always wore these huge, heavy black dresses, even in summer."

Adrienne desperately wanted to know more about her

mysterious great-aunt but took a detour into a more urgent issue. "She visited the town every day? How did she get there?"

"Walked," Beth said. "Always first thing in the morning, too, so that she arrived in town just as the shops opened."

"Wow, she must've been fit. It's a long driveway."

"There's a shortcut." Jayne pointed towards the window and the trees that blocked their view of the town. "Through the woods—it's only about fifteen minutes as the crow flies. We call it Ashburn Walk because she was the only one who ever used it."

Adrienne felt as though a weight had been lifted from her. Fifteen minutes was more than manageable. Provided she could find the walkway, she and Wolfgang would no longer be in danger of starving.

"What other rumours were there?" Adrienne asked. "You made it sound like people were scared of this place."

Jayne shrugged. "Some were, I guess. Others said Edith was just eccentric. Mostly people avoided her because she avoided them. But yeah, there are some strange stories circulating about this house. I don't know how true they are."

Adrienne raised her eyebrows in a silent request for more information. Beth was more than happy to oblige.

"Not to brag, but I'm a bit of an Ashburn expert," she said. "I used to inhale the stories when I was a kid, and I still keep an ear out now. The best-known mystery—and the only one that is undeniably true—is the Friday light."

"We all saw it," Marion continued as she helped herself to another scone. "Every Friday, just after sundown, a light was lit in Ashburn's highest room. Because this place is on a hill, it was hard to miss. It looked a bit like a lighthouse."

Adrienne's mind flashed to the phrase carved into the dining table. IS IT FRIDAY LIGHT THE CANDLE. She suddenly felt cold despite the sunshine coming through the windows. "How long did that happen for?"

"Since way before our time." Beth's dark eyes shone as she leaned nearer. "Dad says it's always happened—every Friday—since Miss Ashburn moved into the house. That's how we knew she was dead. Friday came, and the light didn't appear."

"Oh." Adrienne swallowed the unexpected nausea. She hadn't expected to hear about her great-aunt's death so soon.

Jayne glared at Beth again then gave Adrienne a small smile. "I'm so sorry. She's not all that great at tact."

"No, it's okay. I want to know more about Edith." Adrienne took a breath and returned the smile. "Do you know how… uh… how she passed?"

Glances were exchanged. Beth looked desperate to answer, but Jayne stepped in first, speaking carefully. "Well, she hadn't been to town at all that week. It was a bit unusual but not unheard of; sometimes she skipped days if she was feeling unwell, so no one really paid attention. But when the Friday light didn't come on, people started to talk about going up and checking on her. No one really wanted to approach Ashburn at night, so they agreed to wait until morning. Sure enough, she didn't come to town again, so they sent out a search party a bit before lunch." Jayne licked her lips and squeezed her hands together in her lap. "She was…

61

significantly decayed when they found her, so the post-mortem couldn't be completely accurate, but the doctor said it was most likely a seizure or an embolism. He didn't think she suffered."

"Okay." Adrienne felt light-headed. "Uh, when you say significantly decayed—"

"Black ooze leaking ev-er-y-where."

"Beth! *Please!*"

A hysterical laugh was boiling in Adrienne's chest. She pinched the bridge of her nose as she struggled to keep herself collected. "Do you know—I mean, I guess it doesn't really matter—I know it shouldn't—but do you know where—?"

"Sorry." Jayne shook her head. "I don't know which room."

"Okay. That's okay." She inhaled deeply and took her hand away from her face. "It shouldn't really matter. As long as she didn't suffer." She didn't want to think of Edith's corpse slowly oozing black blood across the floor, so she dragged the subject back to slightly safer ground. "So the light was the best-known mystery. You said there were others?"

"Oh, heaps." Beth, unrepentant, spoke around a mouthful of scone. "Kids would sometimes dare each other to go up Ashburn Walk and see how close they could get to the house before chickening out. A lot of them swear they saw a tall figure pacing back and forth, back and forth behind drawn curtains. Some say they heard manic laughter and hysterical screams. And of course, they all reckon the house is haunted. Terry said he was standing at the edge of the woods when he heard someone breathing behind him, but when he turned, there was no one there. And Michael claims he got right up to the porch when a ghostly face appeared in one of the windows then vanished before he could scream. Those could've been made up, though. Kids love to scare each other."

"Not just kids." Jayne glared daggers at her companion.

"I don't think she was a bad person." Marion was clearly trying hard to inject some lightness into the conversation. "A couple of months ago, I was volunteering at the vet's clinic—I can earn extra credits in my course for practical experience—and Miss Ashburn came in carrying a dog she'd found. It'd been hit by a car and had a fractured leg. We were able to fix it up and find its owners, but it probably wouldn't have survived if Edith hadn't brought it to us, so... yeah. I think she liked animals."

"She came into the library every week too," Sarah said. It was the first time the thin-faced woman had spoken since entering the room, and she seemed to have trouble meeting their eyes. "She never really talked, but she always returned her books on time. I'm not supposed to tell you what she borrowed—we've got confidentiality rules—but they were usually classics."

"Which is pretty much the entire extent of the library's collection," Beth said with an eye-roll.

Sarah pursed her lips. "We bought *three* new releases this month. But, um, yeah. We were founded on donated books, which were mostly old ones."

"What was she like?" Adrienne couldn't stop her curiosity. Her mental image of Edith Ashburn was gradually being filled in, like a jigsaw puzzle that became clearer with each piece of information. "She must have been quite old when she passed away."

"Sure was," Beth said. "At least ninety. No one's really sure when she was born, but Dad thinks she was closer to a hundred."

"And she lived alone?" The image of Edith walking the hallways, delirious or deranged as she carved messages into the walls, haunted Adrienne.

"She was *really* independent," Jayne said. "Some people in town went out of their way to be friendly to her, especially as she got older. My mum actually invited her to have dinner with us one night, and Mrs Western tried to give her a basket of groceries a couple of months before she passed. But she always rejected the offers. And not in a *thank you I'm fine* sort of way. She mostly glared at you then walked away."

"Like I said, she didn't really talk much except when ordering groceries." Beth finished her tea and slid the saucer onto the table with a gratified sigh. "It was like she had a finite number of words and didn't want to waste any on you."

"Huh." The mental representation of Edith Ashburn was coalescing into something far less grandmotherly and far more severe than Adrienne had been hoping for. She glanced around at the furniture—rose-pattern chairs, dark timber tables and bookcases, and the antique patterned wallpaper—and tried to imagine the gaunt, tall, cold woman stalking through the house, occasionally pausing to gaze out of the windows or stoke the fire.

Then a new image interjected itself into her mind: Edith, dead, lying on the wood floor, her blank eyes staring at the ceiling and her mouth hanging open as she bloated and decayed and oozed.

Where did she die? Not her bedroom—the mattress was too clean.

Was it the kitchen? The lounge room? Have I stood on the same floorboards that absorbed her rotting flesh?

Adrienne put her teacup onto the table with a decisive clink that made Jayne jump. She didn't want to let the morbid images stew and grow, so she latched onto a change of subject that she thought her companions would enjoy. "Anyone want a tour of the house?"

Beth's delighted gasp was all the answer she needed.

CHAPTER 10
TOURS

THE IDEA OF SHOWING her guests around the house had been spur of the moment. As she led them out of the drawing room and into the dim hallway, Adrienne found herself hoping the choice wasn't disrespectful towards her late great-aunt. Based on what Adrienne knew of her, Edith wouldn't have welcomed tourists perusing her halls as if they were on some novelty tour.

But Ashburn legally belonged to Adrienne. She wanted to strike a balance between being respectful of Edith's memory and feeling comfortable and confident in her own home.

The hallways and stairwells felt so cold and empty last night. Maybe some fresh feet and voices will chase out some of the starkness. I won't show the whole house—and certainly not Edith's bedroom— but some of the downstairs areas and the hallway of paintings should be okay, right?

She began by showing them to the lounge room she'd slept

in, opening the door and stepping back so that they could enter. "This is where I'm living until I can sort out a proper bedroom. Sorry about the mess."

Beth moved into the centre of the room, her eyes darting about as she absorbed the details. "No skulls, but Edith had a stuffed cat. That's pretty cool."

Adrienne followed her friend's gaze towards the top of the bookcase and burst into laughter. "No, sorry, that one's mine."

Wolfgang, crouched in the narrow space between the top of the bookcase and the ceiling, blinked as though to prove he were actually flesh and blood.

"Oooh, he's magnificent." Marion, more interested in the cat than the room, approached Wolfgang and offered him her hand to smell. "He's part Maine Coon, right?"

"He was a stray, so I'm not really sure." Adrienne gave a sheep-ish grin and shrugged. "Mum said he's just fat."

Wolfgang headbutted Marion's hand in a blatant demand for petting. She was happy to oblige and cooed to him while she scratched around his chin and whiskers.

Beth scanned the books lining the lower shelves, and her mouth creased in disappointment. She seemed to have been hoping for volumes on the occult.

"There's a message in the hallway wall and some paintings upstairs," Adrienne said, knowing those things would give the chill factor the black-haired woman sought. She reopened the door and waited for them to file through. Marion reluctantly left her new friend, who gave a languid yawn and flopped onto his side.

Back in the hallway, they all stopped to read the message cut opposite the lounge room: NO MIRRORS. Light came through the open door and improved the contrast between the scratchings and the wood they were carved into. Sarah made a vaguely unhappy noise in the back of her throat, but the others looked enthralled.

"She's written it all over the house." Adrienne rubbed at the back of her neck. "Anywhere a mirror should logically go. I probably look a bit of a mess this morning because of it."

"Naw, you're fine." Beth was bent over with her hands on her knees as she examined the scratches. "We don't normally look this fancy. It's just our stupid club rule this month."

"Oh, you're in a club?"

"Yeah, Jayne arranged it. She reckons we should do something to improve ourselves each month. In March we had to read a book a week. This month, we're supposed to dress like city folk."

That explained the upper-class clothes and hairstyles that were simultaneously glamorous and not quite right. Adrienne suspected they'd been taking their cues from TV shows and movies; almost no one in her old city had dressed as fancily as they did.

"I catch hell for it at the clinic." Marion, grinning, was already turning towards the staircase. "But it's kind of fun too."

Adrienne waited until Beth had had her fill of the scratched message then beckoned them up the stairs. "That reminds me, Jayne—you told me what everyone else does but didn't say what your job was."

Beth lowered her voice to a deep, sinister whisper. "She works for the government."

"Jeez." Pink tinged Jayne's ears again. "Don't listen to Beth. She'd make you believe I'm with Interpol or something. No, I'm just admin for utilities." She shot Adrienne a sideways glance. "By the way, give us a call in the next few weeks to set up your account, okay? I hooked you up with electricity and water, but I didn't know any of your details, so the account's currently under the name Jane Doe, who was born in the eighteen hundreds."

"Utilities…" *Crap, that was something I should have set up before I moved in, right?* "Thank you—I didn't even think—"

The red tinge spread from Jayne's ears to her cheeks, and she waved the thanks away. "It's nothing. I just heard from Bobby that Sam's uncle heard you were moving in this weekend, so I got it connected for you. Nothing worse than trying to live in a place without power or water."

"Thanks." Adrienne was growing increasingly grateful that she'd opened the door when Jayne had knocked. Her first impression had been so wildly off the mark that she'd almost missed out on meeting the ladies.

Friends, the voice in her head insisted, and Adrienne tried not to grin as she led them into the shadowy hallway. "Have a look at these."

Beth whistled as she scanned the row of portraits. "There's a lot of them."

"And all of the same family," Marion said, frowning. "That's kind of weird, isn't it?"

69

Good; I'm glad I'm not the only one who finds it strange.

"Maybe they were narcissists," Jayne said.

Marion moved from one painting to another, squinting to make out the details in the low light. "Still, artwork this good would have been expensive. And the portraits look like they were done over just a handful of years—see the girl? Here she is as a toddler, and here again she looks about eight. But I can't find any of her as a teenager."

Beth's eyes widened as she looked between her friends. "Wait, you don't *know?*"

"Spill it, Beth," Jayne said.

"Guys, this is Miss Ashburn's family." Beth waved a hand at the portraits. "Mr and Mrs Ashburn, Edith Ashburn as a child, and Mr Ashburn's sister-in-law. The only member of the family not in the paintings is Mr Ashburn's brother, Charles."

She paused, palms held outwards and eyes wide, evidently waiting for a wave of amazement that never came.

Jayne looked about them and shrugged. "Okay?"

"Oh my gosh, you're all uncultured swine!" Beth clasped her hands over her face in melodramatic despair. "Are you honestly telling me you've never heard of Charles Ashburn? The famous artist?"

"Oooh, yeah, I think my mum has one of his landscapes in her living room," Marion said. "Are you saying he painted these?"

"Yes! And there's a bunch more just like them hanging in the museum. How can you have not seen them?"

Marion scrunched her face up. "The museum smells like dead rats, and Mr Benson kicks you out if you talk too much."

"Which is a small price to pay to personally view a deeply significant facet of our town's history." She was pacing as she ranted, and Adrienne had to step aside to avoid being bowled over. "Charles Ashburn wasn't just Ipson famous—he was legitimately well known. He painted for a bunch of lords and such and travelled all over the place before he had a mental breakdown." She stopped, breathing heavily, and stretched one hand towards the nearest image, which depicted Edith as a child. "He came back to live with his brother, Mr Ashburn, and began to obsessively paint his family. He completed close to ninety portraits before his death five years later. The museum has a dozen or so; it looks like the rest of them stayed here."

Jayne was shaking her head as she grinned at her friend. "Wow. I knew you liked urban legends about Ashburn, but I had no idea you were so obsessive."

"Dear, sweet Jayne. We've barely entered the rabbit hole yet." Beth clasped her hands and fixed each of her companions with a deep, lingering stare. "Do you know *how* Charles Ashburn passed?"

"I heard the whole family died in a disaster." Sarah, the quietest of the party, spoke for the second time that day. Her eyes were wide as saucers as they flittered over the images surrounding them. "Everyone except Edith Ashburn."

"Glad to see *someone* here knows their history. Can you tell me what the disaster was?"

Sarah's lips fluttered open, and she shot Adrienne a frightened glance before fixing her eyes on the floor. "M-m…"

"Yes?"

"Murder," she whispered.

Prickles ran up Adrienne's arms as she folded them over her chest. The portraits' persistent stares no longer felt benign but desperate. Accusatory.

"That's right." Beth began pacing around the group, her voice low and sinister. "And you want to know the weirdest thing? No one knows who did it. Was it the artist Charles Ashburn, already mentally unstable, pushed past what he could endure? Was it his wife, so meek and quiet? Or possibly Mr or Mrs Ashburn, stressed to fracturing by their brother's disorder? Or"—she held a finger up to bring their attention off the portraits and back onto her—"was it a stranger who broke into the house and murdered them in cold blood? We may never know."

Adrienne tried to smile, but her cheek muscles felt stiff. "Well, surely—there must be a way to know. What did the police investigation say?"

Beth shrugged. "No one actually remembers. This was way before my time, remember. My granddad's dad was just a little kid when it all went down, so anything I can tell you is coming at least fourth-hand. Some people say the family was hacked to death. Others claim it was a gun. Still others believe it wasn't a murder at all but a disease that swept through the area and claimed almost all of the family. All we know is that Edith Ashburn was the only survivor. She went away for a while then came back as an adult and never left Ashburn again."

"Wow." Jayne looked pale. "I heard her family died, but I had no idea—wow. No wonder she was so strange. That sort of thing would mess anyone up." She grimaced and added in a quieter tone, "I should've been kinder to her. We used to have that stupid rhyme we'd chant when she came into town. *Ashburn, Ashburn, burn Ashburn down.* Oh, wow. I hope she never heard us."

"Eh, she was probably senile by then." Beth seemed completely unconcerned with Edith's well-being and turned back to the images. "She would've been a kid when the murder happened. Maybe she didn't remember much."

Marion abruptly swore, and they all jumped. "Sorry," she squeaked and held up her phone with an apologetic smile. "It's just—I didn't realise we'd been here so long. I was supposed to start my shift at the vet ten minutes ago."

"My fault," Jayne said, turning towards the stairs. "I wasn't watching the time. I'm sorry to leave so suddenly, Addy. Thank you for the tea and for showing us around."

"Thanks for coming," Adrienne said and found she meant it. "It was really nice to meet you. Come back sometime… if, uh, if you want."

"That'd be great." They'd reached the front door, and golden sunlight fell over Jayne's silky blonde hair as she opened it. The others piled out towards the car, but she hesitated on the threshold and tilted her head to one side. "Hey, you said you needed to go shopping. Did you want a lift into town? I can show you where Ashburn Walk starts too."

"Yes," Adrienne said, already turning to fetch her bag from the lounge room. "Yes, please, that'd be great!"

Friends.

73

CHAPTER 11
MEMORY TELEPHONE

JAYNE DROPPED MARION OFF outside the vet clinic then showed Adrienne the narrow opening in the edge of the forest that led to Ashburn Walk before driving them into the town's centre.

"I'd offer to take you out for a coffee or something," she said sheepishly, "but I begged Jerry to cover for me at the utilities centre so that I could come and see Ashburn. I really need to get back before the end of my shift, but maybe another time?"

"Yeah, I'd love that." Adrienne unbuckled her seatbelt as Jayne eased the car into an empty parking space. "Give me a call when—oh, wait, I don't know Ashburn's number. I don't suppose you'd have a way to find it?"

Jayne shook her head. "Actually, I'm pretty sure Ashburn doesn't *have* a number. You might want to get a mobile. The coverage up there's probably going to be dodgy, but putting in a landline would cost a small fortune."

"Oh, yeah, definitely." Adrienne had cancelled her mobile rental the month before. She thought of the lone twenty-dollar bill living in her handbag and how many necessities were clamouring for its favour. *A new phone will have to go on the buy-when-I'm-rich list.* "Until then, visit anytime. You're always welcome."

She slipped out of the car and waved as it eased back onto the main street. She waited until Jayne and her companions had turned the corner before looking at her surroundings.

Ipson truly was tiny, she realised as she rotated in a circle and discovered she could see every shop in both directions. *A hairdresser's… the library… a couple of clothing stores… a second-hand store… a petrol station…*

She fixed on the convenience store not far from her drop-off spot. It was a charming, jumbled sort of shop with more stock than floor space. The shelves were stacked high and deep, and crates and pallets were strategically placed along the narrow aisles. The bell above the door rang as Adrienne entered, and she tried not to pay attention as the other shoppers turned to stare at her.

Everyone here must know each other. She picked up a basket from the stack beside the door and tried not to look as self-conscious as she felt. *I must stick out like a peacock in a pigeon display.*

She edged into the closest aisle and tried to make sense of its order. Dusting cloths were stacked next to the biscuits, and a little beyond them sat a crate of fresh apples. *Is it arranged alphabetically or something?*

"Need any help, dear?"

The voice was so unexpected that Adrienne jumped. She

swivelled and tried to smile at the plump woman with steel-grey hair and a chin that dimpled when she smiled. The name tag pinned to her faded blue blouse introduced her as June Thompson, co-manager.

"Yeah, thank you. I'm just looking for your cat food."

June's smile widened, and bunches of wrinkles formed around her eyes. "'Course you are, honey. Just this way."

Adrienne tried not to notice how June kept shooting her furtive glances as she led her into an aisle that held, among other oddities, tinned beetroot, Chinese finger traps, and watering cans. "Right here, sweetheart. We have a couple of brands. Own a cat, do you?"

"A huge one." Adrienne glanced between the bags. They didn't have the brand Wolfgang preferred, so she picked up one and began examining the ingredients list. She was prepared to compromise on a lot of things, but her cat's protein intake wasn't one of them. "He's got the appetite of a lion."

"How sweet. I've got dogs myself." June tapped her manicured nails on the edge of the shelf, a shining example of indifference, then swivelled towards Adrienne and blurted the questions she'd clearly been trying to repress. "You moved into Ashburn House, didn't you? Is it true there's bloodstains all over the walls?"

That set the tone for the rest of her shopping expedition. June, who appeared to be one of the town's biggest gossips, was desperately curious about the house on the hill. For her part, Adrienne was able to glean fresh nuggets of knowledge about her great-aunt. Apparently, Edith had done all of her shopping in that grocery store. "She never went anywhere else," June said proudly. "Not even the hairdresser. I'd guess her hair must have been down to her thighs at least, but she always bundled it up on top of her head, so it's hard to know."

"Did you talk to her much?" Adrienne asked while trying to calculate how many cups of instant noodles would push her over her budget.

"Ooh, no, not at all." June's expression fell, and she shook her head sadly, her grey perm swishing with the motion. "Not for want of trying, I promise you. She never talked to anyone except to complain if we didn't have the papers in yet. She bought the paper every day, you see. The rest of her shopping seemed to be on whims—some days she'd get vegetables, other days biscuits, or sometimes just a carton of eggs—but she always, without fail, bought the paper."

Adrienne poked around the story of the Ashburn family's deaths as discreetly as she could but was disappointed to find June knew even less about it than Beth.

"That must've been close to a hundred years back, sweetheart." They were checking out by that point, June scanning the items at a glacial speed to prolong the conversation. "I heard there was a big police investigation, but I don't think anyone went to jail over it. I don't know of anyone who remembers the story now. It's like that game the kids play—telephone, I think it's called. One person tells their friend the story, maybe embellishes a tiny bit or forgets some details. That friend then passes their own version on to someone else, and so on, until it's thoroughly garbled. By this point, anything you hear is probably going to be just as much myth as fact."

Adrienne was pausing to admire how insightful this was when June leaned closer, the back of one hand pressed beside her mouth, and stage whispered, "Though if you're curious, I'm partial to Stephen's version where the Ashburns had a second child they kept locked in the attic, and the little darling went insane and killed them in their sleep."

"Oh, wow." Adrienne tried to think of an appropriate way to respond to that. "Uh… wow. That sounds awful."

"Sure does. Twenty-one ninety-three. Thanks, honey."

Adrienne froze as she heard the total, her twenty-dollar note already held towards the checkout. Heat flooded her face. "Oh, uh, better take a couple of the noodles off—"

"Never mind that." June took the money with a grandmotherly smile and pushed the paper bags towards Adrienne. "Welcome to Ipson, honey. I hope you like it here."

I think I will. Spouting awkward thanks, Adrienne took her bags and backed out of the store. The bell jingled at her exit, and once again, glances were shot her way. She knew many of the shoppers had followed her and June around the store, staying an aisle over or lingering a few feet behind, and listened in on the conversation. But the attention didn't feel as unwelcome as Adrienne would have expected it to. It wasn't hostile, and she wasn't being excluded from the tiny community. Instead, she felt sucked into its embrace.

Keeping that happy thought at the front of her mind, Adrienne made a point of nodding and smiling at anyone who made eye contact with her on the walk towards the woods. Most smiled in return, and a few greeted her. Only a couple—mostly wide-eyed children—gawked.

The main street was short, and there was only a brief row of residential properties between it and where the mountainside collided with the flats. She followed Jayne's directions for locating Ashburn Walk—just beyond the blue house with the tyre swing in the front yard—and was soon stepping into the trees' shadows.

The dirt path was narrow. It looked as though it didn't have any regular maintenance but was kept clear of grass and plants simply by virtue of being used twice each day. It took a few twists around large trunks but was mostly straight. *As the crow flies,* Jayne had said. Sure enough, in the infrequent moments when the trees thinned enough for her to see through their boughs, Ashburn always loomed ahead. Only the roof was visible, but the dark wood and its remaining flecks of grey-white paint were impossible to overlook. Ashburn had a presence, she realised, which had probably helped cement its identity as a local fascination. It didn't just look like a house but like a living entity crouched on the hill, glowering over the occupants below.

She shook herself free of the thought and increased her pace. The incline was steep enough to make her breathing laboured but not so bad that she needed a break. She thought it would be easier if her baggage weren't so heavy. Edith's daily walk into town might be a habit she should adopt; that way she would only need to buy what she planned to eat that day.

The path took a sharp turn around a tree, and Adrienne found herself facing a row of zigzagging steps leading up a nearly vertical incline. The stairs were lined with stones but uneven and narrow enough that she had to watch her feet as she ascended. She was thoroughly winded by the time she reached the top of the cliff and returned to following the gentler pathway.

Edith must have been fit to take those stairs every day. Maybe the cardio workout helped prolong her life.

The trees had grown darker and spindlier. When she looked over her shoulder, she could still see the lush emerald greens that grew near the town. It was a striking contrast to the dark-grey woods surrounding her.

The path took one final bend, and Adrienne found herself facing Ashburn House. She hadn't expected to reach it so soon. Jayne's estimation had been right; even at a leisurely pace, the walk hadn't taken much more than fifteen minutes.

When she bumped the front door open, she found two glimmering green eyes in her path. Her heart lurched unpleasantly, then the eyes blinked, and Adrienne laughed as she slumped against the wall. She'd accidentally left the living room door open, and Wolfgang had emerged from his sanctuary.

"Well, I guess you were about ready to see more of Ashburn, anyway," she said as she nudged the front door closed with her foot. "Don't worry—I got more food. Not that you need it, tubbo." She bent to give his ears a friendly scratch then turned toward the kitchen to unpack her haul.

CHAPTER 12
SANCTUARY

NEARLY HALF OF ADRIENNE'S twenty dollars had gone to cat food. She didn't know how soon she was likely to be paid, but it would be less painful to go hungry herself than to see Wolfgang sitting by an empty food bowl.

She'd spent the rest as frugally as she could: six cups of instant noodles, thanks to a buy-two-get-one-free special, plus a bag of rice and a packet of lentils for protein. The cupboard looked less pitiful than it had, but it hardly held a stockpile. Adrienne sighed and returned to the lounge room. She'd sent an invoice reminder to both of her outstanding accounts just two days before, but things were dire enough that she was prepared to dip into aggressive territory and send another.

She sat on the lounge chair, which was still covered in blankets from the night before, and opened her laptop. An angry red "no Wi-Fi" emblem appeared in the toolbar.

"Oh, crap." Adrienne opened the settings. Her laptop was supposed to be its own mobile hotspot, but the unhelpful diagnosis tool told her there wasn't coverage in her area and to call support if she needed additional help.

She snapped the laptop closed, glowered at the cold fireplace opposite, then slid off the chair and returned to the hallway. The Wi-Fi would have a greater chance of working in town, but she was tired and hungry from the walk, and she didn't want to have to retrace her steps so soon. *Besides, sundown is only a few hours away. I should try to figure out a bedroom; I'd rather not sleep on the lounge chair again if I can help it.*

Adrienne fetched herself a cup of instant noodles. Wolfgang followed her into the kitchen, and she watched him nose about the dusty corners as she waited for the kettle to boil and poured the water into the Styrofoam cup. She considered sitting at the head of the table—it was closest to the benches and faced the window—but felt uneasy about occupying Edith's seat. Instead, Adrienne sunk into the chair at the table's side.

IS IT FRIDAY

LIGHT THE CANDLE

She tried not to read the phrase carved into the tabletop, but her eyes wandered back to it anytime she wasn't consciously focussing elsewhere.

I could sandpaper them out if they were shallow, but some of those scratches look too deep. Maybe I could cover them with a tablecloth… when I can afford one. Unless—

She put her fork down and crossed to the drawers she'd looked through when searching for cups the day before. Adrienne gave a small hum of triumph when she found the cloths stacked neatly in the cupboard beside the fridge. She took the top one out and flipped it open. Age had sapped away its sharp white hue, and it was too long to fit the table properly, but Adrienne still draped it over the wood.

It's a shame to cover furniture this nice, but I don't think I can live with that phrase staring at me every time I want to eat.

"Better, right?" she asked Wolfgang. He'd risen up on his back legs to sniff at a stain on the wall and turned to give her a dispassionate stare when she spoke to him.

Adrienne finished her lunch, washed the fork, and returned to the hallway. The sun was already edging close to the treetops, and she wanted to find somewhere to sleep before it became so dark that she needed the lamp.

As she climbed the stairs, Adrienne ran through the possibilities. She was certain she didn't want to move into Edith's room. She'd given it some thought during the walk back from town and had decided it would be best to leave the space untouched as a sort of memorial to the strange, controversial great-aunt she'd never known. She was only one person living in a huge house, after all; it wasn't as though space was in short supply.

But would there be any other bedrooms? If the townspeople's reports were accurate, Edith had never allowed guests into her home, which reduced the chance of a guest bedroom to almost nil.

However, there was a chance that Edith had preserved one or more of her deceased family's bedchambers. If she had, that would create a new dilemma. The family had been killed. She didn't know how, where, and by whom, but Adrienne had to face the possibility that they'd died in their beds. Could she sleep on a mattress where another person had been murdered?

She'd reached the top of the stairs and began opening doors under the paintings' watchful eyes. She'd already looked into several of the rooms when looking for the shower but checked again just to be certain. Storage room, storage room, Edith's bedroom, the office—which looked glorious with the heavy golden late-afternoon light streaming over the desk—the bathroom, empty room, empty room.

Only one door remained at the end of the hallway, next to the flight of stairs that led to the attic. Adrienne expected another empty space and was shocked by what she found when she looked inside: a clean and unexpectedly modern bedroom. Unlike the rest of the building, the walls were covered in eggwhite paint rather than wallpaper. A plush, clean rug filled the centre of the room, and a single bed with a blue-and-purple bedspread sat below the window.

"Wow." Adrienne stepped farther into the room and blinked at the empty bookcase and wardrobe. A bureau was propped against one wall, and although it didn't have a mirror, there were no scratches on the wall behind it. Only a fine layer of dust lay over the surfaces, which meant they must have been cleaned not long before Edith's death. She had found the guest room she'd convinced herself wouldn't exist.

Most mind-boggling was how modern the furniture seemed.

Everything else in Ashburn was vintage, possibly dating to as far back as when Edith's parents had occupied the house. But the bedspread was a modern cotton blend, the desk looked expensive but streamlined, and the rug had a pattern that couldn't have been more than a decade old.

A surreal sensation washed over Adrienne. She felt as though she'd stepped into a different world as she floated about the room, examining the fixtures and trying to tell herself it was too good to be true.

A white square stood out against the pillowcase, and Adrienne approached it. The shape turned out to be a piece of paper that had been scrawled on with a shaky but elegant hand. Her heart gave an uncomfortable lurch as she read the brief note.

Adrienne,

I hope you like your room.

Aunt Edith

CHAPTER 13
CANDLES

AS ADRIENNE REREAD THE note, her shock began to morph into an overpowering, almost painful emotion. She pressed a hand over her mouth and blinked at the wetness in her eyes.

She'd grown to believe Edith had left her Ashburn on a whim or to keep the house from falling into the possession of someone she didn't like. Adrienne had thought that Edith hadn't cared about her beyond dropping her name into her will. But the note proved otherwise.

It meant the decision to give Adrienne the house had been deliberate and premeditated. More than that, Edith had anticipated Adrienne's sleeping dilemma and had prepared a bedroom for her—a room she must have dusted and aired frequently over many years to ensure it would be ready for Adrienne's eventual arrival.

The cold, hostile visage in her mind morphed once more. The severe face shifted to something softer and gentler, and the glittering eyes became warm. Her imaginary Edith smiled, and Adrienne wiped her tears away as she smiled back.

I don't care what the townspeople say about her. Edith was kind. She cared about me. And I love her for it.

She rubbed her thumbs over the short note. Even the fact that it had been signed "Aunt Edith" felt significant. She hoped she wasn't reading too much into it by imagining that Edith had wanted to be a surrogate grandmother to her as much as Adrienne had wanted to have one.

"Thank you," she whispered and propped the note upright on the bureau in place of where the mirror would normally stand. She wanted to remember this kindness.

The window above the bed was large and cleaner than most of the other panes. She crossed to the glass and looked out to see the dark woods that grew near the house. Ashburn had been built at the top of a hill, and the woods sloped downwards for a distance before they rose into the mountain beyond to tower high above the house. Subdued nature sounds filtered through the glass, and Adrienne undid the latch and cracked open the window to let some fresh air in.

Her heart felt full. The sleeping situation had been resolved better than she could have ever hoped. Edith's generosity and forethought meant she not only had a bed but blankets and furniture to go with it.

A sudden desire to see the rest of the house rushed through her. She had a small hope that Edith might have left her more messages. She hadn't seen any loose sheets of paper downstairs or in the other rooms on the second floor, but there might still be something in the highest level of the house—the attic.

She gave her room a final, grateful look before slipping back into the hallway. The stairs rose immediately to her right, but only fifteen steps were visible before they followed the house's corner and turned out of sight. Once again, there didn't seem to be any light switches, but the sun had only just begun to set, and Adrienne thought she could make the trip without needing the lamp.

She jogged up the stairs, one hand pressed to the wallpaper to keep herself stable, and tried not to pay attention to how the house groaned as though her footfalls were almost too much for it to bear. It was a solid building. There weren't any signs of rot or strained supports; the wood was just old and liked to complain.

She turned the corner and found her path flooded with shadows as the natural light from below struggled to refract up the stairwell. She could barely make out a door above her, and it was unlike any other door she'd seen in the house.

Most of Ashburn's fixtures fit their environment: classic, tasteful—though dated—and usually made of deep-mahogany wood paired with light fabrics and rose patterns.

The door she stood in front of had been stained until it was nearly black. It was oversized, taking up the entire width and breadth of the hallway, and Edith had scrawled a new message into its front.

The scratches were more erratic, bordering on frantic, and Adrienne had to climb until she was only a few steps away to make out the words in the gloom.

LIGHT THE CANDLE

YOUR FAMILY
IS STILL
DEAD

She licked her lips, reached for the weighty bronze doorknob, and turned it.

The room seemed to exhale as she opened the door, and a cold breeze buffeted her hair away from her face. The surreal sensation returned. Save for a faint red glow, the room was dark.

Did the sun set so quickly?

The expedition no longer felt exciting. Part of her wanted to run down the stairs, back to where logic and light and warm feelings lived, but she remained rooted to the highest step. Déjà vu crashed over her. The space, although dim enough to blind her, felt familiar; something about the scent, the weight of the air, and the feel of the wood underneath her feet called her back to a moment in her childhood. She tried to fix on the memory, but it slipped away from her as she attempted to catch it.

She blinked, and the moment was gone. It was just the attic, the final unseen room in the house and the most notorious. The townsfolk had seen a light shining there every Friday, acting as a beacon for unknown reasons.

Adrienne stepped over the threshold, hoping her heartbeat wasn't as loud as it felt. Her palms were sweaty, and she clenched them as she blinked at the red-tinted room.

The attic was large, not quite as big as the house's footprint but certainly more spacious than any of the rooms below. Adrienne looked towards the nearest wall and found the reason for the low light. The sun hadn't set after all but had been blocked out by black curtains nailed over the windows. They didn't completely block out the sunset but muted it and darkened it so that a surreal red tinge was thrown across the room's contents.

Adrienne crossed to the nearest window. The cloth had been fixed at its top, but nothing secured the base. She flipped it up, coughing as dust swirled around her face, and managed to catch the lower edge of the curtain on the nails. Brilliant, sharp light cut through the gloom, and she stepped back to see the space.

Close to three dozen crates were stacked around the perimeter. Near the middle of the room was a strange, shiny, chest-high shape, and beyond that, in the exact centre, was a table.

Adrienne's breaths were shallow as she approached the table. Two items waited on its age-stained crochet cloth: a framed photograph and a box of matches.

She turned to get a closer look at the shape between the chair and the table. It was bubbly and odd, like a sculpture gone awry, and had a vicious metal spike sticking out of its top. Adrienne bent closer to squint at it and exhaled a long "Ooh" as she realised what it was: a candleholder.

The stand rose a little higher than the table, the exposed spike waiting for a candle to be impaled on it. What had confused her was a pale, shiny substance flowing from the spike to the floor. When she was close enough to see the individual frozen globules, she realised it was old, melted wax—not from one candle but from hundreds of them; a lifetime of candles all allowed to melt over their holder until the wax stalactites and stalagmites met and it formed a solid mass.

She was looking at the result of Ipson's best-known legend.

IS IT FRIDAY

LIGHT THE CANDLE

Edith had nailed black drapes over the windows to hide her flame, but they hadn't been enough to mask the glow at night. If the curtains had been thin enough to let the sunset in, they were thin enough to let candlelight out.

Adrienne turned back to the table and bent forward, hands on knees, to see the photo more clearly. It was immediately recognisable; she was looking at the same girl who had been recreated repeatedly in the portraits lining the hallway below. The picture showed the girl walking through a garden that towered over her, one hand extended towards a bloom. Her body was angled away from the camera, but her head had turned to see it, and the round eyes and barely parted lips suggested the photo was a surprise.

She was a pretty child. Adrienne smiled at the photo of her great-aunt. The picture was grainy black and white, as was normal for photos from the turn of the century, but it seemed to capture her personality well. Her thick, dark hair cascaded down her back until it brushed her waist, and she wore a pretty striped dress with a plush bow tied around its middle. Her wide eyes and round face hinted at a mix of innocence and mischief, and Adrienne thought she looked like a lively child.

The photo must have been cherished. The frame was ornate and well made and looked heavy. *Pictures taken back then were expensive, weren't they? Edith's family must have been wealthy to risk a candid shot.*

She stood again and scanned the room. The light was failing

quickly, dipping her into near black, but she still wanted to understand the crates stacked about the room. She crossed to the nearest one and found the lid had already been cracked off. She lifted it, hoping she wouldn't collect too many splinters from the rough wood, and squinted inside.

Candles. Dozens of them. Thick and round, they'd been packed amongst wood shavings for protection. Adrienne pulled one out and turned it in her hand. It was unlabelled but looked expensive and was weighty enough to feel like a brick in her hand. She turned back to the candleholder and thought the shades of wax matched.

She carefully placed the candle back in its box and scanned the room. There were dozens of crates, all identical to the one she'd just opened. She crossed to another box and nudged its lid off, just in case, and wasn't surprised to find more candles.

There must be thousands of them. A lifetime of candles. No, more—generations worth of candles. What an odd investment. Even odder that she burnt one every week, and only one—and with no apparent purpose except to illuminate her own photo.

Shivers ran up Adrienne's back. Something had been creeping up on her, but she hadn't even known it was happening until she held her breath and realised how perfectly, completely silent the world felt.

It's like last night. She approached the window slowly, cautiously, her breath held. The sun was seconds away from setting, and the moon and a thousand pinpricks of starlight illuminated the woods outside her house.

She rested her fingertips on the sill and bent closer. Her breath created a small puff of condensation on the glass as she examined the world below. The window faced the town, and house lights created a glowing map of the settlement. The walk had only taken her fifteen minutes, but the village seemed an insurmountable distance from her vantage point.

She tried to swallow, but her mouth was dry. The silence was pressing against her, squeezing her, making her feel feverish. The world was waiting for something, and every second that passed built the tension to overwhelming heights.

Then it happened. Whatever had been building up released, like opening a floodgate, and the silence was shattered as a flurry of birds poured out of the treetops, their screams and beating wings a cacophony. Mixed amongst the shrieks was a screeching that only lasted a second before cutting off abruptly. Adrienne squeezed her eyes closed and waited for the sounds to fade.

Just like last night. What is it? Do the townspeople feel it? Will they know what I'm talking about if I ask them, or will they think I'm crazy?

The flutters and bird calls died away, and the woods were returned to peaceful rest. Adrienne stayed at the window and watched the trees and the town for a long time. The glass did a poor job of insulating against the outside air, and she was shivering when she turned back to the room.

It was too dark to see anything except faint outlines in the moonlight. She briefly considered taking one of the candles to guide her climb downstairs but chose to risk a blind descent.

She still wasn't sure what the attic's purpose had been, but she didn't want to light a single one of its candles.

CHAPTER 14
MISSING LAST NIGHT

THE WOODEN BOARDS WERE gone, clawed through, and her scabbed fingers dug into rich, tightly packed dirt. Her mouth was open, but there was no air left to drag into her starved lungs. The soil was crushing her, suffocating her, filling every crevice around her. It got under her eyelids and filled her mouth and made each twitch of her fingertips a battle. But she kept digging, scratching, clawing, fighting for every inch she gained. She could be patient. The dirt would not last forever.

A loud beating noise pulled Adrienne out of her dream. She started upright and inhaled. She'd been holding her breath as she slept, and a wave of dizziness made her grimace as she waited for the room to steady itself.

What happened? Images of digging through heavy soil flashed through her mind, and she shook her head in an attempt to flick the memory out of it.

She was in the bedroom Edith had prepared for her. The travel case sat in the wardrobe, and the laptop was already set up on the desk. It had been a battle to carry the case up the stairs the night before, holding the lantern in one hand and muttering choice swear words as she navigated the bend.

The events in the attic had unsettled her, and she'd wanted to keep Wolfgang with her that night, but her fluffy monster seemed determined to roam during the witching hours and had refused to be picked up.

The beating noise came again, and Adrienne realised someone was knocking at the front door. She scrambled out of bed and tugged some jeans and a jacket over her pyjamas. *Jeez, I must've overslept. What time is it?*

A glance at the window made her blink in surprise. *Okay, so I didn't oversleep. Maybe this town just wakes up super early.*

The sun had risen but not by much. Wispy, smoggy clouds dimmed what should have been a brilliant sunrise into a faint, apathetic glow. When she leaned close to the glass, Adrienne could see heavy mist gathered about the yard and drifting between the trees' trunks. Amid that was the silvery glint of a familiar sedan. *Jayne?*

The knocks came again, this time beating louder and maintained for longer. Adrienne dashed out of the room, through the hallway of portraits, and jogged down the stairs. "Coming! I'm coming!"

When I told her to drop by anytime, I didn't expect her to take it so literally. Maybe she wants to have breakfast.

Adrienne was breathless by the time she reached the door. Her hair was a disaster, she knew, but there wasn't much she could do for it except run her fingers through it and flip it over her shoulder. She opened the door and grinned at the lady waiting on the porch. "Hey, good morning!"

Her smile faltered. Jayne stood back, out of reach, and had her arms folded across her torso. Her face looked sickly and flat without any makeup, and her glossy hair was mussed from having fingers dragged through it too many times. Her expression held none of the warmth she'd shown the day before but a cold mixture of aggression and fear as she eyed Adrienne. "Is Marion here?"

"Huh? No—uh—" Shock robbed Adrienne of coherency. Underneath the glare, Jayne's eyelids were red and puffy, and dark shadows under them suggested she'd missed sleep. Adrienne took a step closer and extended a hand towards her friend, but Jayne flinched backwards, and her expression hardened. Something glinted in the hand she'd tucked under her other arm. *A knife?*

Adrienne licked her lips. She was still foggy from sleep, but warning bells were starting to ring. "Why did you ask if Marion was here? Has something happened?"

Jayne neither answered the questions nor took her eyes off Adrienne. The silence stretched until it was almost uncomfortable, then she spoke, her tone level and slow, as though she'd chosen the words carefully. "Did Marion come here last night? Have you seen her since yesterday morning?"

"No." The sense of wrongness was growing into hot anxiety. "Not since you dropped her off at work yesterday. Jayne, what's happened?"

The other woman was silent for another moment, then the hard, hostile expression cracked. She dropped her arms, and her face scrunched up as she fought against tears. "She's missing—she said she was going to visit here after work—never came home—"

"What?" Adrienne stepped onto the porch, and this time Jayne didn't flinch away. A glimmer of silver flashed as Jayne pocketed the knife, then the other woman pressed her palms into her eyes.

"I'm sorry, Addy—I just—I don't know what to think—I don't know what to do—"

"Okay. It's okay." Adrienne fought to keep her own fear out of her voice as she put her arm around Jayne's shoulders and patted at her back. "Did she say why she was coming here?"

"Yeah." A drop hung from the end of Jayne's nose, but she didn't wipe it. "She felt bad that you didn't have food and was going to bring you some stuff. Jams she'd made and tinned vegetables and things."

Adrienne scanned the misty yard as she tried to think. The early-morning bird chatter felt subdued to match the muted sun, and the frosty air was burning at her lungs. "Do you know what time she came here?"

"Around seven last night. Not long after her shift finished."

"Have you spoken to her parents?" Adrienne cleared her throat as she realised how little she knew about the veterinary student. "Sorry, uh, does she have parents?"

Jayne raised her head and rubbed the wet circles away from her eyes. She looked ghastly. "Yeah. I didn't know she was missing until they called me at two in the morning. They thought she must have been with me. I've phoned Sarah and Beth and her boss, but no one's seen her since she left work. This isn't like her—she's one of the most reliable people I know."

Crap. "Have you called the police?"

Jayne shook her head.

"You need to call them. Now. I, uh, I don't have a phone. Do you?"

"Yeah." Jayne was already pulling a mobile out of her pocket. She looked at the screen and swore. "No signal. Hang on, one bar—let me try—"

Adrienne pulled the front door closed so that Wolfgang couldn't escape and followed Jayne into the yard as the other woman searched for reception. Frost crunched under her sneakers, and the fog dotted her skin with tiny droplets as she waded through it. The air was intensely cold, and even with the extra layer of pyjamas under her clothes, she began to shake.

Jayne looped across the yard, phone held above her head, as the single bar appeared and disappeared. They were moving towards the front of the driveway. Jayne's car faced the exit, and the driver's door stood open, waiting for its owner to dive inside to make a quick escape.

She brought a knife and was prepared to bolt. What, did she think I murdered Marion or something? Adrienne twisted to see the house's outline, dark and bleak, stretched high above them, and swallowed. *Maybe she did. A stranger moves into the creepy house at the edge of town. Your friend goes to visit and never comes back. It's like the start of a B-grade horror movie.*

Adrienne turned back to the driveway and stopped. A pair of tyre tracks led from the dirt drive to the edge of the forest. They were barely visible in the fog, but Adrienne didn't think they'd been there before.

A horrible, panicky premonition struck her. "Jayne? What time does the sun set around here?"

"Huh?" Jayne had stopped beside her car and was still squinting at her phone. "A bit after seven, I think. Why?"

Marion left work at seven. Sunset comes a little after that. And just after sunset, I watched the birds burst out of the trees and heard a strange screeching noise...

Adrienne ran towards the forest, following the tyre tracks, her heart thundering in her throat and nausea rising in her stomach. Mist billowed around branches that had been snapped in half and trunks that had been scraped. Adrienne followed the path of destruction downhill for close to twenty metres, scrambling and slipping through the fallen leaves, before she saw the faint outline of a compact blue car submerged in the fog.

CHAPTER 15
SEARCH

THE CAR'S HEADLIGHTS WERE still on. They sent twin beams around the tree the vehicle had crashed into, and acted like spotlights through the swirling fog. It would have been beautiful if the implication weren't so horrifying.

Adrienne struggled to breathe. She slowed her descent as she neared the car, grabbing at the trunks to steady herself. The voice in the back of her mind was yelling that she should stay away, that she could be tampering with a crime scene, but the car's door was hanging open, and Marion could still be inside. Adrienne couldn't leave her there. What if she was in pain or—

Some kind of ground-bound bird shot out of its hiding place in the weedy grass and crashed through the underbrush with a cackling, indignant cry. It startled Adrienne so badly that she stumbled, overbalanced, and hit the forest floor. She grunted, tried to roll into a sitting position, and slipped farther down the damp slope until she came to a stop beside the open car door.

The driver's seat was empty. She began to breathe again.

"Adrienne? Addy?" Jayne was still at the top of the hill. Adrienne could see her coral-blue jacket between the trees.

"Did you call the police?" Her voice was muffled by the mist, but it still seemed too loud for the reverential hush surrounding them.

"No. Can't get through."

"Keep trying. I found her car."

"What? Is she hurt?" Jayne began racing down the slope, crashing through the same trees and bushes Adrienne had plunged through a moment before.

Adrienne rolled onto her knees then gained her feet. The area where the car had crashed was mostly flat, but the wet leaves were still treacherous, and she supported herself on the door as she looked in at the driver's seat.

The keys dangled from the ignition, and the internal lights were on, though Adrienne suspected the battery would be close to dead. A covered basket rested on the passenger seat. Adrienne scanned the headrest, seat, and windshield for any signs that her friend had been injured but couldn't see anything out of the ordinary. Then she caught the dull glisten of dried blood on the steering wheel. There wasn't much, but its presence tightened her stomach.

She drew back a little to see the front of the car. The bonnet had crumpled where it had hit the tree but not as badly as in some of the crashes she'd seen on the news. The force had evidently been enough to injure Marion—possibly a broken nose or a scabbed forehead where she'd jerked into the steering wheel—but the windshield was intact, and the airbags hadn't deployed.

Jayne skidded to a halt beside her and leaned through the doorway to examine the scene. Her breathing was ragged as she first locked onto the blood then peered around the front seats to check the back. "We need to look for her."

"Yeah." Adrienne turned to scan the woods around them. "She might have tried to climb up to the house. Or she could have stumbled downhill if she was disoriented... which is kind of likely. We're close enough to the house that I would have heard the car horn or loud yells, but she didn't make a peep."

"I'll go uphill," Jayne said, already turning to begin the climb. "You search downhill. Call if you find anything."

"Okay." Adrienne wrapped her arms around herself. She wished she'd had time to get a warmer jacket, but she wasn't about to go back for one. If Marion were still in the woods, every minute she remained outside increased the risk of hypothermia. So Adrienne set her teeth, huffed in a frosty breath, and rounded the tree.

The headlights blinded her as she stepped into their beams, and she had to feel her way through the trees for the first few paces. That part of the woods was largely made up of tall, thin-trunked saplings and scrubby grass, though she still caught glimpses of the occasional collapsed forest giant. The mist wasn't clearing as she'd hoped it would, and it made her exposed skin sticky and damp.

"Marion!" Jayne's voice floated to her, sounding almost like a wraith amongst the trees.

Following her friend's lead, Adrienne inhaled deeply and called, "Marion!"

She held still, listening, but nothing reached her except erratic, muffled drips and irritated bird chatter.

If I'd just been in a car crash, and it were pitch-black, which direction would I walk in? She turned in a circle, scanning the bushes and trunks surrounding the car, hoping the other woman might have huddled close to the accident. The fog played tricks on her, turning rocks and fallen trunks into humanoid shapes. She tried to remember what Marion had been wearing the day before. She thought it had been orange; that would make her easier to see, unless, of course, Marion had changed after her shift at the vet.

"Marion!"

Please be okay. Adrienne swallowed the lump in her throat and began following the car's headlights. She was working off the idea that a disoriented and lost person would follow the course of least resistance, which was directly downhill. She zigzagged her path as she descended to cover as much ground as possible, peering into hollows and around shrubs and staying alert for any freshly broken branches or crushed grass that would suggest a human had tumbled through them.

"Marion!"

What happens if we can't find her? It would take fifteen minutes for Jayne to drive to town, at least twenty or thirty minutes to muster a search team, and fifteen minutes to come back. That's a long time when the temperature's this low. But is it less of a gamble than what we're doing now?

"Marion!"

A shape caught Adrienne's notice, and she hurried forward, hope blooming through her, only to be disappointed as the mist cleared to reveal it was a stone. She scrunched her face as panic, which had been growing slowly in the background, rose to the surface.

What if she's dead? She only came here because you said you were low on food. You even heard her car go off the road but didn't recognise what it was. If she's dead... it's probably your fault.

"Marion!" Her voice was hoarse and sounded dulled by the mist. She was shaking, and not just from the cold. "Marion!"

She dropped her gaze and saw she'd stumbled onto a little dirt path that snaked through the trees. The scuffed impression of a sneaker lay just past where she stood.

Adrienne frowned and bent low to examine it. The mark was smaller than her own foot, and she doubted Edith had ever worn sneakers.

It could be a child's. Jayne said they sometimes came through the forest as a dare. She raised her eyes in the direction the footprint pointed and saw another just ahead of it. *Or it could be Marion's.*

"Jayne?" No one answered. She'd come farther than she'd thought; even the car lights had faded from view.

Adrienne squeezed her lips together. The footprint was a poor clue but the only one she had, so she followed it, doubling over while she jogged so that she could see the erratic prints. She kept her own feet clear of the marks, knowing that they might be needed for evidence—*Please, please don't let it come to that*—as she followed the dirt trail through the woods.

The path was leading upwards in a slow, meandering course. It seemed to have been designed as a hiking trail rather than a direct route of access to anywhere, and Adrienne struggled to keep track of her location relative to the house. She suspected the building was about a kilometre to her right, higher on the hill, but wasn't certain she could find it if she needed to. The hill was half joined to the mountain behind it, and it would be very easy to climb the wrong slope and end up lost in the deep forest.

Even though it wove and looped erratically, the trail seemed to be curving to the right. It was badly overgrown, and more than once, Adrienne thought she'd lost the footprints before finding them again several metres farther on. The trees were changing. They'd been tall and thin around the crash site but were growing bigger, darker, and uglier the farther she walked. Trunks that had once been straight were gnarled and full of whorls and jagged branches, and although the boughs had fewer leaves, the larger sizes made them more efficient at blocking out the sun. The mist took on a luminescent glow in the few beams of anaemic light that made it through.

Adrienne was so focussed on tracking the footprints that she didn't notice the path was opening up until she was no longer hemmed in by thick trunks. She stopped and straightened, breathing in raw, panting gasps.

She'd arrived in a small, unkempt clearing. The trees grew tightly around its ragged perimeter, creating a natural wall, but the clearing itself was free of plant life; all that existed inside it was a layer of dead leaves and a strange, hulking shape in the centre.

That's not... it can't be...

Only the silhouette was visible through the mist, but the outline was strongly reminiscent of a gravestone. It rose out of the ground to waist height before curving into a rounded top and cast a long shadow ahead of itself. Adrienne, hugging her chest tightly and holding her breath, crept closer.

The mist swirled around her legs, creating little vortexes and eddies as she pushed through it. As she drew closer to the shape, she began to make out the headstone's terrible details, the little chips along its top, the stone's rough texture, and the words carved into its front.

But that was nothing compared to the nauseating squeeze of terror she felt as she saw the woman lying in the tombstone's shadow like a corpse put to rest six feet higher than it should have been.

"Marion," she breathed. The word escaped in a small plume of mist.

The lanky brunette was curled on her side, head turned so that her open eyes could stare at the trees above her. Long hair fanned around her face, which was a ghastly, waxy white save for a smudge of dried blood at her hairline.

She'd dug herself a little indent in the grave. Rich, dark dirt was scattered over the leaves surrounding her, and her fingers were blackened with grime.

Adrienne clamped her hands over her mouth, fighting against a scream that she couldn't completely contain. It came out as a gurgling wail, catching in her raw throat and echoing in her ears.

No, no, not Marion; she can't be dead, please, she can't—

The body twitched, and Marion drew in a single slow, rattling breath.

Adrienne was at her side in a heartbeat. She took the other woman's hand, not caring about the grave's dirt caking it, and rubbed at the fingers. "Marion? Can you hear me?"

The eyes stayed wide and blankly staring. The skin was waxen, and the hand Adrienne held was ice cold. She looked like a corpse.

Please no, come on, breathe again, please—

Adrienne lowered her ear to Marion's chest. She thought she could hear a heartbeat, but it was faint. She dropped the hand and struggled out of her jacket then wrapped it around Marion's torso as well as she could. "Hang on. You're going to be fine. We'll get you back to the house. Just hang on."

"Addy?"

Adrienne turned. Jayne, shivering and pale, stood in a gap in the trees.

CHAPTER 16
CLEAN-UP

ADRIENNE FELT AS THOUGH she were moving through a dream as she closed Ashburn's door. She held a basket in hands that were still smeared with the dirt from Marion's fingers. The peace that had fallen over the house felt entirely incongruous with the previous hours.

The clearing had turned out to be only a few hundred metres from Ashburn. It had been so near, in fact, that Jayne had heard Adrienne's scream from where she'd been searching the brush on the other side of the house. That had been a mercy; Adrienne didn't think she could have carried Marion on her own even if she'd known which direction to take.

They'd had a brief debate when they reached the yard. Adrienne wanted to bring Marion into the house, where she could light a fire while Jayne went for help, but Jayne said it would be safer to take Marion directly to town. Ipson had a doctor's practice but was too small for any kind of hospital or ambulance service. Jayne said her friend would need to be taken to hospital in the next town by car, and the sooner she started the drive, the better.

In the end, Adrienne bowed to Jayne's judgement and helped load Marion into the car. The brunette's eyes fell closed, but she was breathing evenly at least, and Jayne promised to put the heater up as high as it would go. Adrienne had then stood back and watched as the car disappeared down the driveway in a swirl of mist.

She couldn't help but feel that Jayne would have brought Marion inside if the house had been any other than Ashburn.

Adrienne had waited at the head of the driveway for a long time just in case the car returned, but it didn't. She'd turned to enter the house but couldn't get the abandoned vehicle out of her mind. She knew it was a silly thing to worry over, but she hated to think of the seats being ruined by water damage.

The car was easy enough to find; the headlights had gone out as the battery drained, but the sun had risen by that point, dispersing the mist and improving visibility. Adrienne had turned the car off, taken the keys, and closed the door. The bonnet was dented where it had impacted the tree, but it wasn't an especially deep dent. Adrienne hoped the car wouldn't be a write-off.

She was climbing back towards the house when a rumble of engines announced new visitors. A police cruiser and tow truck rolled into Ashburn's yard. It seemed Jayne had stopped off in Ipson to tell people what had happened.

Charles Mackeson was a pleasant, jovial sheriff who slapped Adrienne's shoulder every few minutes and kept laughing at his own jokes. "Nasty accident," he said several times. "She must've lost control of the car."

"Yes." Adrienne's head was filled with a high-pitched ringing noise that made it difficult to think.

The sheriff rolled on the balls of his feet as he tilted his head to look at the house behind them. "Well, this is a treat, anyhow. It's been… oh, nearly two decades since I last saw this place. Was just a rookie back then, scared out of my socks. Can you imagine!" He laughed and slapped her shoulder. She thought she managed a smile in response, though it felt more like a grimace.

The interview passed in a blur. By the time the sheriff tucked his notebook into his pocket, Marion's car was out of the woods and being hoisted onto the back of the truck. Then the sheriff was pressing a basket into her hands and saying, "I think this was meant for you."

"Oh." Adrienne stared at the basket. It had a little tag tied to the handle with her name on in. *The food Marion was bringing me.* "Thanks."

Then both the tow truck and the police cruiser were disappearing along the driveway, leaving Adrienne standing alone on the porch with the basket clasped in her muddy hands.

She threw up. Then she went inside.

Adrienne rested her back against the door and closed her eyes. It was early afternoon, based on the shadows, and she felt exhausted. An irritable mewl came from near her feet, and she blink down at Wolfgang. "Crap. Oh, buddy, you haven't been fed yet, have you? Jeez, I'm sorry."

She staggered into the lounge room, placed the basket on the round table, and took the cat food off the shelf. Wolfgang waited by his bowl, his magnificent tail standing upright like a flag marking Adrienne's destination, and she poured out an extra-generous portion.

"Sorry, buddy." The cat planted its head into the bowl as though he planned to drown himself in food. "Didn't mean to leave you hungry."

Adrienne stood and returned the food to the shelf. She wished she could turn her mind off, but it refused to be silenced.

She looked so much like a corpse. And lying there under the tombstone like that…

Her fingers ached, and Adrienne realised she was squeezing the edge of the shelf as though it were a life buoy. She made herself let go.

Why is there a grave on this property? Who's buried there?

She left the lounge room and crossed to the kitchen. She wasn't hungry, but she hadn't eaten that morning, so she put the kettle on to make some tea and a cup of instant noodles. Then, on impulse, she took the last tin of sardines out of the cupboard, tipped its contents onto a plate, and brought it back to Wolfgang.

"There you go," she said. The cat's tail twitched happily as he switched his attentions from the kibble to the fish. "I'll be more careful from now on, I promise."

Are there other graves around Ashburn? Or was it a cemetery for one?

Adrienne went to press her hands over her eyes then recoiled.

Most of the dirt had brushed off, but her fingers were still coated in a layer of grime.

"C'mon, Addy, pull it together." Back in the kitchen, she washed her hands thoroughly, using hot water and scrubbing until the skin was raw and pink. Dirt was dirt, she tried to tell herself, but it didn't feel right to be touching the ground above where a body rested.

The kettle finished boiling and turned off with a quiet click. She poured some water into one of the dainty fine-china cups and went to fetch the instant noodles from the cupboard.

Why did she crash? It couldn't be a coincidence that it happened at the exact same time as that... I don't even know what to call it. That phenomenon.

She picked one of the containers that promised shrimp, pulled the lid off, and managed a chuckle at the two lonely dried prawns sitting on top of the noodles.

It was some sort of pulse. Invisible but powerful. Strong enough that it frightened both the birds and Wolfgang. Sudden enough to make Marion swerve off the driveway. And localised enough that Beth, the expert on this house, must not know about it—otherwise, she would have said something yesterday.

Adrienne retrieved one of the heavy silver forks from the drawer, sat down, and poked at her swelling noodles while she waited for them to soften.

It's happened twice now, just after sundown. Will it happen again? Is it dangerous? Is there anything I can do to stop it?

Her head ached, and Adrienne abandoned the noodles to sip

at her drink. She'd forgotten to add a teabag but didn't care. She was thirsty enough to gulp down the scalding cup of hot water and pour a fresh one.

The noodles were ready, and she made herself eat them. They tasted like cardboard.

Will she be okay? She wasn't talking or moving. I thought people shook when they had hypothermia, but maybe she was beyond that point.

Her mind built a picture of Jayne driving to the next town, recklessly swerving around traffic, oblivious to the fact that her friend lay dead in the seat beside her...

Stop it. Adrienne stabbed the fork into the container and leaned back in her seat. *She's going to be okay. She's* got *to be okay.*

She let her eyes rove over the kitchen, trying to ground herself by paying attention to her environment. It wasn't exactly a sunny day, but the light that flowed through the window was warming and comforting.

IS IT FRIDAY

LIGHT THE CANDLE

Adrienne's stomach gave an unpleasant lurch. She'd accidentally sat in Edith's chair, and the scratched words were immediately in front of her, just past the cup of noodles. That was a problem. She'd covered the carvings with a tablecloth the day before.

She rose slowly, hyperaware that the chair's legs were scraping through the well-worn grooves in the floor. The off-white cloth had fallen in a crumbled pool behind the table. Adrienne picked it up, shook it out, and gave it a quick once-over.

It's too large to slide off accidentally. There's no wind here, and I'm sure I didn't bump it off myself.

A wet, smacking noise brought her attention to the kitchen doorway. Wolfgang, finished with his meal, was licking his lips and looking very satisfied. Adrienne glanced from him to the cloth and sighed. *Wolf must have jumped on the table and skidded the cloth off. Well, no harm done.*

She threw the covering back over the message, making sure it was centred and balanced, then took her noodles and hot water to a seat at the table's side.

CHAPTER 17
LISTEN TO THE DARK

SHE FINISHED DRYING THE fork and slotted it back into the drawer. The grandfather clock had chimed three times during Adrienne's meal, which meant she had another four hours to fill before nightfall.

She went upstairs and unpacked her suitcase, slotting the clothes and spare sheets into the wardrobe and fussing over how to arrange her book and hairbrush on the bureau. She was low on possessions, and the task took less than twenty minutes. When she finished, she turned in a circle, surveying the immaculate room and feeling completely lost.

Her next ghostwriting job was due the following week. The project was nearly finished and could be wrapped up in a couple of hours, so she grabbed her laptop off the desk and brought it to the second-floor study.

She got as far as placing the computer onto the study desk and pressing the power button before hitting an obstacle. Her laptop was out of power, and there was no electricity on Ashburn's second floor.

Grumbling under her breath, Adrienne carried the laptop downstairs to recharge it in the lounge room. Not having power on the second floor was inconvenient but not completely disastrous for her plan of using the study. The laptop's battery could last a full day; she'd just have to remember to recharge it on the ground floor at night.

She plugged the computer in and watched the screen light up. The round table was at a bad height to write at, so she left the laptop there to charge and began pacing through the house.

Edith didn't own a TV or radio, as far as Adrienne could see, and most of the books in her shelves were printed before the turn of the century. She picked up a scrap cloth from the kitchen and dusted the rooms she passed through, but she didn't know how much good she was doing. The particles just swirled through the air, making her sneeze.

She ended up in one of the upstairs rooms, swiping the cloth over a floating shelf mindlessly as she stared out the window.

Whose grave is it?

Long, wine-red curtains created an elegant frame for the view: a patch of weedy yard, sloping gently downhill, soon merged with the gnarled, blackened trees. The woods were dense and sloped away for a distance before rising up again as the hill joined the mountain. The little clearing and its grave were just a dozen metres past the edge of the woods. Adrienne thought she could even see the narrow opening of the path she and Jayne had emerged from earlier that day.

It's getting late. The sky was darkening as the sun approached the treetops, but it was still a little way from true dusk. *But the grave's so close… there's time to go there and back, surely?*

She glanced behind her, feeling a little like a naughty child about to break curfew, then threw the cloth down.

It's for my own good, she told herself as she jogged down the stairs. *I'll have enough trouble sleeping* without *a mystery on top of everything else. I need some closure about who's buried on Edith's property.*

She snagged her jacket off the back of the fireside chair. Wolfgang, full and content, was sprawled over the rug and gave her a lazy blink before going back to sleep.

Isn't that odd; I still think of this house as Edith's, though it's technically mine now. I suppose it's hard to expunge a lifetime's habitation overnight… but something tells me I'll still be thinking of this as Edith's house in fifty years' time.

She slipped through the front door and rounded the property. That morning's search had been so panicked that she couldn't clearly remember where the pathway was, though she knew they'd emerged near the back of the house. She approached the forest's edge and began walking along its border, looking for the narrow opening.

She found it between two patchy, dying trees. It was unidentifiable as a trail until she was facing it head-on and noticed the dirt track snaking between the great trunks for a few metres before disappearing from view.

One final look at the sky reassured her that, although sundown had started, she still had time to make the journey before night fell. She stepped between the trees and entered the other world of the forest.

The change was instantaneous. While she stood on the grass, the sunlight felt bright and warm. Inside the woods, though, it became muted and greyed. Many layers of shadows wrapped around the trunks and grew over Adrienne's limbs, chilling her. She zipped up her jacket, folded her arms over her torso, and began marching.

It was hard to be certain whether the path had been intentionally created or if feet had worn down the vegetation over decades to create the track. It was too narrow to follow without ducking and weaving, and the tree roots criss-crossing the path were squashed and scuffed as though they'd been trodden on hundreds of times. *By Edith?*

Birds cackled around her. They sounded angry and impatient, and she wondered if they feared sundown as strongly as she did.

The path wasn't long. It widened then abruptly opened into the clearing. Adrienne stopped at the edge of the natural border to stare at the gravestone.

It poked out of the ground like an abomination, the only man-made feature in sight, isolated from the trees as though they bent away from it. No weeds or plants grew there; the only thing covering the clearing's floor was a layer of decomposing leaves.

Adrienne took a step nearer. The dirt immediately ahead of the stone was bare and raw, still dark with moisture from where Marion had scrabbled at it. The indent was shallow, but it really did look as though she'd been digging a hole for a coffin to slot into.

It would have been a lot of work for a freezing and delirious woman, especially after walking so far.

Adrienne pictured her friend lying there, skin waxy and empty eyes staring towards the interlaced boughs above. She shuddered then moved closer to the grave marker.

The stone was deep, sombre grey and looked old, though the forest had protected it from most weathering effects. It had been built in the traditional rectangle-with-curved-top shape, and a decorative groove that ran around the edge kept it from looking too plain.

Words were carved into the stone's smooth face. Adrienne took another step forward and bent to read in the failing light.

E ASHBURN

FORGOTTEN BUT NOT GONE

She mouthed the twisted phrase and felt her eyebrows pull together. Was this a joke? Had some prankster come along and cut the words into the headstone? No, they couldn't have—the grooves were too neat and precise to be made by an amateur.

Did Edith request this epitaph? And for that matter, why is her grave here? I would have thought she'd be buried in town.

Adrienne straightened and rubbed her hands over her sides. The cold was biting at her, which was strange, considering it was a mild day and she was wearing a jacket.

The hairs along her arms stood on end as a prickly, electric sensation touched her. The forest had fallen quiet. The angry bird chatter from earlier had died away, and even the trees' rustling was hushed.

She shot a panicked look upwards to where small holes in the boughs' lattices let her glimpse the sky. It was dark—darker than she'd expected—but not quite black. It was still twilight.

I can feel it. It's like… electricity… conviction… stimulus…

Her mind was struggling to find a way to define the sensation. She felt it physically, in the same way she felt altered when she stood under power lines, but at the same time, the effect was emotionally based—like wanting to scream but having no way to draw breath, or the urge to cry without cause. She understood with absolute certainty that she must run, flee the woods, escape the area before it was too late, but she had no comprehension of why.

And the feeling was growing stronger.

She backed away from the grave, feeling nauseous. Her hands were shaking. She breathed in shallow and laboured gasps as her pulse spiked, preparing her for a fight, pumping adrenaline through her limbs and shorting out the rational part of her mind.

A noise was edging into the periphery of her awareness. She thought she wouldn't have heard it under normal circumstances, but with the sounds of the woods reduced to a deathly hush, the subtle scratching, scrabbling wormed through her ears and into her brain.

Run.

It was the first coherent thought she'd had since the sensation had started. She turned and tore into the forest, neither paying attention to her direction nor searching for the narrow pathway. The woods were thick and tangled. She became caught in branches and fought to break free.

Above her, twilight was fading into night. The tinges of colour on the horizon would cling on for another minute, then the moon would once again reign over the sky.

She was having trouble breathing. Leaves crunched and bushes rustled as she pounded through them, but they weren't loud enough to block out the infernal muffled scratching noise. *Like fingernails being dragged through soil.*

Her whole awareness was focussed on getting inside Ashburn. The house offered safety; a firm wall to withstand attack; shelter and warmth and light. Outside, she was vulnerable. Outside, her ankles could be grabbed at by the fingers that scrabbled, and she could be dragged, screaming, back into the heart of the woods.

She broke through the forest's edge. Her wild run had taken her off course but not by much; the house stood like a monument to her right, and she dashed towards the door, her breath ragged and her heart ready to burst. She turned the handle, fell through the doorway, and kicked it closed behind her.

The birds exploded out of the woods in a cacophony of screams.

CHAPTER 18
GRAVE CONCLUSIONS

ADRIENNE CAME BACK TO her senses slowly. She was lying face down on Ashburn's entryway rug, knees tucked under her and arms thrown over her head. She felt vaguely sick from exertion and fear, and the stinging pain across her hands and face told her she'd scratched herself on the trees.

She rolled back onto her heels and blinked. The house was dark now that the sun had set, and she stretched a hand up to the patch of wall beside the door to turn the light on. Her fingers were shaking, and it took a few seconds to flip the switch.

"What was that?" She stared at her hands. Her heart was slowing, but the jitteriness lingered. She couldn't remember ever experiencing something so frightening. A couple of horror movies had scared her so badly that she'd been shaking as she left the theatre, but they were nothing compared to the feeling she'd experienced in the clearing and during the run back to the house.

She pushed strands of hair out of her face and got to her feet. Her legs were like jelly, but she made it into the lounge room. Wolfgang sat in the centre of the red rug, tail wrapped around his paws and ears tilted back just enough to tell her he wasn't happy.

"You felt it too, right?" She bent to scratch his head, but he didn't lean into it as he usually did. "How about a fire? Looks like you might need it, buddy, and even if you don't, I certainly do. You wouldn't believe how badly I scared myself out there."

She knelt in front of the grate and began scrunching up sheets of newspaper to light the kindling with. There was enough wood in the holder for another few nights, but she was almost out of kindling. She wondered if Edith had a stash of aged wood on the property. A ninety-year-old surely wouldn't be cutting her own.

The thought of her great-aunt returned her to the earlier confusion. *Why was Edith buried on the property? And with that inscription?*

Unless…

The tombstone had looked old, and its markings only said "E ASHBURN." If Edith's mother or aunt had names beginning with E, the grave could belong to one of them. Adrienne also considered the possibility of an even older ancestor, but the gravestone looked less than a century old, which would place it about the time of the family's murder.

That creates another question, though. Why bury one family member here but not the others? If they all died at the same time, wouldn't they be buried in the same place or at least laid to rest alongside the husband?

The newspaper curled up into black soot as the flame licked through it. Soon the kindling, old and well dried, caught as well, and Adrienne began feeding larger sticks onto it as she chewed over her conundrum. Wolfgang came to sit beside her, and she gave him a pat while the flames built.

There's one other option. The grave could be empty. There's no rule saying a gravestone has to mark a body. Edith certainly did many odd things during her lifetime; perhaps creating a fake grave was one of them.

She shivered and shoved a fresh log onto the growing flames. Sparks spat onto the rug, and she used the heavy glove to flick them back into the hearth before they could burn the fabric.

"I'm getting morbid, buddy," she said to the cat poised beside her. "I think this house is a bad influence. Soon I'll start dressing in gloomy clothes and dying my hair and painting my lips black to join the local goth society."

Wolfgang was unimpressed and told her so by ignoring her. She scratched behind his ears, where she knew he liked it, then rose. Her legs were steadier, and her hands no longer shook, but she still felt disoriented. She went to put the kettle on, turning on every light she passed.

She'd gone to the grave to satiate a curiosity that would have kept her awake. But having visited it, she doubted she was going to get any extra sleep. Adrienne exhaled a humourless chuckle as she leaned on the kitchen bench and stared towards the woods. The trees' silhouettes were barely visible against the sky. And hidden amongst the trunks was a gravestone marking a mystery she didn't think she would ever solve.

I'm not sure I want to stay in this house.

It was the first time she'd had the thought. Ever since hearing that she'd inherited Ashburn, she'd imagined herself living in it, integrating into the town, and building a life in her great-aunt's home even if it was cramped or badly insulated or quirky.

But Ashburn went beyond quirky. The wallpaper that had appeared charming on first sight was starting to make her claustrophobic. The groaning pipes and creaking floorboards spoke less of the building's character and more of invisible threats. *And now this twilight phenomenon.*

Adrienne, suddenly exhausted, rubbed her palms into her eyes. *If I don't like the house anymore, should I sell it?*

The kettle finished boiling, but she didn't approach it. Instead, she folded her arms and chewed on her lip as she looked around the kitchen, picking out misshapen faces in the cupboard's whorls and the dents in the pots hung on the opposite wall.

Would anyone buy it? The house is old, and it's a twenty-minute drive from Ipson, which is tiny. Half of the building doesn't even have electricity. And there are all of these rumours about its history: a bizarre owner, murders, children daring each other to climb up to the porch... who wants that?

Except for me?

Adrienne's chewing graduated from her lip to her thumb. As soon as she'd begun thinking about selling, the idea of losing Ashburn struck her as repulsive. Edith might have been strange, but she'd cared enough for Adrienne to prepare her bedroom. And the house wasn't without charm. Adrienne had always liked the old-fashioned-roses aesthetic. Even if Ashburn's fittings were a little dulled from age, there was no denying the antique furniture and fine china were way more decadent than anything she could afford to buy herself.

And if she moved, where would she go? She had no living relatives that she knew of. Her high school friends had scattered across the country in the years following graduation, and she'd lost touch with most of them. Ashburn was the only place where she had any history, incidental as it was.

The nightfall phenomenon, though…

Adrienne looked at her hands. They'd finally stopped shaking, but her chest still felt tight, and the stress had created a low-level headache. Her mind was becoming clearer, though, and with that came doubt about what she'd experienced.

Nothing had been chasing her. She wasn't hurt except for what she'd done to herself by dashing through the trees. And the only physical, tangible manifestation of the phenomenon was the birds scattering out of the trees.

But I've never felt fear so acutely before. That couldn't have been all in my mind, could it?

She looked back at the window. The moon, fat and heavy as it moved towards full, infused the outside scene with a cool, calming glow.

Her brain felt too full to think anything through clearly. Adrienne exhaled a sigh, turned the kettle back on, and focussed on preparing the tea. By the time she returned to the lounge room, Wolfgang had stretched himself out on the rug in front of the fire. The blaze was comforting, and its light helped shake some of the shadows out of the room. Adrienne took the fireside chair, placed the tea on the round table beside her charging laptop, and stretched her legs towards the blaze.

I don't have to stay. She extended the tip of her sneaker to scratch down Wolfgang's back. He arched into the contact and huffed a happy, grumbling purr. *But I think I'd like to.*

She leaned back in the chair and closed her eyes. Her mind was still buzzing, so she made a conscious effort to purge all thoughts and relax. The back of her eyelids were empty for a second, then they filled with the memory of helping to fold Marion—stiff, silent, and cold—into the car.

Fresh anxiety rose through her, and Adrienne moaned. What had happened to the friendly vet student? Was she still at the hospital, back at home, or…?

Not the morgue. Don't think like that.

Adrienne fought the impulse to rise and pace. If she'd had a phone, she could have called Jayne. Instead, she was stuck with her conjectures and overactive imagination until someone drove up to Ashburn to see her, or until she walked to town.

I'll go early tomorrow. I can't afford to buy anything, but at the very least, I can hear how Marion's doing and check my email.

She brought her attention back to the giant tabby at her feet. He'd contorted into what she called his *roadkill pose*: on his back, legs pointed towards the ceiling, head twisted at an awkward angle, and lips peeled back to show two white teeth and the tip of his tongue. Adrienne chuckled. He'd adapted to Ashburn surprisingly quickly. The fireplace upgrade might have helped with that.

Watching Wolfgang's little twitches and shifts let her finally relax, and it didn't take long for her eyelids to feel heavy. Adrienne had only planned on staying in the lounge room until she was calm enough to go to bed, but her limbs felt heavier with every minute that passed, and she was half-asleep by the time the grandfather clock struck nine.

She fastened her bony fingers around a low-hanging branch. Her muscles had atrophied, and she had to expend both physical energy and willpower to drag her withered body forward. She gained ten inches and released the branch. Drew in a rattling, bone-aching breath, though her lungs were far past the point of being able to process air. Reached forward. Gripped a new branch.

Dirt still caked her, filling every crevice in her wrinkled skin. Her hair had been long in life but had grown longer in death. It dragged behind her like a long, matted blanket, catching in the leaf litter and branches.

She hadn't expected to be so weak. But she had been buried much longer than she had anticipated, and she had been interred deep.

Moonlight was not far ahead. She could see it through the trees, glimmering across the lawn and over the face of her dear

Ashburn. The moon would revive her and give her the strength to quell the occupant, that arrogant child, to drag her down, peel the skin from her frame, drown her screams in flowing blood, crack her bones, and taste her still-pulsing flesh.

She drew her lips back from rotting teeth as anticipation quickened her breath. Fixed her fingers around a new branch. Pulled.

CHAPTER 19
STRANGERS

ADRIENNE CLAWED AT THE air. A scream gurgled in her throat, but her lungs didn't hold enough breath to give it form. The terror had returned, but this time it had a source.

A woman was coming. She was withered, her body twisted and malformed, her teeth like yellow stubs in black gums, her hair a river of tangles and heavy with dirt. And she was coming for Adrienne.

The room was dark. Slivers of moonlight highlighted the edges of the furniture, but the fire had crumbled and exhausted itself. Adrienne held herself still, posed awkwardly in a position that was half sitting, half lying, and tried to absorb her surroundings.

The house seemed silent at first, but the longer she listened, the more she began to pick out tiny sounds of life. The grandfather clock's ticking, inaudible during the day, created a steady pulse. The wood contracted as it cooled in the night air, creating muffled cracking and groaning noises. She could even hear the rustle of trees outside.

Then there was a low exhalation as something moved in the shadows. Adrienne's heart stuttered, and she opened her mouth to cry out.

The figure turned towards her, and two round, sea-green eyes caught the moonlight. *Wolfgang.* The scream died on Adrienne's tongue, and she slumped forward, arms held around her torso, and finally gained enough control over her muscles to breathe.

It was a dream. That's all. She tilted her head to meet Wolfgang's eyes and began to chuckle. "You nearly gave me a heart attack, buddy."

Her laughter petered out. The house felt too empty and too quiet to allow for levity. Wolfgang continued to watch her for a moment then turned back to face the window. Adrienne licked at dry lips and sat back in the chair as chills began to run through her, starting at the top of her spine and working their way down her back.

She tried to remember the dream. It had felt intensely real, but within seconds of waking, the details had begun to slip away. *There was a woman. An old and contorted woman. And the moon was somehow important.* But every other detail fled as soon as she reached for it.

Wolfgang's silhouette was barely visible in the gloom. He sat pin straight, bushy tail wrapped around his paws, and faced the window. That unnerved Adrienne. Her cat rarely paid attention to the outside unless he could see something moving.

It was too dark; the longer she sat, the easier it was to imagine a thousand horrors creeping through the shadows. Adrienne pushed out of the chair and felt her way through the room, running her fingers over the wallpaper as she neared the door. She touched the plastic light switch, flicked it, and felt her courage wither. The light didn't turn on.

Did the bulb blow? Jayne wouldn't have cut power to the house, would she?

The black was pressing against her, weighing her down like a thick blanket. Adrienne made her way across the room to the fireplace and knelt on the rug ahead of it. She found the newspaper with trembling fingers and wadded up several sheets, placed them in the cooling ash, then ran her fingertips across the mantel until she found the box of matches.

The first match broke when she tried to strike it, so she threw it into the fireplace. The second flared nicely. She touched the flame to the newspaper and released her breath when it caught and the blaze began to grow.

She turned towards the kindling bucket, and her heart dropped. It was empty except for a few small twigs; she'd forgotten she'd used the last of the kindling for the previous night's fire.

"Crap." She dropped the twigs onto the newspaper, but it was clear they wouldn't be enough to catch any of the larger logs. She watched as the flames licked the sticks, converting them into ash, and her malformed fire died before it had a chance to live.

Adrienne turned. Instead of chasing away the dark, the fire had made her blind; when she'd first woken, her night-adjusted eyes had been able to pick out shapes in the moonlight, but now she couldn't see anything.

There's the lamp in the hallway. Adrienne's chest was tight, and she rose carefully. *As long as I can find it and light it.*

She thought she saw a flicker of motion in the room's corner. *Wolfgang?* The moon was nearing full, but the windows' grime smothered its glow. She crossed the room, hands held ahead of her to guide her way through the furniture, and touched the door.

The handle felt stiff, as though it hadn't been used in a century. It whined when she turned it, and Adrienne slipped through the opening.

With the two small windows on side of the front door providing the only light, the hallway was even darker than the lounge room. She was closer to the entryway than to the staircase, so Adrienne moved to the door first and felt for the light switch. It turned, but the light stayed dead.

The whole house is affected, then.

On the other side of the door, just past Adrienne's reach, the porch's boards groaned. They were shifting as though a person moved across them. Adrienne squeezed her lips together, her heartbeat staccato, and tried to banish the idea of company prowling just outside.

She turned to face the hallway and retraced her steps towards the stairs, waving her arms ahead of her as though swimming through air. Floorboards creaked with every step. Her ragged breathing quickened to match the clock's tempo. *Tick, tick, breathe. Tick, tick, breathe.*

Adrienne hit the bannister and grunted. It had passed between her waving arms and bumped her firmly enough to bruise, and she held onto it for a moment as she regained her bearings.

The lamp was on the table to the right of the stairs. There were matches beside it.

She felt towards the table, moving slowly for fear of knocking the lamp over and smashing its glass, but touched the table's edge first. She ran her fingers along the hand-stitched cloth—tacky from old dust—then found the bronze holder. It took several agonizing moments to remove the glass then another minute to find the small cardboard box, remove a match, and strike it.

The light, although small, was an intense relief. She touched it to the wick, waited for the tiny flame to stabilise, then replaced the glass.

It was easier to breathe once she had light. The lamp's glow didn't extend far; a few precious feet surrounding Adrienne were illuminated, but its effect diminished the farther it stretched, and the front door was still heavy with shadows.

Something outside the door moved.

Adrienne jolted backwards. The lamp flickered, but its light held. She stared at the two small windows set on either side of the front entrance, her eyes skipping between them as she searched for motion. She could have sworn she'd seen a dark figure shift behind the glass as it moved along the porch.

I heard the floorboards groan earlier too.

Fear returned, curling like a cold serpent through her stomach. Someone was outside.

Her first instinct was to run for help, but no help existed. She had no phone. She had no mother. It was just Adrienne and whoever or whatever lingered outside.

"Crap." She mouthed rather than spoke the word. *Is the door locked? No, I don't think it is. What about the back door? I can't even remember where to go to find it.* "Crap!"

The choice was terrible. If she stayed where she was, the stranger could break into the house through any of its entry points: not just the doors but also multiple unlocked windows. She wouldn't even know which direction to face to defend herself. But her heart shrivelled at the idea of confronting the person outside.

Don't be weak. She took a step towards the front door. *Whoever's out there won't go away unless you make them.* Another two stumbling steps. She kept her eyes shifting between the narrow windows, searching for motion, but outside was dark and still.

It might have just been a trick of the light. She reached towards the doorknob with one hand and held the lamp high above her head with the other. *The flame might have reflected off the glass oddly and given the illusion of motion.*

She touched the bronze handle. Squeezed it. Twisted it. The sound of grinding metal strummed on her taut nerves. Then she released the handle, raised one foot, and kicked the door open.

There was motion. Fear and panic blurred Adrienne's vision; she tried to catch a glimpse of the moving shape, but it was gone before she could fix on it. It had crashed into the woods, disappearing amongst the thick black trees, and its footsteps were already fading from the cold night air.

Adrienne took a long, slow breath, light held high, as she stared at the point where the figure had disappeared. The bushes rocked from the disruption and gradually fell still. Silence returned to Ashburn. And logic slowly crept back into Adrienne's mind.

Beth had said children dared each other to approach the house. It was a test of bravery to see who could get closest to the porch or linger there the longest before fear forced them back to the woods. And with a new owner in the house, those dares were undoubtedly being passed around with fresh enthusiasm.

Adrienne looked upwards. The moon, just a few days away from being full, was clear and bright. It was well after midnight but still a few hours before dawn. Whichever child had braved the Ashburn ghosts was also risking their parents' wrath.

She turned back to the forest and scanned its edge again. The lamplight didn't quite reach the trees, but she could see that the shrubs and weedy vines were still except for where the breeze tugged at them. Adrienne tried to tell herself that the intruder wouldn't be coming back.

She locked the door behind her then methodically moved through each downstairs room, making sure the windows and the back door were locked before finally settling back into the lounge room.

Wolfgang had returned to dozing on the rug. Without the fire, he'd curled into a compact bundle with his tail tucked around his head. Adrienne placed the lamp, still lit, and the bottle of refill oil onto the round table. She propped the fire poker at her chair's side then sat, wrapped her jacket about herself, and waited for dawn.

CHAPTER 20
A RELUCTANT VISIT

BY THE TIME MORNING spread its golden light over the treetops Adrienne was cold and stiff. Wolfgang had moved to her lap in the early morning. She was grateful for his presence and drew her fingers through his thick fur to reassure herself.

She'd stayed alert all night, listening for any groaning floorboards that might indicate the stranger had returned, but the only noises the house produced were when the wood shifted as it cooled.

Dawn brought relief and also a twinge of embarrassment. She felt silly for sitting up all night; the longer she thought about it, the more convinced she felt that the figure outside had been a child visiting Ashburn on a dare. She'd probably scared them just as much as they'd scared her. She could picture them backing away from the porch as the lamp's glow grew brighter in the windows then fleeing in terror when she kicked the door open. The image almost made her laugh.

Almost.

She felt sore, tired and irritable. The stress had brought her headache back, and her limbs were numb from cold. She scratched Wolfgang's head to wake him then carefully shifted him to the floor and went to get his breakfast.

How often is this going to happen? Am I going to have to panic over kids coming up to the house every month, every week, every night…? She poured the kibble, replaced the tin, then extinguished the lamp's flame. The sun wasn't quite high enough to light the room on its own, but her eyes had adjusted so that she was no longer blind. *Honestly, I can understand Aunt Edith being a little crusty if she had to put up with this.*

Adrienne shivered and returned the lamp to the table beside the stairs. Tiredness weighed on her, but she was also acutely aware of how dirty she'd become. She'd washed her hands after the race through the forest the previous evening, but little bits of dirt still clung to her clothes and her hair, and her skin was grubby with dried sweat. She trudged up the stairs, retrieved a change of clothes from her bedroom, and ran the shower.

She'd been looking forward to a scorching-hot bath, and was crushed when the water didn't heat. *Of course—no power means no hot showers. Or cups of tea for that matter. Terrific.*

She showered as quickly as she could. The icy water coupled with chilled morning air woke her up better than a litre of coffee could have, and by the time she bundled herself into her warmest clothes, she was too alert to consider going to bed.

Instead, she returned downstairs to prepare breakfast. She

suspected she would need a nap come afternoon, but in the meantime, she hadn't forgotten her resolution to go to town early. Worry for Marion continued to eat at her.

She was washing her bowl when she heard the car engine resonating as it moved up the driveway. A mixture of hope and fear sparked through her, and she dropped the washing back into the sink.

She ran down the porch and towards Jayne's car as it drew to a halt at the top of the driveway. Jayne must have seen Adrienne's expression because her face was scrunched into an apologetic smile when she stepped out of the car.

"I'm so sorry, Addy. I should've come to visit last night. It was just really late by the time I got home—I didn't mean to make you worry."

She looked much more collected than the day before. Her blonde hair was straightened and styled, and the red lipstick, not quite the right shade for her, shimmered in the morning light. The panicked, haunted expression was gone, and that reassured Adrienne enough that she could catch her breath and ask, "How's Marion?"

"Fine. She's already back home." Jayne closed the car door. "Doctors said she had mild dehydration, mild hypothermia, and shock, but they discharged her last night."

"Thank goodness." Adrienne felt like a heavy, painful rock had been removed from her back. "Thanks for letting me know."

"'Course." Jayne gave her a bright smile, but something about it was slightly off. Adrienne was trying to identify what was wrong when Jayne turned and opened the car's back door. "Oh, I brought you something, too."

She pulled a large cardboard box out and held it towards Adrienne. "It was Marion's idea. She remembered that you didn't have any mirrors, and said you could have some of hers. I thought it was a great idea, so the rest of us—Beth, Sarah and I—all chipped in as well. If you want them."

"Seriously? Thank you!" Adrienne took the box and was shocked by how heavy it was. She staggered under the weight and began carrying it towards Ashburn's front porch. "This'll save me from looking like a homeless person all the time. I mean—are you sure it's okay? I don't want to take all your stuff."

"Don't worry about it!" Jayne laughed, but the same hint of not-rightness hung in the chuckles. "They're what we had in storage. We weren't using them."

"This is great. Thanks." Adrienne dropped the box onto the porch and turned. Jayne lingered a few feet away and was peering around the clearing. "Want to come in for some tea?"

"Oh, uh, I'd love to, but—well, my parents are expecting me back so I can help them clean the house. Maybe another time?"

The tiny hints of uneasiness coalesced into an understanding. The excuse was fake. Jayne was being friendly because she felt obligated towards Adrienne because of her help the previous day, but she wasn't comfortable lingering at Ashburn. In the same way she'd refused to bring Marion inside the house when they'd found her, she didn't want to step any closer to the building than she absolutely had to.

That hurt Adrienne more than she would have expected. Jayne was clearly trying very hard to avoid offending her—she had even brought the mirrors as a peace offering—but her visit was out of duty and nothing more.

Why? Did I do something wrong? Is it because of what happened to Marion?

Adrienne tried to swallow the hurt and smiled. "Sure, well, you're always welcome to visit, and hopefully I'll see you in town sometime."

"Yeah, definitely!" Jayne was already backing towards her car. "Give me a call if you need anything, okay?"

You know I don't have a phone. Adrienne felt as though she'd become trapped in a stage play where they both pretended they couldn't see the giant elephant sitting between them. The still-young friendship was dying in front of her, and there was nothing she could do except smile as if nothing was wrong.

Jayne was halfway into the car when Adrienne remembered that her power had been turned off. She jogged towards the car, one hand raised. "Hang on, wait a moment!"

Jayne's smile held a hint of panic as she looked up. "Yeah?"

"My lights stopped working last night." She searched for a polite way to ask her question without sounding as if she was accusing the other woman. "Um, are there any problems with my account?"

Jayne held still for a moment, one leg inside the car and hands on the door to maintain her balance. Adrienne could almost see the mental battle being waged, then Jayne inhaled, lifted her chin, and stepped out of the car. "Not that I've heard about. Let's have a quick look at your fuse box."

"Oh, right, thanks." Adrienne felt immensely grateful for Jayne's response. It would have been easy for Jayne to say she couldn't help and then leave. The friendship might not be as doomed as she'd thought.

Jayne led the way around the house. She walked quickly, arms tucked around herself and back straight, as she scanned the outside of the house. The fuse box was on the side wall, half-hidden behind scrubby weeds, and she waded through the plants to reach it. "Right. This is weird."

Adrienne moved forward to see what Jayne was looking at. She had the box's top open and was running her finger across the switches. "What happened?"

"All of your breakers are tripped. Did you plug in any new equipment yesterday?"

"Uh… yeah, my laptop."

"Nothing else?"

"No."

"Weird." Jayne scowled at the switches. "That might have tripped one but not all of them."

Adrienne glanced towards the forests surrounding them and cleared her throat. "There was someone outside last night." She thought about mentioning the strange phenomenon but didn't know how to broach it without sounding insane, so she stuck with tangible facts. "I think it might have been a kid."

"Ugh, probably those Crowther brats." Jayne began flicking

the switches on, still scowling. "They get zero supervision from their mum, and their father basically lives at the pub. They would have thought this was a hilarious prank. If they come around again, threaten to call their dad. They don't care about the police, but Mr Crowther terrifies them."

"Okay. Will do."

Jayne flipped the last switch and began walking back to the front of the house. Adrienne followed, and grinned as they passed the lounge room window. The light inside had turned on, and its glow shone through the foggy glass. "Ha, it worked! Thanks!"

"Anytime, Addy." Jayne's smile still held a hint of tightness, but Adrienne thought it was more genuine than earlier. "See you around, okay?"

Adrienne waited as her companion got back into the car then waved as it turned into the driveway. She kept her hand up until the car had disappeared from sight then lowered it and let her smile fade.

Something had upset Jayne enough that she didn't want to spend any time around Ashburn. Adrienne ran through their interactions, searching for any instance when she might have inadvertently caused offense or hurt Jayne's feelings, but she didn't come up with anything. They'd been fine when saying goodbye after that first meeting; then when Jayne had arrived the following morning to search for her missing friend, she'd been stand-offish.

More than stand-offish. Adrienne picked up the box of mirrors and backed through the front door. *She brought a knife.*

That had been understandable, at least. Marion had gone missing after visiting a house with an awful history. Jayne would have been foolish to visit alone without any kind of protection.

But they'd found Marion, and it had been clear Adrienne wasn't responsible for the crash. So why was Jayne still wary?

Adrienne placed the box on one of the hallway tables and began sorting through the contents. It contained nearly a dozen mirrors in various sizes and states of cleanliness.

The gift was a good sign. If Jayne's objection had been against Adrienne herself, she wouldn't have brought the mirrors... or even visited, for that matter. It suggested her dislike was directed towards the house, not the owner.

Maybe I can understand that. Her friend nearly died here the day after her first visit. Combined with the rumours and legends, it must have unnerved her. She might be the sort of person who doesn't believe in coincidences.

Which meant the friendship might be salvaged with a little time and hard work. Adrienne hoped it could, at least.

Wolfgang sat on the lowest step of the stairs, and the tip of his tail twitched as he watched his owner.

"How about it, buddy?" She held up one of the larger, cleaner mirrors for him to see. "Reckon we're ready to abolish the no-mirrors rule?"

CHAPTER 21
CAKE

JAYNE HAD BEEN CONSIDERATE enough to leave a small jar of nails and a spool of wire in the bottom of the box, and Adrienne spent an hour fixing her new mirrors about the house. Most of them were placed directly over the NO MIRRORS inscriptions, not because she intended it that way but because they naturally tended to be the most appropriate places to hang the frames.

She fastened one onto the wall opposite the lounge room's door. One went into the bathroom in the space above the sink and another onto the bureau in Adrienne's room. A smaller mirror sat on the mantel, and a gilt frame fit perfectly into the larger guest room.

The last mirror—the largest in the box and framed with heavy, dark wood—gave Adrienne some trouble over its placement. Initially, she put it in the kitchen, but it didn't feel natural there. It would have blended perfectly into Edith's bedroom, but while she was okay with hanging mirrors through the rest of the house, she felt it would be rude to install one in Edith's domain. She was hesitating in the upstairs hallway, glancing up and down its length with the mirror clutched to her chest, when it struck her that the dark wood frame would blend amongst the family portraits perfectly.

She hung it halfway along the hall, where there was a bit of a gap between a painting of Edith's parents and one of Edith as a child. When she stood back, it almost looked as though it were a painting of her. She stuck her tongue out at her reflection, laughed, then returned downstairs.

The paintings had disturbed her when she'd first seen them, but she was gradually growing accustomed to their presence. The eyes continued to follow her, and the repetition still unnerved her, but it was becoming easier to walk past them without noticing they were there.

Morning was edging towards midday by the time Adrienne put the empty box away and stretched. It was her fourth day in Ashburn, and she was starting to feel guilty about how little she'd accomplished. The laptop waited for her in the lounge room, so she went to it, intending to spend a few hours on the incomplete project before walking to town in search of Wi-Fi.

She opened the lid, pressed the power button, and felt her good mood wither as the computer failed to respond.

"C'mon." She checked the cord where it connected to the laptop and the power socket. "Even if you didn't charge yesterday, you had plenty of time this morning!"

She pressed the power button again but got the same result: the screen stayed dead. Even the little light that normally winked to tell her the battery was charging remained black.

Adrienne began muttering as she tried pressing more buttons, tapping the touchpad, and pressing her ear to the keyboard to see if she could hear the fan. Nothing worked. She slumped back in the chair, pressed her hands to her face, and groaned. Her laptop was dead.

"This can't be happening." Her mind was already jumping through every incomplete task and document that hadn't been backed up as she tried to assess how big of a disaster it was. She couldn't contact her outstanding clients, and if they didn't pay of their own volition, she'd be facing an empty cupboard in about five days. Her work-in-progress document wasn't due for a week but would amount to about forty hours of lost work if she couldn't retrieve the partially completed file.

And of course, she had no money for repairs or for a new laptop.

She groaned. *Whatever knocked the power out must have killed the laptop. Thank goodness I don't have any projects due in the next couple of days... but I really, really could have done without this.*

She unplugged the laptop, snapped its lid closed, and tucked it inside its carry bag. The best she could do was ask around town to see if anyone would repair it for a trade—she could edit any website or offer to do manual labour such as gardening. Or maybe they would even take an IOU.

She was halfway to the door when an idea came to her. Jayne

147

had said Marion was back home. She should visit, not just to check on how she was but also to thank her for the basket of food. Adrienne dropped the laptop bag on the side table and ducked into the kitchen. She sorted through the cupboard and grinned when she realised the fresh eggs, milk, and jam Marion had brought the day before could be combined with Edith's flour and sugar to make a small, basic cake.

It took less than forty minutes to mix and bake the cake then another half hour for it to cool while Adrienne cleaned up. She wished she had some icing sugar to decorate it, but beggars couldn't be choosers, so she wrapped the cake in a towel and placed it in the basket Marion's supplies had come in. Then she returned to the hallway, took up the laptop, and stepped outside.

The midday sun was warm and bright, and Adrienne had to tie her jacket around her waist before she'd reached the forest's edge. Descending into town was a lot more fun than climbing away from it had been. Sunlight came through the canopy in dappled spots, and as she moved lower and began to cross into the greener, healthier woods, the bird chatter and hum of insects increased. She was breathless but happier by the time she reached the street. The walk had shaken off her morning grumpiness and even erased some of the stress caused by the broken computer.

She didn't know Marion's address but knew she volunteered at the local veterinary clinic. Her hope was that one of the staff there might give directions to Marion's house or at least agree to pass the cake on to her.

The vet was surprisingly easy to find. It was on the main street a little past the town's only bank and advertised itself with a big white sign that held silhouettes of a rabbit, cat, dog, and horse arranged in a row.

The building had been a house before being converted into a clinic. As Adrienne entered the small waiting room, the screen door squealed. An elderly woman sat in one of the two chairs, an overweight pug held in her lap, and a frizzy-haired receptionist was tapping at the computer behind the front desk. She turned a toothy, eager smile on Adrienne. "Good morning!"

"Hi." Adrienne shuffled to the desk, leaned close, and briefly explained her reason for the visit. To her surprise, the receptionist grabbed a notepad and had begun scribbling an address before she'd even finished her story.

"Here we go. Tell her Peggy said hi, okay?"

"Oh." She felt a little stunned as she took the messy street address. Peggy had kindly included directions on how to reach it from the clinic. Adrienne hadn't expected it to be that easy. "Thank you!"

"No worries!" Peggy's smile stretched a little wider, showing her gums. "Anything else I can help with?"

Adrienne hesitated then glanced towards her laptop bag. "Actually, yeah. Do you know anyone around here who can repair laptops? Mine died this morning."

Peggy looked as though her day had been made. She stretched her hands towards the bag. "Yeah, my brother's visiting this week. He works in tech; I'll get him to have a look for you."

The bag was out of Adrienne's hands before she knew what

was happening. Her first impulse was to ask for it back—to fear for her computer's safety in the hands of a stranger—but she had to stop herself. This wasn't the city, and Peggy had already demonstrated that Ipson had a high trust threshold. Adrienne let the bag go.

"Okay, that would be great." She leaned a little closer and lowered her voice so that the pug's owner wouldn't overhear. "I, uh, I can't afford much right now, but would he let me pay him back over the next month?"

"He will if I tell him to." Peggy tucked the bag under the desk. "I'll see if he can have a look at it tonight. Pop back in tomorrow if you like."

"Great. Thank you." Adrienne picked up the basket with the cake and turned towards the door. "Uh, I'm Adrienne—"

"From old Miss Ashburn's house—of course." Peggy's grin was so unguarded and free that Adrienne couldn't help but return it. "Nice to meet you at last, Adrienne."

"Ha. You too, Peggy."

Adrienne left the clinic, walked twenty paces, and had to stop to get her bearings. The whole exchange had been so rapid that she felt dizzy. But—and she hoped this wasn't a one-sided impression—she felt as though she might have just met another friend.

CHAPTER 22
BOXES AND DIRT

MARION'S HOUSE WAS EASY to find. It was a neat suburban two-story property just a block off the main street with an unruly garden spilling over the fence.

A broad, muscly woman answered Adrienne's knocks. She seemed relieved that Adrienne had come to visit.

"Maybe you can talk her 'round." The woman—who'd introduced herself as Marion's mother, Kris—led Adrienne up the stairs to the second floor. A little like the garden, the house felt overfull and disorganised but in a homey sort of way. "She's been moping about all morning. Acting like that crash was the worst thing ever. I even told her she could borrow my car until hers is fixed, *but...*" She punctuated the last word with an eye-roll and knocked on the first door at the top of the stairs. "Well, maybe she'll cheer up with some company. Oy, Mar, that girl from Edith's house has come to visit."

Kris turned and started down the stairs without waiting for a response from either Adrienne or her daughter. The door remained closed. Adrienne dawdled in the hallway, feeling uncomfortable, but when a minute had passed without any sounds suggesting she was going to be let in, she turned the handle and nudged the door open. "Marion?"

The room was dim. A pink-tinted lamp beside the bed was on, but the curtains were drawn, blocking out all natural light. The space was a little neater than the rest of the house but still filled with a plethora of clearly loved possessions. Two mismatched dressers were pressed against one wall, above which hung a cluster of posters and animal-healthcare charts. Colourful scarves were thrown over the wardrobe, and the bed's quilt didn't match the pillowcase.

A figure sat in front of the window, facing away from the door and staring at the closed curtains. Adrienne cleared her throat, gently shut the door, and stepped towards the woman. "Hey, Marion? It's Addy. I came to see how you were."

There was no response. Adrienne's skin began to prickle, but she tried not to let her discomfort show. *She's not long come home from hospital, and the doctors said she had shock. She probably doesn't feel well.*

"I wanted to thank you for the food basket you made. That was incredibly sweet of you." She moved to stand at the other woman's side. Marion didn't look well; the waxy pallor she'd had at the gravesite lingered, and dark circles under her eyes suggested she hadn't slept. She didn't look at Adrienne but kept her attention focussed ahead, seeming to watch something intently despite the drawn curtain.

Adrienne didn't know what to do. Her instincts were telling her to get out of there, that something was very clearly wrong, but she didn't want to leave Marion if she needed help. She carefully placed the basket on the ground beside the chair and tried to smile. "And—and the mirrors as well. Jayne said that was your idea. Thank you."

Marion twisted to face Adrienne, and the blank expression contorted into shock and anger. "She gave them to you?" she asked, her voice raw and cracked. "I told her to bury them."

"I..." Adrienne glanced towards the door, wishing Kris would return, but no one came.

Marion held the gaze for a minute, then her features relaxed as her eyes slid back towards the curtains. "I suppose it doesn't matter. She was in the box when I saw her. But I don't think she's still there."

Adrienne tried to swallow, but her mouth was dry. "I don't understand, Marion. Do you feel sick? Would you like me to call the doctor?"

"She was in the box, covered in dirt." Marion spoke slowly, her words slurring, as her eyes glazed over. "I saw her in my mirror. Made me swerve. Hit a tree. But I don't think she's there now."

"I'm going to get your mother, okay?" Adrienne hated how high her voice was. She began to back towards the door, but Marion's next words froze her.

"Do you want to know what Jayne said?" She turned in her

chair as a humourless smile tugged at her lips. "I know you saw us laughing when you passed us in that taxi. D'you want to know what she said?"

Adrienne shook her head. Her heart was thumping against her ribcage, and she felt as if she might be sick. The room was stuffy, and stress was digging into her mind, compromising her ability to reason.

"She said, 'That'll be Ashburn's new owner.'" Marion's body began to shake with silent laughter as her eyes, flat and dead, arrested Adrienne. "'I wonder how long it'll be before she goes mad, too.'"

"I have to go." Adrienne felt behind her for the doorknob. She didn't want to take her eyes off the other woman or turn and make her back vulnerable. Marion remained in her seat, hands held limply in her lap, her lips frozen into a lifeless smile.

Adrienne found the doorhandle and turned it. She ducked through and made a final attempt at conversation. "I made you a cake. I-I hope you l-like it."

No answer, but the joyless smile twitched a little larger.

Adrienne closed the door and stepped back from it. Her heart thundered as though she'd been running, and a high, ringing pitch filled her ears. She took the stairs carefully, her legs feeling too tense to move smoothly, and found Kris blocking the hallway leading to the front door.

"Well, how was she?" The older woman was drying her hands on a dishcloth and looked weary. "Did she show any signs of coming out of that lair?"

"I think she needs a doctor." The words spilt out of Adrienne in a rush. "I don't think she's well."

Kris's tight smile collapsed into a scowl, and she flipped the cloth over her shoulder. "Nonsense. She only got a little scab from the crash. She's making a fuss over nothing."

"I think something's wrong." Adrienne glanced over her shoulder, towards the stairs and the closed door at their top. "She wasn't like this a couple of days ago."

"You haven't been upsetting her, have you?" Kris looked disgusted. "She needs to move on, not dwell on it like some shrinking violet. I already told that Jayne girl not to keep harping on about the accident."

"I'm sorry." Adrienne didn't know what she was apologising for as she edged around the irate woman, but she felt partially responsible for what had happened to her friend. "I need to go."

Kris huffed but didn't stop Adrienne as she hurried to the front door and let herself out.

The sun was still bright and hot, but it did very little to warm Adrienne's clammy skin. Her arms felt empty and useless now that she didn't have the basket or the laptop to carry, so she wrapped them around herself as she hurried back towards the street that would lead to Ashburn Walk.

At least it explains why Jayne didn't want to come back here.

Adrienne had stopped just inside on the house's threshold

and stared down the length of the hallway as she organised the thoughts that had been swirling through her mind during the walk home. The house was silent around her, almost as though it were holding its breath to let her think. *She's not upset because her friend crashed here. She's upset because Marion has been acting strangely ever since.*

The grey tabby, silent and elegant as a shadow, slipped out of the kitchen, fixed his sea-green eyes on her, then turned to climb the staircase. Adrienne watched his fluffy feather-duster tail bob with each step until it disappeared from view. She wondered where he was headed. He might have found a warm spot with a good view of the yard, or perhaps he was in the mood to explore more.

Is Marion still in shock? It shouldn't last this long, should it? And if it did, the doctors wouldn't have discharged her from hospital...

The house was at least ten degrees colder than the outside. Adrienne pushed away from the door and went into the kitchen to turn the kettle on.

IS IT FRIDAY

LIGHT THE CANDLE

She stared at the words for a long moment then exhaled. Wolfgang had knocked the cloth off the table again. She picked it up, shook it out, and replaced it. There was an empty glass vase in one of the higher cupboard shelves, and Adrienne half filled it with water then placed it on the table to act as a weight. It looked odd without flowers.

The kettle finished boiling, but Adrienne left the room without touching it. *If it's not shock, then what's wrong with her?*

Depression? Bipolar disorder? She was so bright and cheerful when she came to visit. And so proud of the jam she'd made.

Adrienne collected the empty kindling bucket from the lounge room and carried it outside. There were still a few hours until sunset, but she didn't ever want to be caught without light again. She turned and circled the house before approaching the woods. Dry sticks littered the ground, and she was able to let her thoughts wander as she filled the bucket.

Jayne said Marion had donated her mirrors to me. But it sounds like that was a sanitised spin on what actually happened; Marion asked for help disposing of her mirrors, and Jayne decided to pass them on to me.

It didn't take long for the bucket to grow heavy. A flowering vine ran up one of the trees nearby, and Adrienne picked a few of its blossoming tendrils to fill the kitchen vase then turned back to the house.

Marion said something about seeing a woman in her mirror before the crash. She must have meant her car's rear-view mirror. But who did she see?

Something crunched under Adrienne's boot as she crossed the porch, and she stepped back to see what it was. Clumps of dirt littered the surface. She'd been so wrapped up in her thoughts during the walk home that she hadn't noticed them.

Must have come from the kids who scared me last night.

She scuffed the larger clumps off the porch's edge with her sneaker then backed into the house. It was growing dimmer as the sun lowered, so she turned the hallway light on and sighed at how little it helped.

As she carried the bucket of wood towards the lounge room, she turned to look at her own reflection in the hallway mirror she'd hung the day before. She looked pale and unhappy and tried to smile at her visage. In the reflection, it looked more like a grimace. She turned into the lounge room, placed the bucket in its space beside the fireplace, then gathered the flowers and returned to the hallway.

Why did Marion want to throw away her mirrors? Why didn't Edith have any in her home? How likely is it that those two choices are connected?

Adrienne stopped in the kitchen doorway and let the flowers fall from her hands. The off-white cloth lay in a heap at the end of the table, its creases sagging as it soaked up the water from the smashed vase.

CHAPTER 23
UNNATURAL

ADRIENNE MADE HERSELF A promise as she collected the broken glass shards and used the tablecloth to mop up the water: she wasn't going to be the girl who investigated creepy noises in the basement at the start of horror movies, nor would she be the one who said, *It's probably just the wind,* while a serial killer tried to kick his way into the house.

The combined events from the previous days—the sunset phenomenon, Marion's accident and change in personality, the intruder the night before, and the sliding tablecloth—weren't enough to definitely say there was something wrong. But they were warning signs, and she suspected she'd already ignored them more than was wise.

She had no idea what those warning signs might be point-ing towards, though. The rumours circulating about Ashburn focussed on ghosts, but she didn't put much stock in that idea.

She'd watched her fair share of ghost-hunting documentaries and had ultimately concluded that if the professionals couldn't gather clear, definitive proof, then ghosts either didn't exist or were so intangible that they wouldn't bother anyone who wasn't looking for them.

But that didn't mean there was nothing to worry about. She was a somewhat unfit, unarmed woman living alone. Her only knowledge of self-defence came from a two-hour class she'd taken as a teenager and could barely remember. And as idyllic and calm as Ipson seemed, bad things could happen in the most unlikely locations.

As a child, she'd read about a German family who had been murdered with a mattock in their remote, snow-bound farmstead. The police investigation had revealed that someone had been hiding in the barn for days before the murder. The story had lingered with her, and she wasn't keen on experiencing a re-enactment.

And so, as she dropped the last glass shards into a bag, she promised herself she would face the situation with equal doses of caution and pragmatism. There was a good chance her fears were unfounded. Coincidences were common, and strange things happened every day.

But she would be careful.

Adrienne threw the bag into the outside bin she found near the fuse box. She dried her hands on her jeans as she re-entered the house and checked the grandfather clock in the hallway. It was a little after four, which meant she had a few hours until sundown.

That would be the first stage of her investigation. It was too late to risk walking to town and making it back before night, but she would document the phenomenon that evening as carefully as she could and then speak to the townspeople about it the next morning. There was a good chance they wouldn't know what she was talking about, but even that was valuable data. It would mean the situation was localised.

Next, she wanted to learn everything she could about the Ashburn family. Not just Edith, who was an enigmatic paradox in her mind—hostile yet kind, reclusive but welcoming—but also Edith's parents, aunt, and uncle. She wanted to know when they'd moved to Ashburn, whether they'd built or bought the house, and how they'd died. Beyond that, there wasn't much she could do except be cautious and wait until she could afford a mobile phone.

Adrienne returned to the kitchen and chewed at her lip as she surveyed the bare table. She didn't think there was anyone in the house—she'd been careful to keep all doors locked since the encounter the night before—but the horror story of the snow-bound family unwittingly harbouring a killer flashed through her mind again, so she took the largest, sharpest knife she could find in the kitchen drawer and began to search the house.

She checked both ground-floor doors and any window a human could fit through as she passed them. They were all still closed and locked, and none showed any signs of forced entry. Keeping the windows closed had the unfortunate side effect of making the house stuffy and claustrophobic, but she would have to live with that until she was certain she was safe.

161

As she passed through the rooms, Adrienne looked inside wardrobes and cupboards as a precaution and hunted for any signs that someone other than her and Edith had been in the house. She found nothing.

The last room she checked was the attic. Just like the first time she'd seen it the message cut into the huge black door made chills ripple along her back.

LIGHT THE CANDLE
YOUR FAMILY
IS STILL
DEAD

What happened, Edith? What made you write these messages?

She slipped into the room and gave her eyes a moment to adjust to the dim light. It looked different during the day; the wax-coated candleholder was easier to identify, and the shadows felt less suffocating. Even so, the black curtains hung over the windows did a good job of blocking out the sun's warming effects.

Adrienne skirted around the room, checking behind the candle boxes, before returning to the table that held the matchbox and photo. Child-Edith stared up at her, eyes widened in slight surprise, a mischievous upturn to the corners of her mouth, long hair swinging behind her as she explored the garden. It was amazing how well Charles Ashburn, her uncle, had captured her likeness. Beth had said he had been a famous artist and in high demand, and Adrienne could see why. The child in the portraits hung along the hallway below was almost a perfect copy of the photo.

Adrienne moved to the only window without a black cloth

cover and looked towards the town. It was harder to see during the day when the lights weren't glimmering like beacons in the black. Ipson had a lot of trees along its streets, and while she could make out roofs and even a few roads, the town almost looked like an extension of the woods.

There didn't seem to be an easy way to climb up the house's exterior to reach the attic, but she locked the windows just in case before returning downstairs and putting the knife back into its drawer. Searching the house had taken nearly an hour, but there was still time to burn before nightfall. Adrienne tried to distract herself by tidying the already-clean rooms, but she couldn't keep her eyes from wandering towards the windows every few minutes.

She finally gave up, threw down the cloth she'd been mechanically rubbing across a shelf, and went back to the lounge room. It was early for a fire, but she started one anyway. She'd considered watching the phenomenon from one of the upstairs rooms where she would have a better view, but she doubted it would reveal much. She'd been in the attic during the second night's sunset, and the only thing she'd seen were the birds scattering from the trees. And if the phenomenon caused the same panicky sensation she'd felt the previous three nights, she wanted to be somewhere safe and familiar.

Once the fire had caught on a larger log, Adrienne turned the room's light on, collected a pen and paper, and drew her seat close to the window. She sat patiently, watching as the sun dipped closer to the treetops, and waited to feel the creeping, anxious sensation she'd learned to associate with nightfall.

Shortly after the pale-blue sky started to fade into dusky purples, Wolfgang sauntered into the room and flopped in front of the fire. Adrienne flashed him a tight smile. "Aren't you worried? Sun's almost down."

He ignored her but stretched out to his full, impressive length to expose maximum belly surface to the heat. Adrienne tried to chuckle, but the laughter died quickly as she turned back to the window.

Nightfall was only a few minutes away. If the previous days' routine repeated itself, the woods outside would fall still and quiet, and the anxiety would begin any second. Adrienne searched her emotions, but she felt nothing except nervous anticipation. She tapped her pen on the paper, impatient, as she watched the sunset fade into darkness.

The birds continued to chatter as they settled down for the night. Wolfgang remained sleeping on the rug. The trees swayed gently in the breeze, and day transformed into night.

Adrienne stayed seated for nearly ten minutes more, held in suspension for the event that never came. By the time stars began to spread over the sky, she was forced to drop the pencil in disbelief.

"I didn't imagine it," she said to the sleeping cat. "It really happened."

He flicked his ear. Adrienne gave the forest one final, confused look, frowning at the placid trees and quietening birds. "I didn't imagine it," she repeated in a softer voice. "Did I?"

CHAPTER 24
UNWELCOME FORAY

SILENCE PRESIDED OVER THE house as Adrienne ate her dinner. She'd tried to prepare herself something special by boiling two of the remaining eggs and dipping biscuits into them, but the result was a sad, lonely meal for one.

She wished she had company. Anyone would have been welcome—Jayne and her friends, Peggy the vet's receptionist, or even chattering June from the grocery store. Without the laptop, she couldn't even visit one of the forums she haunted. She had never felt so thoroughly *alone*.

The biscuits tasted like sand, and she dropped the final one back onto the plate half-eaten. She would have given her right arm for some form of mindless distraction. A TV, some light-hearted romance novels, or even a radio would have provided a welcome relief from her thoughts. But Ashburn offered no diversions except to wander its halls and gaze into the empty, musty rooms that had housed a woman who had dedicated her life to solitude.

"Pull yourself together, Addy." She shoved away from the table and made a conscious effort to keep her eyes off the now-familiar inscription carved into its wood. "You're tired. You're stressed. That's all this is. Get some sleep, and things will seem a million times better in the morning."

She dropped the eggshells and uneaten biscuit into the bin and began washing the plate and spoon. Moonlight dappled over the yard outside, and Adrienne leaned forward to admire it through the window while she waited for hot water to run through the taps.

The yard and forest beyond looked hauntingly beautiful that evening. As the moon edged closer to full, it brought the shapes into sharper relief. Adrienne could make out the individual branches in several trees and one bush that stood a little ahead of the woods' edge that looked like a hunched, twisted woman. *It's amazing how much night-time can change something. I never noticed that shrub before; it probably looks just like any other plant in the daylight.*

Hot steam misted up from the sink, and Adrienne turned her attention to scrubbing the dried scraps of yolk off her plate and cutlery. It was still early in the evening, but her lack of sleep the night before was starting to weigh her down. *I'll go to bed early and wake up in time to walk to town just as the shops are opening. Ipson is bound to have a local historian or similar—someone who collects newspapers and maintains records of the town's occupants. I'll just have to ask around to find them.*

She lifted the clean plate, shook the excess water off it, and glanced towards the window. The odd, human-shaped shrub was gone.

Adrienne's heart lurched unpleasantly. She dropped the plate back into the sink and pressed close to the glass.

It was right there; I'm sure of it.

The patch of weedy grass she scanned was empty. She leaned farther forward, pressing so near the window that her nose bumped the cold glass and her ragged breathing spread plumes of condensation.

It must be one of the children. Who did Jayne say it would be? The Crowther boys, wasn't it? Adrienne stepped back from the sink. Sweat beaded over her palms, and she rubbed them against her jeans. *I've got to make them leave. Show them this is no joke.*

But even as she turned towards the hallway, an anxious voice began chattering in the back of her mind, reminding her not to take risks, not to ignore the red flags. It was almost certainly the Crowther boys. But there was also a tiny chance it was something else. And she couldn't afford to take chances.

Adrienne retrieved the long, serrated knife from the kitchen drawer and clutched it close to her chest as she entered the hallway. Ashburn was ponderously quiet around her. She could hear the grandfather clock's ticking interspersed with her own quick, panicky breaths, but the house itself lay still, silent, and waiting.

The moon is bright but not bright enough. I need some stronger light.

She kept her attention focussed on the front door and the two little windows on either side as she backed up the hallway till she reached the little lamp beside the stairs. The match caught with a quiet hiss, and she transferred the flame onto the wick, replaced the glass top, and began pacing back towards the door.

She couldn't see any motion through the windows or hear any telltale creaks from the porch boards, but she still wasn't able to shake the thought that someone might be lingering on the other side, hidden in the blind spot between the windows, waiting for her to unlock the door. She slowed as she drew closer and held her breath, listening, waiting, then pressing near the distorted windows to see through.

With only the moon to light it, the porch appeared as a ripple of muted blues and greys. There didn't seem to be anything outside the door, so Adrienne braced herself, raised the knife, disengaged the lock, and turned the handle.

The lamp's yellow glow pressed against the shadows, forcing them back into the forest and lighting up the lawn. She wished it were brighter. Its circle wasn't strong enough to reach through the trees to where the dark coagulated like an impenetrable wall.

She searched for any motion or human sounds, but the air held nothing except insect songs and the groaning trees. Adrienne swallowed, took a deep breath, and prepared to call a warning.

A strange hissing, whining noise stopped the words in her throat. She twisted towards the house in time to see its lights flicker and fail. Suddenly, her lamp became her only source of illumination, and its circle of influence felt claustrophobically small.

Adrienne tried to speak, but fear squeezed the breath out of her. With its windows cold and black, Ashburn no longer felt like home but seemed to transform into a monstrous, incomprehensible shape towering over her. The forest lost any sense of familiarity she'd developed for it, and its sounds changed into a slow, ponderous, threatening symphony.

Stop it! You're going to be fine. Think this through—the lights are out. You can turn them on at the fuse box just like Jayne showed you yesterday.

But the fuse box was around the side of the house. She would have to wade through the blackness to reach it.

You have a lamp. You're not blind.

Something was out there, though—something that had come back for the second night in a row to rob her of light.

It's just kids. They probably think this is hilarious. It's frankly surprising that you can't hear any laughter.

She turned in a circle to survey the area. She couldn't see far; the porch was a small haven of light, but the lamp's glow only brushed the edges of the forest, and long stretches of yard to either side were invisible.

It was probably just children. But *probably* wasn't *certainly*. She clutched the knife closer.

She had two options: turn the lights back on—which would involve circling the house—or retreat inside and wait for dawn.

Adrienne squeezed her lips together at how unappealing the choice was. She'd locked every door and window, but that didn't guarantee the house was impenetrable. And although the lamp gave her a small measure of protection at that moment, it wouldn't last more than an hour before needing to be refilled.

Take a risk to regain the light, or hide and wait in the darkness?

It wasn't a fair choice. She couldn't survive another night like the one before, when she'd sat stiff and cold during the early hours as she waited for dawn. Adrienne forced her spine to straighten, lifted the lamp a little higher, and yelled, with every ounce of force she could muster, "I know you're there! And I'll call your dad if I catch you coming back! Don't think I won't!"

Good job sounding like a cantankerous old woman. Maybe you should shake your cane at them while you chase them off the lawn.

Adrienne held still, listening and searching, but neither heard nor saw any sign of motion.

They might have already left. Or they could still be out there, watching. They'd be well hidden in the dark, but thanks to the lamp, I must stand out like a beacon.

She filled her lungs with air again and took a chance on a lie. "I have a gun, and I'm not afraid to use it. Tell your friends—I'll shoot the next person who comes here without an invitation!"

Again she waited and again heard nothing but creaking trees and bat chatter. She blew air out through cold lips, locked the front door, and stepped into the yard.

The weedy grass reached her knees, and Adrienne was suddenly struck by how easy it would be for someone to blend into the shadows if they crouched in just the right place. She tried not to dwell on it as she hurried around the house's corner.

She hadn't put her jacket on, and the wind bit as it swirled past her. Adrienne kept her eyes moving, scanning the space surrounding her, but her thundering heart and the scrape of her feet through the grass drowned out all other noises.

The fuse box, a plain grey square against the house's dark wood, was still closed. She waded through the weeds and shrubs surrounding it, put the knife between her teeth, and raised the lid.

Just as the day before, all of the switches were off. Adrienne glanced behind her a final time then rested the box's lid on her head so that she could flick the switches up. As power returned to the house, lights appeared in the windows, and the squares of gold helped bring the outside world into relief. Adrienne felt as if she could breathe again as she lowered the lid back into place.

She would have liked a padlock to keep the fuse box closed but didn't know if Ashburn had any. Instead, she put the lamp on top of the box, bent, and pulled the shoestring out of her sneaker. It fit through the little hole in the lid that had been designed for a padlock, and Adrienne threaded it through several times before tying it into a tight, complicated knot. It wouldn't stop a dedicated vandal but should at least discourage them. Her shoe no longer fit properly, but that was a small price to pay for keeping the lights on.

Adrienne retraced her path back towards the porch. She felt calmer now that the windows created regular blocks of lighted sanctuary. The house was no longer a foreign entity; it was her home. She climbed the porch, unlocked the front door, entered, locked it again, and tucked the key safely into her back pocket.

Wolfgang crouched at the end of the hallway. His eyes were

flashing circles, his ears flattened to his head, and his fur had bushed out.

"Hey, buddy. Shh." Adrienne kept her voice soft and gentle as she approached him. "It's all right. It's just me."

Wolfgang's mouth opened as he expelled a low, rumbling yowl. The fur along his back prickled up even farther, and he shuffled backwards into the wall.

Adrienne stopped walking. She'd never seen her pet so frightened before; he looked as if he was about to start frothing at the mouth.

"Hey," she whispered and lowered herself to the floor. She put the still-lit lamp and knife to one side and stretched her hand towards her pet so that he could sniff it. "It's just me. Everything's all right. Shhh."

That was when she realised Wolfgang wasn't focussed on her, as she'd first assumed. His round, bulging eyes stared at something over her shoulder.

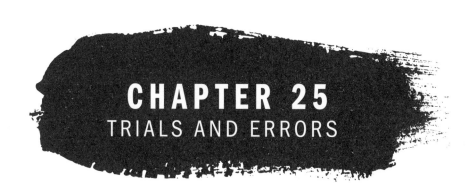

CHAPTER 25
TRIALS AND ERRORS

ADRIENNE TURNED AND SAW motion.

Her mind, stretched thin and taut with fear, struggled to identify all of the shapes along the cluttered hallway. The tables, stands, clock, and shelves all took on a terrible importance, and they harboured strange shadows about their bases where neither the dim ceiling light nor the lamp could penetrate. Adrienne's eyes darted over each object in turn, searching them, trying to locate the motion that had turned her heart to ice.

The hallway was empty.

She shifted forward an inch, hardly believing it, and caught the motion again. It was her own reflection in the mirror she'd hung opposite the lounge room. Adrienne exhaled and clutched at her chest, where her heart was beginning to beat again.

Behind her, Wolfgang's growls settled into silence. She peeked at him over her shoulder and saw that the fur was starting to deflate and his ears weren't clamped down so fiercely.

She turned back to the hallway and slowly, shakily regained her feet. As she picked up the lamp, the light glittered over the windows on either side of the door, and a mark on the left-hand one stunned her.

Is that…?

She moved closer, breath held, to examine the smudgy handprint.

That wasn't there when I came inside.

Chills trickled through her. The print was a little smaller than her own hand, but the fingers were longer and thinner. The outline was created out of condensation that evaporated into nothing even as she watched.

"Who…?"

A quiet fizzling echoed from deeper in the house, but she didn't realise what was happening until the lounge room's light clicked out. A second later, the hallway's light died, and she was once again stranded with only the lamp.

Wolfgang hissed when she ran towards him but didn't try to fight as she scooped him up. She clutched the cat against one shoulder, gripped the knife between her teeth, took the lamp in her spare hand, and ran up the stairs. All she could think about was getting them into a room that only had one door and was small enough to light properly. Ashburn had never felt so gloomy before.

The portraits tracked her progress with silent glee as she ran past them. The lamplight caught on the paint, making them seem almost alive, as though they would shift and turn in their frames as soon as she took her eyes off them. Wolfgang's claws punctured her shoulder as he clung to her, but Adrienne bit the inside of her cheek and held him tighter.

She kicked open the door at the end of the hallway and dived through. When she turned, she fully expected to see something following her down the hallway, but it was empty save for the eerily lifelike paintings. She closed the door with a hard shove, locked it, and lowered Wolfgang onto her bed. He shot her an offended glare then hopped onto the floor and began examining the new room.

Adrienne dropped the knife and lamp onto the bedside table then ran her hands through her hair. She was struggling to breathe. A mantra ran through her mind, but it was becoming increasingly difficult to believe. *It's just kids. It's just kids. It's just kids. I hope.*

She couldn't remember any of her childhood friends being creative, clever, or dedicated enough to pull off some of the frights she'd experienced that night—certainly not without breaking into giggles or exchanging stage whispers.

What are you saying, Addy?

The townspeople joked that the house was haunted. They spread tales about incorporeal creatures whispering into their ears and spoke of seeing disembodied faces in the windows.

Whatever this is, it isn't a ghost. Spirits can't cut through shoelaces to turn the power off or leave wet handprints on the outside of windows.

But why would someone go to such effort to scare her? They hadn't vandalised or burgled the house and were apparently trying not to be seen.

Is someone trying to frighten me away?

It was one of the simplest explanations. The cut lights and handprint were incredibly effective fear tactics. But the *why* stumped her. If there was someone in town who had been close to Edith—a carer or relative—they might have had a sense of entitlement to her estate. But all accounts suggested Edith had lived a solitary life.

Well, if someone is trying to chase me out, they're going to have a tough time. I have nowhere else to go. Like it or not, Ashburn is my home for the immediate future.

Wolfgang, his examination of the room complete, leapt onto the bed and sat with his paws tucked neatly under himself. Adrienne settled beside him and buried her hand into his fur for comfort.

No one could get into the room without breaking through the door. She had a knife for self-defence, but the lamp's oil wouldn't last more than an hour. She suspected it was going to be another long night.

Adrienne woke to sunlight cutting across her face. She felt groggy and sore and tried to roll over, only to discover her legs were draped over the edge of the bed. She moaned, shifted fully onto the mattress, then flinched as something heavy fell and clinked on the floor. *The knife.* Wolfgang sprawled beside her, contorted so that his head was upside down, and deep, rumbling purrs serenaded her.

The previous night felt like a bizarre dream. She'd sat on the bed's edge with every intention of staying awake through the night but had fallen asleep even before the lamp's flame died. Judging by the sun's angle, it was several hours past dawn.

"Why'd you let me sleep so late, buddy?" She scratched under Wolfgang's chin, making him shiver happily. His purrs were easing away her anxiety and stress. It was as though he were saying everything was good with the world again, and it was hard to argue.

Her problems weren't gone—far from it—but with the sunrise, she'd been given twelve hours of daylight to figure something out.

"I'm going to have to figure real hard, Wolf." She stared at the ceiling but kept her fingers stroking his fluffy cheeks. "Last night took stuff past simple coincidences and into legitimate-threat territory. Best-case scenario, this town has some really dedicated pranksters, and I'm going to have to talk to their parents. Worst-case scenario…" The rural snow-bound family, butchered with a mattock and not found for days, flashed into her mind again, and she grimaced. "Well, anyway, I'm thinking the original plan is still my best option. What d'you think?"

The original plan—to document everything, be cautious, and research what she could—was truthfully less of a *best* option and more of an *only* option. But Wolfgang didn't need to know that.

True to form, the tabby didn't respond. Adrienne inhaled deeply, huffed the breath out, and rose.

Her shoulder ached, and she had to feel the little droplets of dried blood to remember Wolfgang's claws had dug in there. A small headache lingered in the back of her skull, a remnant of the stress, and her hip and leg muscles were stiff from where they'd been draped off the bed, but otherwise, she felt surprisingly good. Not even an icy-cold shower could break her new enthusiasm.

She fed Wolfgang and boiled Edith's half packet of pasta. There wasn't any sauce to go with it, but that didn't bother her. While she ate, she walked through the building and checked the windows and doors. She wasn't surprised to find them all closed and intact. Whoever came onto her property at night didn't seem to care about actually entering the house.

Once she'd finished eating, she went outside to check on the damage to the fuse box. She'd had no qualms about searching her home, but stepping outside was another matter. The window beside the door was now clear, but she couldn't forget the handprint with its long, narrow fingers pressed into the glass.

Adrienne stood on the porch for a long minute before stepping into the grass and circling around the house. The fuse box waited at the side, half-hidden behind weeds and shrubs, and Adrienne swallowed an unpleasant lump in her throat when she saw it.

The shoelace was still threaded through the lock hole. She bent close to examine it in case it had been undone and replaced, but she recognised the complex, lumpy knots she was so fond of.

They turned the power off without touching the fuse switches. How?

She slowly, painstakingly untangled her knot. The sun beat down on her back as she worked at it, and she was sweating by the time the lace came free. She opened the lid, flicked all of the switches up to restore power to her house, then slammed it closed and turned to survey the woods.

If the stranger had an alternate method for cutting her power, there was no point in locking the box again; it would just delay her when she had to turn it back on. Adrienne knelt and returned the dirty lace to her shoe.

She would have to ask Jayne how else the power could be cut. The fact that she could turn it back on meant the wires were intact, fortunately. Jayne had said one section of the house could be blown by a bad appliance, but that didn't explain how they could all be knocked out in a matter of seconds.

Adrienne sighed, filed the problem into her increasingly full mental box labelled "How and Why?" and turned towards the woods.

She'd overslept that morning, courtesy of a disturbed sleep the day before, and the sun told her it was late morning. She needed to move quickly if she wanted to chase all available threads of enquiry.

CHAPTER 26
THREADS

SHE HIKED ASHBURN WALK quickly, running down the steepest slopes and jumping over the edge of the stairs rather than zigzagging down them. She counted through her tasks as she walked, and she tried to prioritise her time.

She wanted an update on Marion's condition. Visiting again didn't seem like a smart option, but she hoped that, in a town as small as Ipson, news would spread quickly and someone could tell her how her friend was faring.

A higher priority, though, was to find out if anyone in the town had an abnormal obsession with Ashburn. The culprit could be someone who had developed a fixation on the building as a child and grown into a not-quite-mentally-right adult. It could be someone who felt entitled to the land in some way; perhaps their parents had helped build the house. Or it could be someone who simply wanted a home on the mountain and was prepared to go to great lengths to buy the property cheaply.

No matter the cause, Adrienne hoped the perpetrator would have left breadcrumbs. They might have talked about Ashburn a little more than was normal or dropped hints to friends. If she spoke to enough people, she felt she had a good chance of finding something.

But she didn't have any leads on where to begin her enquiries, so she decided to combine that goal with another priority: learning about Ashburn's history.

Once she reached the main road, Adrienne followed it until she found the library in one of the side streets. It was a surprisingly modern and clean building though not especially large. Ferns hung in baskets around its door, and the coat of egg-blue paint was just messy enough to make Adrienne think it was a volunteer job.

She used her fingers to brush her hair back, hoping she didn't look too windblown after the dash down the forest path, then slipped through the front door.

The library was cool and blissfully quiet. The reception desk sat against the right-hand wall near the door, and a row of tables and comfy chairs were set up under the windows to the left. Past them, rows of shelves filled the rest of the room. They'd been arranged carefully but weren't very full. Beth's comment about the library being starved for recently published books seemed accurate.

Adrienne approached the front desk and waited for one of the two librarians to notice her. The taller of the ladies turned, and her face lit up with a flash of recognition.

"Oh! Adrienne!" Sarah hurried forward, a stack of books clasped under one arm and her eyes wide with surprise. "I'm so sorry; I didn't see you come in."

"I almost didn't recognise you." Adrienne laughed. "You look so different!"

Sarah kept her long, sandy hair out of her face with a hairband, and large glasses magnified her eyes. The suit she'd worn when visiting Ashburn had been swapped for a cardigan and slacks, and she wasn't wearing makeup. Adrienne liked the new look.

"Jayne says I look better with contacts." Sarah adjusted the glasses self-consciously as the hint of a shy smile appeared. "But these are more comfortable."

"They suit you."

The second librarian, an older woman with a dark perm, shot them a warning glare. Adrienne lowered her voice to a whisper. "I'm glad you're here, actually. Have you heard from Marion today?"

"Oh." Sarah's sigh deflated her whole person. "She's, um. She's not feeling very well. Jayne and I tried to visit this morning, and Beth visited last night, but she doesn't want to see anyone."

"I'm really sorry," Adrienne said. It was an impulsive statement, but Sarah seemed to understand. She took Adrienne's upper arm and steered her towards the back of the library, where they could talk without incurring the wrath of the older librarian.

"It's not your fault," Sarah said after checking over her shoulder to make sure they weren't going to disturb anyone. "Jayne told me you helped look for her. That was so brave."

Adrienne shrugged awkwardly. "Not really. Do you know what's wrong with her? Has her mother taken her back to the doctor?"

Sarah shook her head with a tight-lipped grimace. "Kris is… um… she's not…" She paused to gather her thoughts then continued in a rush. "Kris is really, really strong. And I think she expects everyone else to be the same. When she heard that Mar had thrown her mirrors away—" She stopped herself and shot Adrienne an anxious glance.

"It's all right; I knew. It was very kind of Jayne to give them to me."

"Okay, good." She exhaled and shrugged. "Well, Kris wasn't happy with that at all. Apparently, she bought new mirrors, and Marion smashed them, so she bought even more, except this time they're break-proof and she glued them to the walls."

Her friend's expression showed that she didn't approve of Kris's methods. Adrienne agreed. After seeing how strongly Marion had reacted to just the mention of mirrors during her visit, she could only imagine how distressing it would be to have them permanently fixed in her room.

"Is there anything I can do?" She already knew the answer, but Sarah's hopeless shrug was still crushing.

"She has our numbers," Sarah said. "We've been friends since we were toddlers. I know she'll call when she's ready to talk. Until then, maybe the best thing we can do for her is to give her some space."

"Okay." Adrienne glanced through the shelves towards the seating area of the library. Half a dozen patrons lounged there while they read, and a couple more were browsing. It felt surreal to see people living their lives so normally when hers had turned into a wreck of confusion and mystery and indecision. She rubbed at the back of her neck. "There's something else I'm hoping you can help me with."

Sarah's flat expression picked up. "Yes?"

"Do you keep copies of any old newspapers?"

"Oh! Um…" Sarah chewed her lower lip. "Some. Not recent ones, I'm afraid. Ipson used to have its own newspaper written and printed by the Pearson family. Gregory Pearson was the last editor, but he passed away about forty years ago, and his son shut the printing press down soon after. It was a labour of love and never made much money, as far as I can tell. Since then, the town has brought in the national papers as well as the local papers from two nearby towns, but we don't have one of our own."

"I was hoping you'd have some papers from when Edith was a child."

Sarah's eyes widened. "To find out how her family died. Of course! Let me think—that would have been at least eighty years ago—so our town would have been producing its papers around that time. Yes, we should have copies of most of them. But they're in storage and not arranged very well, I'm afraid. We inherited them from a… a… collector." She cleared her throat and added in a whisper so low that Adrienne could barely hear, "He was really more of a hoarder, to be completely honest."

"That's fine! I'm just glad you have them. Would it be okay if I had a look through them?"

Sarah took a step back to peek around the shelves. None of the patrons had moved since the start of their conversation. She gave Adrienne a nervous little smile. "I'll help. I don't think Pam will notice if I take my break a little early."

Sarah led her back to the reception desk. The other librarian, Pam, was returning books to their shelves, so Sarah unlocked a door behind the desk and ushered Adrienne inside.

"I'm not really supposed to bring patrons in here," she whispered. "You won't tell, will you?"

Adrienne mimed zipping her lips, and Sarah beamed. Adrienne had the distinct impression that this was the most excitement the other woman had experienced in a long time.

The room seemed to be a sort of storage area. There were no windows, but a single uncovered bulb hung from the ceiling. Industrial shelves covered all walls, and a small table sat in the centre. Sarah paced through the room, mouthing words as she traced the rows of filing codes with her fingers. She stopped near one of the box-filled shelves at the back of the room and knelt to read the labels on the lowest crates. "Here they are. What year did you want to start with?"

Adrienne did the math quickly. Assuming Edith was in her nineties when she passed away, and her family had been murdered when she was eight or nine, which was the oldest she appeared in the portraits… "Let's start in the mid-1920s. We might need to cover a few years, I'm sorry to say."

"No problem at all." Sarah smiled as though she meant it as she pulled one of the boxes out. "The papers were weekly, as I recall, so there won't be more than fifty-two in a year."

Adrienne nodded as she helped carry the box to the table. "And we probably only need to look at the front page of each paper. A local family's murders aren't likely to be buried inside."

Sarah pulled the box's lid off. A small puff of dust exploded out with the motion, and she waved it away as they peered inside. The papers were badly yellowed, and some looked stained. Sarah carefully pulled a bundle out, laid them on the table, and flipped through. "They're not in chronological order, but at least they seem to be from the same year. Want to work through a stack each?"

"Sounds like a plan." Adrienne took out a pile of her own and scanned the first paper's headlines. "Crop Blight Returns: The McGregor Family's Grief." "Young Crime: Officer Stacey Expresses Concern Over Increased Incidence of Loitering."

The paper, the *Ipson Chronicle*, seemed to feature local news exclusively… of which there was very little. Each paper was between three and five pages long and occasionally included a eulogy, a house-for-sale notice, or a birth notice as the town's population shifted.

They worked in silence, scanning a paper's headlines before placing it into a separate pile. Occasionally, there was news of a violent crime—most often, a fist fight outside the pub—but the only reported deaths were accidental or due to old age.

Once the first box had been read through, Sarah refilled it

with the papers, returned it to its spot on the shelf, and brought out a new box. The papers inside had been exposed to water, and some of the ink had bled. Adrienne was still able to read most of the articles, but it slowed her progress.

They were nearing the end of the year 1929 when Sarah gasped. Adrienne looked up, hopeful. "Did you find it?"

"It's not a story about the murders—but it's about the house. Here, read it."

CHAPTER 27
MONOCHROME VANDALISM

SARAH SWIVELLED THE PAPER to face Adrienne and pointed to a tiny article in the lower-right corner.

ASHBURN HOUSE TO BE REOCCUPIED?

Since the tragedy that transpired in our town's most notorious house in the summer of 1918, the Ashburn property has lain dormant. Recently, however, there have been rumours of reoccupation. Mr Paul Grover reportedly sighted labourers carrying timber to the property. When asked what their purpose there was, they claimed to be hired to renovate the house. Some suggest the sponsor and intended occupant may be Miss Edith Ashburn herself, who would have recently turned eighteen and so inherited the property.

"You're kidding," Adrienne muttered and glanced at the paper's date: June 18, 1929. *But that would make Edith over a hundred years old when she passed.*

Sarah was already kneeling beside the boxes and reading their faded labels. "It was a lucky find. Without it, we would have just kept going forward without realising we needed to look earlier."

Adrienne stacked the papers back into their box so that there would be room for the new crate Sarah carried over. She took the lid off, pulled the stack of papers out, and laid them on the table. This time, they searched through the yellowed sheets together.

They only had to sift through four papers before they found what they were looking for. As Adrienne had suspected, the story filled the front page. The title, in huge bold font, read, "GRUESOME SLAUGHTER AT ASHBURN HOUSE."

But the text below made no sense; from what she could figure out, it was talking about a sheep-herding competition.

Sarah lifted the page, and Adrienne's confusion turned to surprise as she saw a rectangular hole in the paper. Someone had carefully, meticulously, sliced out the article's body. The sheep-herding story Adrienne had been reading belonged to the page behind it.

"Unbelievable," Sarah hissed. "Someone must have cut it out as a souvenir."

All that was left of the front page was the title and a smaller article near the base: "Town In Shock." Adrienne read that story, but it only contained interviews from neighbours expressing grief and alarm. There was no information about the deaths, probably because they'd been exhaustively covered in the main article.

"Look in the next paper," Adrienne said. "I'll bet there will be articles following the investigation."

"Good call." Sarah shifted the newspaper to one side, and they both made little upset noises when they saw the tabloid below had been vandalised as well. That paper didn't even contain a heading; nearly half of the front page had been cut out. All that remained were unrelated articles.

Sarah leafed through the paper while Adrienne moved on to the next, and then the one after that, and the one after that. Each *Ipson Chronicle* had been altered. Sometimes large chunks had been carved out, sometimes just a small side column. In every case, the cuts were surgically precise and straight.

With each subsequent paper, the excised sections grew smaller as the story provided less new material, until at last, Adrienne reached a paper that hadn't been touched. She flipped through every page, but there was no mention of Ashburn House.

She turned back to Sarah and saw her face had grown pale and her lips quivered with quiet, restrained anger.

"This is reprehensible," Sarah whispered as she stared at the damaged papers. "These are historical documents—possibly the only copies left. To butcher them this way—if I ever find out who did this—"

Adrienne didn't know what to say. Sarah stared at the papers for a minute then exhaled and gave her a tight smile. "Would you like to keep looking?"

"I don't think there's any point." Adrienne peeked through a few more papers and saw another space where an article had been removed. She dropped them back into place. "Whoever did this was incredibly thorough."

Sarah rose. "I'm really sorry, Addy. I'll ask around town to see if anyone else might have some copies, but—well, it was so long ago—"

"Just shy of a hundred years," Adrienne said as she helped stack the papers back into their box. "That's a long time to keep old newspapers."

They slid the crate back into its space in the shelf, and Sarah turned towards the door. "I'd better go back out. Pam's usually good about letting me take breaks, but I've been gone a while, and her patience has its limits."

"No problem. Thanks for helping me out." Adrienne rubbed at the back of her neck. She also needed to know who was terrorizing her at night, but it was a difficult question to phrase. "Ah, as an aside—do you know of anyone in town who's shown, uh, an abnormal interest in Ashburn?"

Sarah's eyebrows rose. "Well, Beth loves researching it, just like she loves all of Ipson's mysteries. Few that they are."

Adrienne couldn't imagine bright, cheerful Beth attempting to drive her off the property. "Anyone else?"

"Not that I know of. People sometimes talked about Edith if they saw her in the street, but I think mostly they forgot about the house." She tilted her head. "I hope this isn't too rude, but is there a reason you asked?"

Oh yeah, I think someone's trying to frighten me away from my house. Either that, or there's a serial killer who likes playing with their victims. No biggie. It sounded crazy even in Adrienne's mind. She opted for a sanitised version of the truth. "Someone's been coming around the last couple of nights. I'd like to know who so I could talk to them, if possible."

"Huh." Sarah looked a little surprised but nodded. "I can ask about that, as well, if you like."

"That would be great. Thank you. I don't have a phone yet, but, um, I'll pop into town as often as I can. Or send a carrier pigeon or make a smoke signal or something."

Sarah laughed. She went to the door, opened it a crack, and peeked out. "Okay, Pam's tidying the shelves. I'll go out and distract her. Wait a minute, then sneak out and close the door behind yourself, okay?"

Adrienne gave her a thumbs up, so the young librarian slipped out, wearing a smile that was equal parts nervous and excited. Adrienne counted to thirty before cracking the door open. Pam, the older librarian, was facing away and speaking to Sarah, who was gesturing to a book enthusiastically. Adrienne made eye contact with her friend for a split second while creeping out of the room and to the main door.

After being in the cool library for so long, the sun felt beautiful on her skin. She took a deep breath, savouring the clear air, and tried to formulate a plan.

She'd been able to ask after Marion, at least, but the more pressing threads of enquiry had led to dead ends. Someone had gone to great lengths to remove the articles pertaining to the Ashburn deaths. That seemed significant, though she wasn't sure in which way. The thoroughness with which the stories had been clipped spoke to a dedication that went beyond wanting a simple memento. Did the vandal have a motive for erasing the event from the town's memory?

Sarah also hadn't known of anyone who might be a suspect for the nightly visitations. She would need to keep asking about that.

Without any other clear course of action, Adrienne returned to the main street and followed it to the vet's clinic. She'd suspected it might be too soon for the laptop to be returned, and she was correct. Peggy, the vet nurse—just as enthusiastic as she'd been the day before—said her brother was still working on it.

"He says it's something to do with the hard board or mother drive or something." She was talking to Adrienne at the same time as filling out a form for a bug-eyed terrier called Lieutenant Doug. "He reckons he can save all of your documents but needed to order a replacement... oh gosh, it was, uh, a replacement... a replacement... *thing*. He says it should arrive tomorrow."

Ordering *replacement things* sounded expensive. Adrienne laced her fingers together and tried to avoid the terrier owner's curious stare. "Um, did you get a chance to ask him about payment?"

"Oh yeah, that's the best part!" Peggy swivelled back to the computer and began typing the terrier's details into the clinic's database. "He says no charge—but he wanted me to ask for a favour."

A trade—that's good. Trades are good. "Yeah?"

"Well, there's a shortcut to the next town that goes through the mountains. It saves, like, fifteen minutes off the highway. But the first part of it goes along Edith's—that is, uh, *your* driveway. And Edith never let anyone use it. She'd block the road and, in my brother's words, rain a hellfire of a lecture onto you. He wants to know if you'd be cool with him using that path."

Adrienne couldn't believe her luck. "Yeah! Yeah, absolutely!"

Peggy's face opened into a huge grin. "Sweet. Pop back in the day after tomorrow, and your computer should be ready. Here we go, Mrs Carrow," she said, addressing the terrier's owner. "Lieutenant Doug's all set."

Mrs Carrow thanked Peggy, gave Adrienne a polite nod, and carried her dog out. Adrienne waited for the squeaky hinges to subside before leaning closer.

"Peggy, you probably know a lot of people around town, right?"

"Anyone who owns a pet," Peggy said, scribbling on the form. "Which is literally almost everyone. Oh, I hear you have a cat! We do free dental check-ups on the first Tuesday of every month. You should bring him in sometime."

"Great, I'll do that." Adrienne wondered how the news had reached Peggy. Was she friends with Jayne or her companions, or had it gone through multiple mouths? "I was wondering—is there anyone in town who's shown an... er... *unusual* interest in Ashburn?"

Peggy's face scrunched up. "Well, like, most everyone's at least a *bit* curious about it. But mostly in a *glad I'm not its neighbour* sort of way, if you know what I mean. People were really interested when you moved in. They wanted to know if you'd be much like Edith, being her granddaughter and all."

"Grand-niece actually," Adrienne said. "I'm afraid I never met her. Did you?"

"Nah." Peggy's face fell as though it were a great tragedy. "Saw her in town a few times but never talked to her. Apparently, she used to bring injured birds in when she found them, but that was before I started working here."

Everything Adrienne learned about her great-aunt was a contradiction. *She never had guests. She prepared your room. She chased cars off her driveway. She rescued injured birds.* The concepts were having a tug of war in her mind, and the rope felt dangerously close to snapping.

She risked being candid. "I think someone's been coming onto the property at night. But they won't let me see who they are. If you had to guess who it could be, who would you say?"

"Oooh!" Peggy was so excited she almost shot out of her chair. "It could be the ghosts!"

Laughing felt painful, but Adrienne managed to chuckle. "Yeah, it sure could be. But, um, other than that...?"

The vet nurse propped her elbow on the desk and leaned her chin in her palm. "Huh. Wow. I honestly don't know. Mr Truscott asked me if I'd met you when he came in yesterday. He has a lovely Maine Coon. And I heard Suzy Delaney—she's got a horse; we sometimes make house calls—had a bet with Rachel who owns the rabbits."

"A bet?"

Peggy looked faintly embarrassed. "About… about when Edith was gonna die. I didn't approve, you know? I thought it was pretty, uh, mor… mor… what's the word…?"

"Morbid?"

"Yeah. Morbid. And not very kind. But Miss Ashburn wasn't all that well liked, and she was getting kind of old and… yeah." She huffed a sigh. "Sorry. Literally almost everyone in this town has talked about Ashburn at one point or another. But I wouldn't call any of them preoccupied."

"That's okay. I really appreciate you helping, anyway." Adrienne turned to leave but caught herself. Jayne had already suggested some suspects for the night-time visits, and as hard as it was to imagine children being so obsessive, she needed to follow every lead she had. "One other thing—do you know the Crowther boys?"

"Oh yeah, sure! They have two pit bulls."

Adrienne couldn't shake the feeling that Peggy identified people by the animals they owned. "What are they like? Do they pull a lot of pranks?"

"I don't really know them well, sorry. But I don't think they could be visiting Ashburn, if that's what you're wondering. They're both staying with their grandmother in the city this week."

CHAPTER 28
SUN'S ARC

ADRIENNE WANDERED WITHOUT PURPOSE for several minutes. The good news about her laptop had cheered her, but the lack of answers on everything else was becoming frustrating. *All I want is to know whether I'm going to be murdered in my bed tonight. Is that too much to ask?*

The sun had passed its zenith and was beginning the slow glide towards the horizon. Adrienne needed to be back at Ashburn before sundown, which only gave her a handful of hours in town. She'd spoken to Sarah and Peggy, two people whose jobs put them in contact with large segments of the town's population, and had zero leads to show for it. And she had precious few other acquaintances to impose on.

She came to a halt and looked up. Her feet had carried her to the bank, not far from the vet, so she pulled her wallet out of her pocket. Without her laptop, she wouldn't have any notification when her outstanding accounts were paid, but she could at least check her balance.

It had been $3.49 when she'd left her friend's house for Ashburn, and Adrienne felt relief bloom through her chest when the ATM told her she now had a little over sixty dollars. That meant the smaller of the two accounts was paid, bailing her out of immediate crisis.

She withdrew the money and tried to plan a budget for it as she resumed her walk. There were a lot of items on her wish list, but she could only afford a few of them. The biggest priority was a mobile phone. At the moment, she had no way to contact the outside world if she got into serious trouble, and that was a terrifying idea.

Her pantry had enough food to last a few days, but she felt that it would be wise to get more while she had the funds. And she needed some way to defend herself. The knife was better than nothing but would be close to useless if the stalker had a gun, an axe, or any other weapon that extended their range.

Everything else on her wish list—including shampoo, new toys for Wolfgang, and socks that didn't have holes in them—could be pushed back until the next couple of accounts were paid.

Adrienne found her way to Ipson's only phone provider outlet thanks to directions from two men playing chess outside a café. The store clerk rolled his eyes when she asked for help, so Adrienne leafed through the company's brochure instead. The cheapest plan would take fifty-five out of her sixty dollars. She cringed.

Getting a phone is really damn important. But so is not starving. Jeez, jeez, jeez.

Adrienne eventually left the store empty handed. She'd forced herself to think through a worst-case scenario—a crazed axeman breaking into her house—and had come to the grim decision that owning a phone likely wouldn't save her. The police station was in the town's centre, which meant help would take nearly twenty minutes to reach Ashburn. She'd be chopped into mince by then. Finding an effective weapon was a greater priority.

A gun would have been ideal, but at that point, she couldn't even afford the license. Adrienne found the next best thing in the back of the general store, though: mace. The canister was small enough to carry in her pocket and had the bonus of being able to blind an attacker as well as hurting them.

She also collected an armful of budget food, a cheap keychain torch, and batteries, and she splurged on a tin of wet cat food for Wolfgang. *He deserves it after last night.*

June, the chatty store assistant, was more than happy to gossip about the town's occupants. Disappointingly, she couldn't offer anything except an increasingly long list of people who had spoken about Ashburn. She didn't think anyone had shown an exceptional preoccupation with the house, and she hadn't heard anyone talk about one day owning it. Adrienne thanked her and left the store, fifteen dollars remaining in her pocket. She looked at the sky. The sun was dropping much faster than she was comfortable with.

Adrienne retraced her path up the main street and stepped

into the café on the corner. She couldn't afford to waste money on a meal, but a cheap coffee would buy her space at a table for an hour or two.

She chose one of the larger tables, sat straight and alert, and made eye contact with everyone who entered the store. Her hope was that at least a few people would be curious enough about Ashburn to take notice of her. Staring at complete strangers was awkward and embarrassing, but it worked. Within a few minutes a portly, middle-aged gentleman stopped by her table with a cheerful, "Well, you're the new girl from Ashburn House, aintcha?"

Adrienne responded enthusiastically and invited him to sit for a chat, and soon a small crowd had gathered around her table. With so many other people there, Adrienne was able to sit quietly and listen to them swap stories.

A few talked about Ashburn fondly, and a couple sheepishly admitted that they'd sneaked up to the porch as children. One woman with large, horn-rimmed glasses insisted that she'd felt a ghostly hand land on her shoulder once when she was walking past the driveway.

"Spookiest thing I've ever felt," she said. "Like ice running down my spine. I turned around, but there was no one there."

One of the older men gave a snort of disgust. "Ashburn is a lot of things, but it's not haunted."

"How would you know, John? After that poor family got murdered there, I would be surprised if it didn't house a whole coven of ghosts."

A tall, spindly man piped up. "Ghosts don't have covens. Only witches. The correct group noun is a 'fraid' of ghosts."

"No one cares, Jerry."

Adrienne could feel the discussion being derailed and tried to save it. "How did the family die, anyway? I never heard the full story."

A chorus of answers came to her. "Cholera."

"A serial killer attacked them while they slept in their beds. He was never caught."

"Poison in the sugar bowl."

"They all went insane and killed each other."

"I heard it was Edith's father who went through the house and shot them before they could escape."

Adrienne managed a thin smile. "Oh… I, uh, I guess there's not really a consensus, is there?"

The portly man who'd first stopped at her table huffed as though he'd just heard a bad joke. "They're just a bunch of sanitised tales these lot were told as children. They seem to forget that my grandfather was a policeman during that time. I'd say I'm one of the only people in town who knows the real story, but nobody ever bothers to ask me about it."

Adrienne leaned forward, her heart thundering. "Your grandfather was there? What did he tell you about it?"

"Oh, plenty. He went into dementia in his last years, which wiped his memory, but he was staying with me during the early stages and loved to talk about it. Mostly about how much of a botched job it was. It was the first proper murder Ipson had ever seen, and neither he nor his partner knew what to do. They were touching things with their bare hands and moving bodies around and ruining evidence. A few people from the public even traipsed through before backup from one of the larger towns arrived and took over. He said he didn't know any better at the time but wished he could have gone back and smacked himself. He had this idea that, if he hadn't contaminated the evidence, the killer might have been caught."

"It was definitely murder, then?" Adrienne didn't even try to keep the excitement out of her voice.

"You sure you want to hear about this stuff?" The man leaned back in his chair and scrunched his mouth up as he appraised her. "Don't want to give you nightmares."

The chatty woman gave his shoulder a slap. "Come off it, Greg, and just tell us."

Greg raised his eyebrows and looked around. Close to a dozen people had crowded into the little café's corner, some sitting and some standing, to listen in. He surveyed the large audience, and the corners of his mouth twitched up. He laced his hands together. "All right, since you're all so darn curious, I'll tell you what my grandfather passed on to me. I don't think he even shared this stuff with my dad. People didn't really like to talk about the deaths back then; I think they found it too close for comfort. That's why, when kids asked about it, they were given all of these ridiculous half-truths. Cholera, my foot."

The woman who had suggested cholera scowled.

"Like I said, my grandfather was a policeman at the time—one of only two in this town. Ipson was a little larger back then but not by much, so people talked when the Ashburns stopped coming into town. They were the richest family about, which doesn't sound important until you remember that this was just after the turn of the century. We hadn't long moved past the strict social classes of lords and dukes and whatnot; when Ashburn House was established, the Ashburns would have been the most-important family in the neighbourhood."

And perhaps they hadn't adjusted to the twentieth century as well as other families. Adrienne thought of Edith's wardrobe, filled with black silk dresses that would have been outdated even when she was a child.

Greg paused to sip his coffee as he looked about the group to ensure he had their attention. "So when the Ashburns stopped coming into town, people noticed, and it didn't take long for one of their friends to check in on them. My granddad said she came running into the station screaming, 'They're dead, they're dead, my God, they're all dead.' He said she was so hysterical that he had to shake the family name out of her.

"He and his partner left for Ashburn immediately. He reckoned he could feel something bad in the air as soon as they crossed the property bounds. Like a foul smell but one you felt rather than tasted."

"Come off it, Greg," the chatty lady said. "Stop embellishing."

"I'm not! That's how he described it."

They glared at each other for a moment, then Greg sighed and waved a hand as though it weren't important. "Well, regardless, my grandfather said he could smell the blood before he even opened the door. And what he found inside is the reason why the story has been so thoroughly distorted through the last few generations: the truth was too grisly for the teller to want to recount and too horrible for the listener to believe."

He paused for effect, and Adrienne had to squeeze her hands together under the table to stop herself from shaking him. "Yes?"

"The Ashburns had been torn apart. Blood was sprayed over nearly every room in the building, and limbs were scattered everywhere. My grandfather threw up on a dismembered arm. He said that one of the Ashburns seemed to have been trying to escape but was caught just before they reached the door. A red trail of blood ran down the hallway where the body had been dragged back into the house. Mrs Ashburn—Edith's mother— had her whole lower jaw torn off. One of them had been burnt alive. Charles Ashburn's heart was found three rooms away from the rest of his body. He said—and no"—he glared at the chatty woman—"I'm not embellishing this part—he said it was like the house had been baptised in blood."

He still held the crowd's attention, but the expressions of fascination had morphed into revulsion and doubt. The tall, spindly man who'd corrected the use of *coven* looked faintly green.

Greg paused to sip his coffee again. He seemed to be enjoying the story's effect. "To make everything worse, the family had been dead for a couple of days by the time they were found, and were decaying. He said the smell was worse than anything I could imagine, and he was sick all over the crime scene."

"This is ridiculous," the chatty woman interjected. She threw her hands up as though trying to break some spell they'd been pulled under. Her tone was brisk and exasperated, but Adrienne could see beads of sweat developing on her face. "You're an appalling liar, Greg."

Greg just shrugged. "And this is why none of you ever got to hear the real story. You were told lies. Your parents were told lies. Your grandparents were told lies. Because the truth was just too awful to spread."

"I don't understand." Adrienne had her hands clasped around her cup. The coffee inside had cooled to lukewarm, but she couldn't bring herself to drink it. "If the murders were really as awful as that, and if the crime was unsolved, the story would spread. There'd be books written about it. Or it would be in those 'Top Ten Unsolved Murders' lists that float around online. People love mysteries like this."

Greg made a small noise of annoyance in the back of his throat. He held up his hand and began ticking points off on his fingers. "Well, to start with, the Internet wasn't even a pipe dream when the Ashburns were murdered. News spread slowly back then. Ipson was a small town, and its occupants didn't put much effort into record-ing their history. And those top-ten lists you're talking about? Don't think they include every noteworthy unsolved crime. Heck, I doubt they list even a small percentage of them. They just parrot the best-known stories. How many hundreds of thousands of mysteries exist in this world? How many will you hear about, and how many are left to rot in the cold-cases section of some two-man police station?"

Adrienne didn't have any answers.

"Exactly," Greg said, nodding as though he'd won a vital debate. "For a story to spread, people have to hear about it. Ashburn's massacre never reached the greater world, never got circulated, and its place on those top-ten lists was taken by some murder from a town with an actual journalist." He sighed and flexed his shoulders. "Now, let me finish my story. We're almost there, I promise.

"As you'd know, Edith was the only Ashburn to survive the massacre. She'd been hidden in a locked cupboard—probably by one of her parents—and escaped the encounter with just a couple of scratches. She was nonresponsive when found. The police tried to interview her, but she wouldn't say a word. Shock, my grandfather said. I guess nowadays it would be classified as PTSD. She'd listened to her family die then been trapped in a lightless box for two days while her loved ones decayed just metres away."

A tight, painful ache rose in Adrienne's chest as her mind reconstructed the scene. A few people in the crowd began muttering—some in disbelieving shock, some in anger—but Greg continued as though he hadn't heard them.

"Because she was the only survivor, Edith was naturally a suspect in the murders but got cleared pretty quickly. She was only eight at the time, for starters. And the cupboard had been locked from the outside, meaning at least one other person had been alive to hide her in there. She got shipped off to her grand-parents' the following week, her relatives' corpses were cobbled together and buried, and the case went cold. Eventually, the event faded enough from people's memories that they no longer double bolted their doors at night, and they stopped hiding guns under their pillows. And here we are, near to a hundred years later, and people are trying to claim the Ashburns died of cholera. The end."

"You're a real ass, Greg." The chatty woman's face was contorted in anger. "A lying shock jock of an ass."

The tall, weedy man cleared his throat. "Actually, the term shock jock only applies to radio presenters."

The chatty lady was too furious to respond. She turned, threw her half-finished coffee into the bin, and stormed out of the coffee shop. Greg lifted his hands as if to say *What can you do?* then also rose.

"Hope I didn't ruin the house for you," he said to Adrienne. "Don't worry—Edith had the whole thing remodelled when she moved back in. New floors, new walls, the lot. So if you see any weird stains, it's probably not blood." He winked. "Probably."

The crowd was disbanding. Adrienne had the impression some of them would have liked to talk with her, but Greg's horror story must have left such a bad taste in everyone's mouths that they wanted nothing more than to leave and purge it from their minds. *Maybe Greg was right,* Adrienne thought as she made herself drink the cold coffee despite her churning stomach. *Maybe some stories are just too horrible to spread.*

CHAPTER 29
IMPLICATIONS

ADRIENNE SIGHED AS SHE exited the café. The sun was far lower than she'd expected. There wasn't any more time to hunt for answers, but she could still make it back to Ashburn before sundown if she hurried.

Greg's story hung with her, particularly the image of young Edith trapped inside a windowless box while her family was murdered. Nauseating anger churned up her stomach. She realised she hated the town for how callous it had been towards her great-aunt. The ostracisation, the rumours, and even that mean little bet about how soon Edith would die were like thorns digging into the back of her head. Edith clearly hadn't been well, and she might have had a prickly, stubborn personality, but the community should have been kinder to her. It couldn't have been easy for Edith to live in the house where her family had died.

Then why did she?

The question came out of nowhere, but Adrienne couldn't answer it. Greg said the Ashburns had been wealthy, and Edith clearly hadn't been friendless if she'd been raised by her grandparents. So why had she chosen to return to Ashburn House?

"Addy!"

She'd even had the money to fully renovate the building. And if the reconstruction had depleted her fortune, she could have sold the property and moved to a smaller house in a different town.

"Addy! Please, wait!"

Adrienne pulled up short. She'd been so engaged in her puzzle that she hadn't heard the voice or the pounding footsteps. She turned and blinked at Sarah, who clasped a folder to her chest as she ran up the street. "Oh, jeez, I'm so sorry, I didn't hear you!"

"It's fine! Fine!" Sarah, caught up, doubled over and wheezed in laboured breaths. "Oh, wow. Okay. I didn't realise I was so unfit. And Jayne wants us to take up Pilates next month. It might just kill me."

Adrienne laughed and patted Sarah's shoulder while she caught her breath. "It's okay, take your time." *But please not too long; the sun's close to setting.*

"I was about to give up looking for you." Sarah straightened and rubbed wisps of hair out of her flushed face. "I thought you must have gone home."

"You caught me just in time. What happened?"

Sarah was still breathless, but she seemed excited too. "After you'd left, I couldn't stop thinking about those newspapers and how the articles had been cut out. So I asked Pam if she remembered if anyone asked to see them. She's worked at the library for, oh, longer than I've been alive. She was surprised but said yes, that Edith had come in to see them nearly a decade ago."

"Ooh." Adrienne wasn't as surprised as she would have expected to be. She found it easy to picture Edith sitting at the papers with a scalpel and carving out the stories with brisk, precise cuts. "I wonder what she took them for."

Sarah shrugged. "I asked Pam why she didn't stay in the room with Edith. She became flustered and told me she'd been too busy and to mind my own business, but I think she was scared of Edith and didn't want to be around her for too long and—sorry, I'm rambling!"

"No, no, it's fine!" Adrienne's mind was still churning through the news, and she gave Sarah's shoulder a gentle squeeze. "I'm glad you told me."

"That's not all." Sarah raised the folder, and a jittery smile lit up her face. "I thought that the paper might have published another story to recap the deaths when Edith moved back to town—it had been ten years, and memories would need refreshing—so I looked through the papers from around that time. Sadly, they'd been vandalised, too. Edith must have really, really wanted to hide the story. I was about to give up when I found this."

She opened the folder. Inside was one of the newspapers, and Sarah turned it around to show Adrienne. "Read this. It's from two weeks after Edith moved into Ashburn House."

BODYSNATCHERS STRIKE AT IPSON CEMETERY

The family whose name has become synonymous with tragedy has experienced another blow. This past Wednesday, sometime between the hours of 6:00 p.m. and 7:00 a.m., a bodysnatcher exhumed the late Eleanor Ashburn's body.

Groundskeeper Stanley Horvath claims the grounds were undisturbed when he closed the cemetery gates at 6:00 p.m. on Tuesday evening. But when he reopened the graveyard the following morning, a hole had been dug into Eleanor's grave and her remains removed.

"Lord knows why they'd want to do that," Mr Horvath is quoted as saying. "She's been dead these ten years. Wouldn't be much of her to take, you know?"

The culprit is as yet unknown. While many people have voiced suspicion regarding the body's removal so soon after Miss Edith Ashburn's return to town, Constable Bluet says he has both interviewed the heiress and searched her home and is satisfied that she has no part in the body's theft. Investigation is ongoing.

Adrienne had to read the story twice before she could meet Sarah's eyes. Her mind was moving so quickly that she found it difficult to latch onto a single idea. "They didn't say who Eleanor is—was she Edith's mother or her aunt?"

"I don't know. Sorry. Beth might; I'll ask her next time I see her."

211

Adrienne closed the folder and handed it back to Sarah. "Thank you. That was a great find."

"It was, wasn't it?" Sarah grinned and clasped the folder against her chest. "I'd better put this back before Pam locks the library. Visit again soon, though, so I can tell you if I find anything else."

"I'll do that." Adrienne glanced at the sun. It was sinking behind the treetops. "Thank you!"

Sarah raised a hand in farewell then began jogging back down the street. Adrienne turned in the opposite direction, hiked her shopping bag up, and started to run. The delay had been important, but it had turned what would have been a brisk walk into a mad dash. Even if the phenomenon didn't return that night—and she was praying it wouldn't—she didn't want to be stumbling through the woods in the dark.

So Edith is responsible for the missing articles. Why? I could understand it if the stories had become a curiosity in the town and people were reading and gossiping about them, but it sounds like no one had touched the newspapers since they were donated to the library. That means Edith wasn't stopping a problem but... preventing one? Was there something in those articles that could incriminate her in her family's deaths?

Adrienne, winded, slowed to a brisk walk as she started along the forest trail. She couldn't believe her mind had jumped so quickly to considering Edith's guilt. *It goes to show how powerful circumstantial evidence can be. Edith was the only surviving family member, and she removed the evidence from the newspapers, and that's enough to implicate her. But Greg already said the police discounted*

Edith as a suspect. Besides, it stretches believability to think that an eight-year-old could kill and butcher four able-bodied adults.

Daylight had morphed into twilight, but she was making good progress along the path and soon reached the zigzagging steps. She jumped up them, paused to catch her breath at the top, then set off at a jog.

The missing body is another matter. It seems too coincidental that it was removed within weeks of Edith's return to town. Unless... unless there was someone in Ipson who wanted to torment her. Digging up a loved one's body would be a horrible but creative way to do that.

It was growing hard to see. Adrienne followed the zigzagging path as well as she could, but shapes blended together in the twilight. She was still five minutes from the house when she realised she'd gone off the trail.

She turned, bent, and hunted for the path. *It's already so dark. How long until sunset? One minute? Two?* Anxiety made her breath come in quick, low pants. She tried to retrace her steps but suspected she was going in the wrong direction and couldn't guess which way to turn to correct herself.

The house is on top of the hill. As long as I keep going up, I can't miss it. Unless I end up on the mountain instead...

A bird burst out of a tree ahead of her. It spiralled into the sky in a flurry of wings and squawks. Adrienne froze, shoulders hunched and shopping clutched against her chest, as she waited for the phenomenon to shake the rest of the birds from their boughs.

It didn't.

She blinked at her surroundings and realised night had fallen. For the second day, the sunset panic hadn't returned.

Thank mercy.

With no deadline looming over her, Adrienne could afford to take a few minutes to find the torch in her shopping bag, tear the packaging off, and load its battery. The torch was designed to clip onto a keychain, and its beam was narrow and weak compared to the store's more expensive brands. But it would be a small and handy substitute for the lamp in case the power was cut again, and it would work well enough to guide her through the forest.

Even with the light, she was forced to move carefully. The moon was as good as full, but very little of it permeated the canopy, and the forest floor was littered with debris. On several occasions, she stepped on a pile of dead leaves, expecting solid ground below, only to have her foot plunge into a hidden hole.

The daytime birds were near silent, but night creatures were waking up. A colony of bats chattered behind her, and she even caught a faint, high-pitched wail that she thought might be a fox.

She was just starting to worry that she'd trekked past the hill and was climbing the mountain when she started noticing the darker, sickly trees that she associated with Ashburn. She began breathing a little more easily and quickened her pace.

Something shifted to her right, and Adrienne turned her light towards it. The narrow beam danced across a patchwork of foliage and shadows, but she couldn't see anything sentient. She licked at her dry lips and kept walking.

The startle had planted the idea that she was no longer alone, and it was hard to shake. Adrienne started imagining she could hear leaves crunching barely ten paces behind her, mixed with low, ragged breathing. She turned, panning her light in a slow arc, hunting amongst the gently moving boughs and trailing vines. *There—the dull glint of an eye!* She fixed the light on the area, but it was empty. Her skin turned clammy, and her heart knocked against her ribcage.

Being careful not to remove her light or gaze from the forest, Adrienne reached into the shopping bag and searched for the mace amongst the food.

A branch snapped to her left. Logic fled. Adrienne turned, ran, stumbled, righted herself, and ran again. The light arced wildly as she moved her arms, providing stuttering glimpses of her surroundings. She was making too much noise to hear if she were being followed, and she no longer tried to point herself uphill but aimed for any gap she could see between trees, her only goal being to put as much space between herself and the stranger as possible.

Her foot caught in a vine. She cried out, fell, and rolled down a shallow incline. Branches stabbed at her. The crunching leaves sounded like a storm in her ears. Adrienne felt as though her heart might explode, but then she slumped to a halt, and the world was still and quiet once again.

She didn't move for a minute but kept her eyes closed and focussed on her surroundings. The heavy taint of organic decay came from the leaves and filled her nose. An owl chattered nervously behind her. Unlike in the earlier, cramped sections of the wood, she couldn't feel any branches or bushes touching her. She lifted her head, opened her eyes, and saw why.

Her fall had landed her in a clearing. The canopy was thinner and allowed more light through, which rained down in slanted cold-blue columns. Several hit the headstone; they made the aged rock look as though it were almost glowing.

A cemetery for one.

Adrienne rose carefully. She tried to assess herself without taking her eyes off her environment. Her ankle felt sore. It had twisted but not too badly. She could put her weight on it at least. The torch lay behind her, its beam uselessly directed at a tree trunk, and the shopping was scattered from where it had spilt out of her bag. She retrieved the torch first then shook the bag so that she could see inside. It only contained two bowls of instant noodles, so she dropped it and began searching around the area, moving the light slowly to pick out shapes and colours amongst the detritus.

Whenever she found a piece of her shopping, she threw it back towards the bag, but stopped when she uncovered the mace. She tore it out of the packaging and squeezed the canister in her palm. The weight, small as it was, reassured her, and she allowed herself a few minutes to let her pulse slow.

"This is good." Her voice sounded strange; it was tinny and thin and seemed to be sucked into the woods. "It's less than a minute to home from here, and we know which direction to go. We're going to be fine."

She returned to her bag, shovelled all of the shopping she'd found back inside, and hooked it over her elbow. She thought she was still missing a few packets of food, but they could stay there until morning.

A branch snapped, and Adrienne backed into the clearing as stress choked her. She tried to tell herself it was fine, that branches broke by themselves all the time, that no one could approach her without her hearing them, that the mace would protect her from anything that stalked through the night. But the primitive, instinctual part of her screamed for her to run.

The forest was eerily quiet. She hadn't heard anything since the owl's anxious cry several minutes before. There were no bats, no birdcalls, not even any insects. It was horribly, nauseatingly similar to the calm that had come in the minutes before the sundown phenomenon.

She turned back to the clearing, desperate to get her bearings and find the path that would lead home. The glittering tombstone drew her attention, and Adrienne frowned as she stepped closer. There was something wrong with the gravestone's shadow. It stretched long and black ahead of the marker, but its angle didn't match that of the rest of the shadows, and it was far darker than it should have been.

Terrified prickles spread over Adrienne's arms as she stopped at the shadow's edge. She tried to swallow, but her throat wouldn't work.

She wasn't standing at the side of a shadow after all. Spread out ahead of her was a deep, black hole.

The grave had been exhumed.

CHAPTER 30
UNEARTHED

SHE LIFTED HER EYES to the tombstone. *E ASHBURN. Forgotten But Not Gone.* The gravestone was too old to belong to Edith but would be a close match for the Ashburn massacre. *Eleanor.*

Or perhaps it was just the right age for a grave robbery that took place a decade later.

Adrienne wet her lips. Pieces of the puzzle slotted into place, but the picture left her more confused than ever.

Who dug up the grave?

Disturbed earth had been scattered around the clearing. It was dry; the removal had to be at least a few hours old.

Why?

Her mind grabbed for an answer but found nothing. She couldn't see a single reason for a grave to be exhumed when nothing of the corpse would remain and when the only person it held significance for had passed away.

Unless…

It was a stretch, but she couldn't stop her mind from going there.

Unless Edith was buried here after all. If she'd made a request to be interred with her mother's remains, would it be honoured? Not in a city, probably, but in a small and personal town like Ipson…

Leaves crunched as though flattened under heavy feet.

Adrienne turned and slowly, cautiously raised her torch towards the forest's edge.

A woman stood there, chin elevated, gaze fixed on Adrienne.

No. Not a woman.

A corpse.

Her steel-grey hair flowed behind her in horribly long, matted strands. Her skin, ancient and rippled with a lifetime of wrinkles, still held remnants of the grave's dirt. She was naked, but her figure was so crooked and malformed that the shock of her nudity paled in comparison to the terror her form inspired. Death had not been kind; her limbs were set at crooked angles, and her spine had warped like a twisting river. Bones protruded under the draping flesh. Hips jutted out, and her flat, sagging breasts couldn't hide the sharpness of her ribs.

Adrienne took a stumbling step back. Her legs had locked up. Her mind screamed. But she couldn't drag her gaze from the dead woman.

Edith had no embarrassment for her nakedness or her contorted form. She held her head high, and a powerful, self-assured arrogance lived about her heavy-lidded eyes. They were bleached white, empty of iris and pupil but alert and aware regardless. She released a breath, the sound guttural and rattling and permeating Adrienne's bones.

She tried to run. The shopping bag's weight disoriented her, so she dropped it. She had barely enough mental presence to maintain her grip on the torch and the mace. Her legs wouldn't work the way she wanted them to; they felt as though they were tangling on each other, stumbling her, and her arms pinwheeled as she tried to catch her balance.

A glance over her shoulder confirmed that she was being followed. Edith seemed to be in no hurry but strode forward in long, patient paces, her limbs' awkward angles accentuated as they moved. Adrienne faced forward again and focussed on making her legs move in the right order, and quickly.

She was amongst the trees in five paces. The forest tried to slow her, but she wouldn't allow it to. She could hear Edith's movements between the painful, sharp gasps that stung her throat. The corpse made a strange clicking noise, as though the cartilage had worn away from her joints, and the bones scraped together with each step.

Adrienne prayed she was running in the right direction. Her path carried her uphill, which taxed her shaking muscles and made every breath scorch her lungs. Fear and adrenaline kept her moving, pushing her to make every pace longer, every turn faster.

Branches stung as they cut into her face and arms. Her legs were jarred with nearly every step as she misjudged where to place her feet. But she couldn't slow down; the clicking was drawing closer.

How? She was only walking before—

Adrienne risked a look over her shoulder then yelped as her foot caught on a root and tumbled her forward. She let the momentum flip her over, regaining her feet as they touched ground, and launched herself forward without caring how badly her muscles screamed.

She'd only glimpsed the dead woman for a fraction of a second, but that sight had seared itself into her mind and refused her any respite.

Edith had been *scuttling*. She'd moved on all fours, her twisted frame writhing as she pressed through the trees, using hands and feet simultaneously to grip the trunks, branches and roots to propel herself forward. Her head had been raised, eyes directed at Adrienne, jaw stretched wide in a hungry leer.

The trees cleared, and suddenly, Adrienne was running across the open lawn. Ashburn, her sanctuary, blotted out the stars ahead of her, and she raced for it, begging her legs to carry her, praying that her heart would hold up for another dozen beats.

Searing, burning pain cut into her ankle. It threw Adrienne to the ground, and both the torch and the mace skidded out of her grip.

Too slow. Her mind was stretched to breaking, and she wanted to laugh. *Too slow, too slow.*

She turned to face the source of the pain. Unlike in the forest, there was nothing to smother the moon's cold light, and it brought the area into terrible relief. Edith, crouched and looking more like a leathery animal than a human, had sunk her teeth through Adrienne's jeans and into her ankle. The corpse's long, bony fingers tightened around Adrienne's foot and calf to reinforce its hold. Her flesh was cold, as though she'd stepped out of a fridge, and that sickened Adrienne more than anything—more than her protruding bones, more than her opaque, bloodshot eyes, more than the yellow teeth that had grown far out of their gums.

She thrashed, twisted, and tried to kick free. Edith only tightened the bite, cutting through muscle, and Adrienne screamed. She threw her head back and saw Ashburn. Its porch was only ten paces away. It taunted her, offering salvation but asking her to fight for it.

Closer than the house, though, was a small canister of red and white plastic. Adrienne threw her hand back, touched the mace, and coiled her fingers around it. Edith's jaw continued to tighten, squeezing, drawing rivers of blood until Adrienne's foot felt as though it had been dipped in acid. She aimed the canister at Edith's face and squeezed.

Even in the moon's cool light, she could see the spray burst over the cadaver's face. Edith's grip loosened, her teeth coming free from Adrienne's ankle, as she lifted her head. Adrienne waited for the wails of pain, but no noise came. Droplets of mace settled over the corpse's opaque eyes, but they did not blink.

She can't feel pain. Of course she can't; she's dead.

The mace had confused, but not harmed, Edith. Already, she was returning her attention to the bleeding ankle. A long black tongue extended over her white lips, licking up the hot red liquid smeared there, and her dead eyes flashed as they focussed on the soaked jeans.

"Please." Adrienne tried to pull free, but the fingers only tightened, digging into her harder every time she flinched. "Please, let me go, Edith, please!"

The corpse froze, a flash of shock twitching at the wrinkled skin hanging on its face.

Adrienne took advantage of the second's confusion and fought with the only weapon she had left. She raised her uninjured leg, channelled all of her strength into it, and kicked the corpse. Her sneaker hit Edith's jaw and snapped the head backwards.

The fingers released their grip. Edith's neck twisted horrifically, far past the point of where it should break, until the vertebrae were visible through her throat. Then it began to tilt forward again, righting itself, allowing the white eyes to fix on Adrienne.

She didn't hesitate. As soon as the fingers' pressure relaxed, Adrienne began scrambling back, kicking and hobbling and dragging herself to Ashburn's porch with everything she had.

The clicking noise told her Edith was following. Adrienne's leg hurt enough to make her scream, but she pushed the pain back as well as she could, telling herself she had to ignore it, had to move past it, if she had any hope of survival. The clicking was close enough for the bony fingers to grab her again, the teeth to bite, but she was already pulling herself over the porch's top step, crawling to the door, stretching to reach the knob.

"Eeeeeediiiiiiith…"

The word was like dead tree branches rattling against each other. The stench of decay was thick. The handle wouldn't turn; she'd locked the door when she'd left that morning. Adrienne bit back a terrified cry as she scrambled to pull the key out of her pocket.

Fingers touched her. She flinched against them, but they didn't try to grab her. They tapped and nudged and prodded over her legs and back as Edith's corpse crept up to hover above her.

The key was in the lock. It was at a bad angle and difficult to turn.

The cadaver was so close, and its stench was overwhelming. Lips, cold and wet and rotting, brushed her ear. "*Weeeeeep for Eeeeeediiiiiith,*" the corpse whispered.

Then the door was open. Adrienne pitched herself into the house. Edith tried to follow, the moon's light shining off her bulging, laughing eyes, and Adrienne kicked the door into her face. It created a horrible crunching noise as it hit her skull, but Adrienne only kicked harder and harder, pushing against the pressure until the latch clicked closed.

Everything was quiet and dark and calm for a handful of seconds. Adrienne drew in gasping, sobbing breaths, her eyes squeezed closed to block out both pain and terror. Then a low, steady scrabbling began as Edith clawed at the door.

Adrienne wanted to lie there forever, to close her eyes to the world and never move again, but the scratching sound was moving higher as Edith lifted herself up the door. Adrienne rolled over, flinching against pain, propped herself up, and turned the lock.

The handle twitched as Edith tried to turn it, then a pale, grimy hand pressed against the window. The head rose beside the hand, and a single bulging white eye peered through the glass and fixed Adrienne under its repulsive stare. Edith held the pose for a moment then slid out of sight, leaving a hand's outline made of condensation.

CHAPTER 31
A NIGHT OF HIDING

ADRIENNE WOKE AND IMMEDIATELY wished she hadn't.

She ached all over. The worst was her leg, which was caked in drying blood and mud and felt as though it had been shredded. But a thousand secondary pains dragged her away from sleep as well; scrapes from tree branches, exhausted and strained muscles, a dull but persistent stress headache, and the throbbing in her chest that came from a taxed heart and exhausted lungs.

It was still dark. Two rectangles of moonlight cascaded through the front door's twin windows, but they were her only illumination. Adrienne tried to swallow, and a horrible acidic taste reminded her that she'd thrown up before passing out.

A small, fluffy shape danced around her legs. Adrienne had to squint at it for a moment before she identified it as Wolfgang's tail waving in the moonlight. Something prodded at her injured leg, and she groaned. "Get away, Wolf. You're not allowed to eat me unless I'm dead."

Wolfgang turned his sea-green eyes on her and made an innocent chirruping noise. Adrienne stretched an aching arm forward and scratched his head.

"Is she gone, buddy?" The question came out as a whisper. Wolfgang appeared calm. She hoped that was a good sign; he'd warned her against the corpse's presence before, hadn't he?

She turned towards the door and the windows set on either side. She could still picture the hand pressed there, just below the bulging eye. *She wanted to come inside. That's the only reason she didn't kill me: so that I could let her inside.*

Adrienne leaned back against the wall. She felt sick, cold, and miserable. Too many thoughts were pressing into her at once, and she didn't have the energy to face them all.

Ashburn House is haunted.

She shifted forward and tried to check her leg. The light was too dim to see anything except a mess of blood, torn cloth, and dirt.

I have no phone, no laptop, no way to contact the town.

Adrienne reached a hand behind her and ran it along the wall until she felt the light switch. It turned, but the bulb hung from the ceiling didn't respond.

Of course. Now I have no light, either.

She'd dropped the torch outside, and there was no way she was unlocking the door to retrieve it. She groaned and pulled herself up to standing then, using the side tables and furniture as support, hobbled down the hallway. Her ankle screamed even though she held it above the floor, but she limped to the stairs, to the lamp, and rested her forehead against the shrivelled wallpaper as she lit the wick.

The golden glow spread down the hallway as the flame grew. Adrienne waited for it to stabilise before picking up the lamp and hobbling back the way she'd come.

Wolfgang, his feather-duster tail twitching, followed. He was hungry and made little purring cries as she entered the kitchen.

"In a minute. Be patient, buddy." Adrienne placed the lamp on the table then filled the kettle and put it on to boil. She fetched a bowl from the cupboard and found an assortment of dishtowels in one of the drawers. She sniffed them. Except for being a little musty, they seemed clean.

She eased into the nearest chair, moved the lamp to the floor, and bent over to examine her leg. It was a mess. She clenched her teeth as she prised the sneaker off. Blood had run into it and soaked the sock, which she took off and discarded as well.

The drawers were close enough that she could lean across the walkway and open them. She hunted through until she found a pair of kitchen scissors designed to cut bones and used them to trim the jeans' leg to a little below her knee.

She reached for the kettle, but its water was still cold. *Of course—no power means no boiled water. All right. I'll work with what I have.*

Adrienne poured the water into the bowl, dipped a washcloth into it, and set to cleaning her leg.

When she was done, she slumped back in the chair, panting and trying to ignore the wet tracks running down her cheeks. The idea of cleaning the cuts had seemed straightforward enough when she'd started. She'd watched plenty of movie stars clean themselves up in blockbuster action films, but hands-on experience had forced her to admit that the reality was a lot messier and involved considerably more crying and whimpering.

"I'm a total baby," she told Wolfgang. He waited in the room's doorway, tail thrashing and good mood dissipated now that he had realised food wasn't Adrienne's top priority. "Don't cast me in a survival movie. I wouldn't make it past the first twenty minutes."

He opened his mouth in a silent, cranky meow, and Adrienne sighed.

"Okay, okay, I know. Food's coming."

She took three clean, dry towels and wrapped them around the ankle. She'd had very little experience treating injuries, but the cuts didn't go too deep. The area had swollen and turned red, and if she cleaned too deeply, it just started bleeding again. She knew infection would be the biggest risk, but with so little to work with, she would have to wrap it as well as she could and wait until she could get to a hospital. She'd heard that human mouths contained a huge amount of bacteria, and she could only imagine how bad a dead human's mouth would be.

Adrienne choked on a thin, strangled laugh at the idea. *I can't believe I've accepted the idea of ghosts so easily. I can't believe there are ghosts. Oh hell, this is such a phenomenal mess.*

She tied the makeshift bandage off and stood. It still hurt too much to put weight on the injured foot, so she carried the lamp in one hand and used one the other to brace herself on furniture and walls as she hopped out of the kitchen and into the lounge room.

Wolfgang, infuriating as always, wove about her legs and threatened to trip her until she'd found his food. Adrienne was past the point of worrying about her cat's waistline and emptied the entire tin into his bowl. It overflowed the sides and created a little mountain of kibble. She watched the tabby mash his face into the feast and sighed. *At least now, if anything happens to me, you should have enough food to last until you're found.*

Provided Edith doesn't get you first. An image flashed across Adrienne's mind: Wolf, writhing and yowling, being squeezed in Edith's long, bony fingers as she bit through his fur.

Adrienne bent over, certain she was about to be sick again, but there was nothing left in her stomach. She stayed doubled over, one hand braced against the piano, as she sucked in ragged, painful breaths.

No one's going to hurt Wolf. I won't let them.

She blinked, trying to clear her stinging eyes, as she watched the cat eat. His bushy tail flicked happily as he attempted to drown himself in the food, and Adrienne managed a shaky, uneasy smile.

As much as she complained about him, Adrienne loved Wolfgang. She'd found him as a straggly, half-drowned clump of wet fur on the side of the road one rainy autumn afternoon. He'd only been a kitten and so malnourished that not even his thick fur could hide it. She remembered staying awake well past midnight, watching the sleeping kitten with his newly bulging stomach, and promising herself he would never go hungry again.

"And look where that got us, tubby," she said fondly. One ear flicked in her direction, but Wolfgang's priorities were firmly cemented on his meal.

The room felt too gloomy, and the windows were too dark for Adrienne to feel comfortable. She shuffled to the fireplace, dragged the chair close so that she could keep her foot off the ground, and busied herself with building up a fire. The task kept her hands busy but not her mind.

Ashburn really is haunted. Imagine that—the rumour that everyone laughs about but no one really believes is true. At least... I think it's haunted. That wasn't exactly the picture-book variety of ghost. She was dead, sure, but not transparent. Not intangible. Nothing like those orbs, cold spots, and flashes of light that they chase after in the ghost-hunter shows.

She continued feeding sticks into the little blaze and watched the flames eat through them and reduce them to ash.

She's closer to a zombie—undead and hungry for flesh. But that doesn't fit, either; zombies are mindless. Edith clearly wasn't. She spoke and was startled by the mace and wanted to come into the house.

Adrienne sighed, shoved a new log onto the flame, and shuffled her chair back so that her legs didn't get too hot. After a moment, Wolfgang sidled up to her, gave her good leg a single headbutt, then lay down on the rug at her feet.

Whatever Edith has become, she used to be dead. Or maybe she still is dead but just never stopped moving. And she hunted me. And hurt me. Why?

Against the townspeople's advice, Adrienne had built up the idea of a quirky but benevolent great-aunt who had longed for a family as strongly as Adrienne had. But the signs that Adrienne had taken as welcoming—being bequeathed Ashburn and finding a room prepared for her—had started to take on a sinister light.

All right, I'm going to have to assume a few things. Firstly, that the corpse outside is Edith. It's got to be. She's the right age, has the right hair, and responded to her name. And if the corpse is Edith's, we can assume the grave was hers too. I discounted that earlier because the headstone was decades old, but what if she prepared it as a burial place when she was younger? What if it's a special location that's enchanted to raise the dead? She snorted and massaged her closed eyes. *Not too long ago I would have laughed at myself for thinking this sort of stuff. It's amazing how much a brush with a corpse can change you. I didn't even believe in ghosts yesterday. Now—curses, spiritual hotspots, the Loch Ness Monster, whatever. Bring it on; I'll believe it.*

Adrienne twisted in the chair. The aches and pains were making it difficult to get comfortable, and her reeling mind didn't help.

If we can assume all that to be true, then we've also got to think there's a very strong possibility that Edith was responsible for her family's murders and Eleanor Ashburn's exhumation. Maybe it ties into whatever brought Edith back from the dead. Some kind of satanic sacrifice, possibly.

And all that rolls together to suggest Edith wasn't a very nice person. She frowned at her leg, where blood was staining the towels pink. *Not that it's a surprise or anything. But if all of that logic is sound, I've got to accept that Edith wanted me here for a reason. She prepared a room for me. She left the house to me in her will. All to lull me into a false sense of security while she dug her way out of her own grave.*

Why me, though? Does she need me to complete whatever messed-up sacrificial stuff she did to the rest of her family? Is it because I'm a relative? No, not just a relative—I'm her only remaining living blood relative. That's got to be significant.

A memory surfaced: thunder crashing and heavy raindrops beating on her arms as her mother—wide eyed, mascara running, and cheek dotted with blood—carried her out of Ashburn.

That has to be related to what's happening now. But what did Edith do? Was she trying to hurt me? My mother? Both of us?

She remembered being thrown into the car and the door slamming behind her. She'd watched Ashburn in the rear-view mirror and seen Edith, tall and proud and dressed in one of her heavy black dresses, come and stand in the doorway. The woman's stately, composed stance gave the impression that she could have stopped them from leaving if she'd wanted but had voluntarily let them go.

Because she knew I would move into Ashburn after her death? Why didn't Mum ever talk about Edith or mention Ashburn or tell me what happened that night? What did she see inside these walls?

Wolfgang startled and sat upright. Adrienne's nerves were so tense that she stood up with him. She hadn't thought to bring a knife with her, and her clammy hands felt unpleasantly empty, so she limped to the fireplace and took up the poker.

Adrienne turned back to her cat and watched him for telltale signs of distress. There were plenty: his eyes dilated, his fur bristled out, and he exhaled a long, low warning yowl as he backed towards the room's shadowed corner. His eyes were fixed on the farthest window, and Adrienne turned towards it. The moon had passed over the house, and she couldn't see anything through the dark pane.

But she could hear the clicking.

Edith moved outside, shifting around the building's exterior, hidden in the infinite blackness that engulfed everything beyond the lounge room. Her bony fingers touched the house's walls and windows, prodding and tapping much as she'd prodded and tapped at Adrienne. The noises blended with the clicking bones. Adrienne rotated to keep her attention focussed on the sound. It moved along the lounge room's wall, drawing closer until the women were no more than two metres apart, then it was passing by and grew fainter until Adrienne couldn't hear it at all.

The clock in the hallway chimed one.

Adrienne wanted to remain standing, but her balance was shaky and her muscles exhausted. She kept a tight grip on the poker as she slid back into the chair.

After a few minutes, Wolfgang crept out of hiding and returned to his place beside her. She scratched his head to comfort him but could feel the tension lingering in his muscles. He was just as frightened of the walking corpse as she was.

We're going to be okay. The doors are locked and the windows bolted. There's no way for her to come inside.

It wasn't the only time Edith came by that night.

Every hour, just before the clock's chimes, the clicking noise returned. The first two times, Adrienne rose and Wolfgang scrambled into a dark corner, but as the night wore on and their exhaustion mounted, they both learned to keep their place and silently listen as the tapping passed them by.

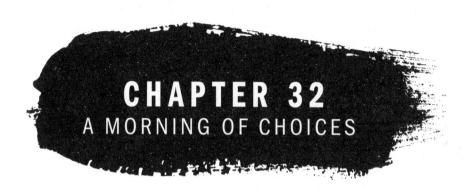

CHAPTER 32
A MORNING OF CHOICES

ADRIENNE MANAGED TO SLEEP in patches of thirty and forty minutes between Edith's visits. Her naps were fitful, though, and she dreamed repeatedly of her mother, her eyes wild as she clutched Adrienne close and fled Ashburn, six drops of red glistening on her chin.

By the time dawn rose, the physical and mental tiredness weighed so heavily that Adrienne felt as though she might drown under it. One minute, she was watching the blood-red sunrise creep over the treetops; the next thing she knew, she was startling awake as the grandfather clock chimed. The sun's angle had changed. Adrienne held still, breathing quickly as she counted the rings. *Eleven. How did I sleep so late?*

She looked down. Wolfgang napped at her feet, his back to the dying fire embers. He looked languid and content.

Edith must have left at dawn. Maybe light hurts her. Maybe it's her weakness.

Adrienne peeled herself out of the chair. The pain in her ankle had settled to a dull ache, but she was careful not to put weight on it as she clambered into the kitchen.

She hadn't eaten since the previous day's breakfast and suspected hunger was responsible for the lingering nausea and weakness. She collected two packets of instant noodles, a pot, more dishtowels, a bowl, and a fork and bundled them in one of the crocheted tablecloths for easier carrying. She then filled the metal whistling kettle with water, looped the tablecloth's tie over the crook of her elbow, and carried the kettle in her other hand as she brought them all back to the lounge room.

The fire was nearly dead, but some kindling and careful tending revived it. Adrienne waited for the blaze to grow then hung the kettle on the metal rod to boil. She slumped back into the seat and ran her fingers through her hair as she tried to think.

Wolfgang stretched, flexing his claws, then sauntered to the overflowing food bowl. Adrienne watched him eat. He seemed happy again, which she assumed meant they were alone.

We're safe right now, but I can't assume that will last.

She turned towards the nearest window. The woods shifted and rocked in a gentle wind. The glass was too dirty to pick out details, but it was easy to imagine a hunched, angry figure waiting just inside the forest.

Adrienne felt as though something inside of her had broken the night before. She would have thought she'd be a hysterical, shivering mess over the idea of having a dead—*or undead or whatever she is*—woman stalking her. But she felt as though the entirety of her tears and fear had been burnt up during the night, leaving behind a small, smouldering coal: single-minded determination to get herself and Wolfgang out of Ashburn.

I need to decide on my priorities. Top of the list is physical safety. Edith wanted to get into the house; the fact that she didn't, despite circling Ashburn all night, suggests she can't break through locked windows or doors. Thank mercy. But it means I'll need to be cautious when going outside or not leave the house at all.

The kettle was hissing. Adrienne pulled it off the fire, took the lids off both noodle cups, and added the liquid. She was supposed to leave them to cook for two minutes but began scooping food out of the first cup immediately. The noodles were crunchy and the water hot enough to burn her tongue, but she was too hungry to care.

The second priority is to get out of this place. Maybe someone in town will let Wolf and me stay with them for a night or two until I can find a more permanent place to live. With no money. No relatives. Very few friends. She grimaced around the noodles. *We'll figure it out somehow. Anything's got to be better than staying here.*

She discarded the empty noodle cup and picked up the full one. *How I'm getting out of here is a different kind of puzzle. Edith might not like light, but I don't know how badly it affects her. Am I safe during the day, or is she still out there, waiting for me to emerge?*

That came back to the first priority: physical safety. For the time being, until she had evidence suggesting otherwise, she needed to assume Edith was still active during daylight.

She was able to chase me down while I was flat-out running, which makes me a sitting duck with this leg. I need transport to get out. If I'm lucky, someone will drive up here to check on me. Both Peggy from the vet's clinic and Sarah are expecting to see me within the next few days. How long will I have to be absent for them to worry?

That tied in with her next two priorities: food and infection. Both the dwindling pantry and her ankle were ticking countdowns to death. Adrienne finished the second noodle cup, got up, and hopped back into the kitchen to check the pantry's stock. It was enough to last a day and a half, or a little over two days if she rationed it. She could probably last another couple of days after that before weakness from hunger became a serious concern. At least water was unlimited, provided Jayne didn't cancel her account.

Jayne didn't want to come back here. And Sarah listens to Jayne, even down to what she should wear. I can't count on Sarah to visit.

Adrienne sighed and rubbed a hand over her face. She needed the bathroom, but that involved navigating the stairs to the second floor. She hopped into the laundry behind the kitchen and found a broom. The bristles were soft from decades of use, but the wooden handle was worn away and rough. Adrienne took one of the smaller tablecloths from the kitchen and twisted it around the handle before tying it off tightly. The result was a silly-looking walking stick that worked surprisingly well, and Adrienne used it to get upstairs and into the bathroom.

While she washed her hands, she stared at her pale reflection in the new mirror and let her mind wander. The second major worry, besides food, was infection. She'd done a poor job of cleaning her leg and was limited in how much more she could do. *I'd need disinfectant or at least some clean bandages—*

An idea struck her, and she opened the cabinet below the sink. Like the rest of the house, it had been kept immaculately clean. Adrienne found a large wooden box behind a stack of handtowels and pulled it out. It hadn't occurred to Adrienne before but now seemed obvious: Edith had lived alone at Ashburn for more than eighty years. She would have been an idiot to not own any emergency medical supplies. And Edith definitely wasn't an idiot.

Adrienne looked inside the box and exhaled in relief. It was overflowing with bottles, bandages, and little vials of pills. Most of the packaging looked modern too.

As she lifted her head, a flash of motion in the mirror caught her attention. As soon as she tried to fix on the shape, it disappeared. Adrienne turned to examine the room over her shoulder. She was alone. Frowning, she hoisted the box and turned to the door.

She was grateful for the makeshift crutch on the climb downstairs. The kit was heavy and threatened to overbalance her, and she had to lean on the railing and the wall a few times to keep herself upright. She put the kit on the lounge room's small, round table, returned the kettle to the fire, and opened the box.

The only thing missing was a guidebook. A few of the bottles were unlabelled, and Adrienne discarded them, but most of the other packages had instructions on them. There were unexpired painkillers, so she dry swallowed two of them then took out bandages, a bottle of antiseptic, and a pack of swabs.

Adrienne then returned to the problem of escaping Ashburn while she watched the fire lick at the kettle's base and waited for it to boil.

She couldn't count on Sarah or her three friends visiting, especially not within the first few days. The only other person who would miss her was the vet nurse, Peggy, and she was a complete wild card. She'd been interested in Adrienne and seemed to enjoy being helpful, but would that helpfulness extend to visiting Ashburn if Adrienne was a day or two late picking up the laptop?

Probably not.

The kettle whistled. Adrienne chewed at her lower lip as she poured the boiling water into the bowl. Sarah's group of friends and Peggy were long-shot chances but nothing she could count on.

The pain tablets had started to work when she began cleaning her leg, but it still hurt like crazy. The swelling hadn't gone down, but at least Adrienne was able to bathe the cuts in antiseptic and wrap them in clean bandages. The old towels were crusty with dried blood, so she put them to one side to throw out.

She was starting to piece together the puzzle that had been growing since she'd moved into Ashburn. Almost certainly, Edith was responsible for the sunset phenomenon, Adrienne's torment over the previous two nights, and the power cutting out—all events that had happened after nightfall. Even that day's encounter hadn't started until after the sun went down.

Adrienne repacked the kit carefully then glanced towards the window. The early-afternoon sun was bright and warm, though precious little of it was allowed into the house.

I promised myself I wouldn't take unnecessary risks. But if Edith is dormant during daylight hours, it would be insanity to stay here and give her another night to hunt me. Even carrying Wolf in the cat case and with my leg like this, there'd be plenty of time to walk to town before nightfall.

Wolfgang had jumped onto the windowsill to watch the outside world. His silhouette was almost perfectly still except for the occasionally twitching ear, and he was the cutest, fluffiest sentry Adrienne had ever seen. She blew her breath out and went to join him.

"Whatcha think, buddy?" She scanned the forest. The dark trees rustled in the breeze, but she couldn't see any unnatural motion amongst them. "Take a risk and run to town, or stay put and hope for rescue?"

True to form, the cat ignored her. Adrienne scratched behind his ears while she thought through the choice. Running to town was almost painfully tempting. Once she was outside the property's bounds, there was nothing that could bring her back. She would never have to face Edith or the house again.

But it also carried the greatest risk by far. She could picture herself running through the woods, cat carrier clasped to her chest, as Edith hunted her, snagged her foot, and toppled her to the ground. She would be eaten, or worse. And then what would happen to Wolfgang? *Would he be left in the case—mercy*

241

forbid—to starve, or would Edith carry him away to add him to her simmering witch's brew?

No, don't get carried away. Edith is a ghost, and that tall man in the café was adamant that covens of witches were distinct and separate from fraids of ghosts.

She snorted and buried her face in her hands. Wolfgang, blissfully ignorant of the horrific fates he'd been doomed to in his owner's mind, flicked her an irritated glance.

No matter how much I want to get out of here, and despite the evidence that suggests Edith may be harmless during the day, the risks are far heavier than the rewards. I can't leave. At least, not today.

But that doesn't mean I have to stay inside the house.

Adrienne couldn't see the front yard from the lounge room's window, but she could picture it: the weedy patch of dirt just ahead of the porch where she'd dropped the torch.

It was close enough to the house that she could run back inside if Edith tried to leave the forest. And the torch would be an invaluable boon during the night.

Ten steps past the door. It should be safe enough. Adrienne limped into the hallway and faced the front door. *Right?*

CHAPTER 33
SORTIE

NO MATTER HOW SMALL the risk of the brief sortie, it was still a risk, so Adrienne prepared herself as thoroughly as she was capable of. The mace had been useless against the corpse, but she figured a knife would be able to chop bits off it as well as it could with a regular human, so she took the large, wickedly sharp blade out of the kitchen drawer. She also brought the broom-turned-crutch, partly to make the trip faster and partly to use as a weapon if it came to it.

She pressed against the door's narrow windows and scanned the yard. Everything was still and quiet. Slowly, moving with care in case noise attracted Edith's attention, she turned the handle and nudged the door open.

It groaned on its hinge, and Adrienne cringed. She waited in the opening for several minutes, one hand on the doorknob, prepared to pull it closed again if a shape burst out of the forest. It didn't. Nothing was out there except still, quiet solitude.

Adrienne took a quick breath and stepped onto the porch. Her footsteps sounded unpleasantly loud on the aged wood. She left the door open, in case she needed to run for it, and approached the porch's edge. Her nerves were buzzing and her senses on high alert as she followed the steps one at a time until her feet landed in the weed-clogged yard.

She felt vulnerable with the stairs separating her from the door, so she increased her pace as she retraced her path from the night before.

I was facing the house head-on when I came out of the forest, which means the attack would have happened in line with the door. It wasn't far away. It should be somewhere around—ah.

Dried blood stained a clump of weeds. The area around was scuffed up from the fight, brief though it was. Adrienne gave the treeline a final scan then bent and began hunting amongst the weeds.

A minute of searching revealed the torch. It was small, but its black plastic stood out against the natural browns and greys. She picked it up, pressed its button, and wasn't surprised when the light didn't come on. *The battery would have drained during the night. Hopefully, Edith will have spares somewhere.*

Adrienne lifted her eyes to the forest edge. It would take less than a minute to cross the yard, and the burial site was only two minutes past the treeline. Her shopping, including spare batteries and food, waited on the forest floor. She swallowed the saliva that had built in her mouth. It was too risky; if Edith didn't return, she might risk a trip into the woods when her supplies ran low. But not before.

She tucked the light into her pocket and turned back to the house. A second temptation struck her as she thought of the power box waiting on the building's side. A short walk and a handful of flicked switches would give her light, a hot shower, and a working kettle. She knew better than to think it would last; Edith was capable of nixing the electricity with just her presence. But Adrienne was tired, stressed, grimy, and sore, and a hot shower promised to solve all of those problems.

Adrienne took a step towards the house's corner. She could reach the switch box in less than a minute, even hobbled with a bad foot.

But a lot can happen in sixty seconds. And you promised you wouldn't take risks.

She wrinkled her nose in resignation and turned back to the front door. *Fine, fine. Stupid conscience. We'll just have to deal with another day of cold showers.*

Movement caught her attention, and she raised her eyes. Suddenly she was very, very grateful that she hadn't tried to turn the power back on.

Edith crouched on the roof.

She was only a silhouette against the overcast sky, but the twisted body was unmistakable. She held completely still, crouched like a predatory animal on the spire near the chimney. Her thick hair ran like a river onto the roof tiles, and her eyes flashed as Adrienne met them.

"Oh—oh, crap—"

Adrienne dashed towards the door in the same instant as Edith threw herself forward. The woman scraped over the roof's slates, half running and half plunging towards the gutter, her lips peeled back from her teeth.

Climbing the stairs would waste precious seconds; Adrienne threw herself over them. She hit the porch hard and rolled, trying not to scream as her injured ankle buckled.

A heavy, crunching *whump* told her Edith had flung herself off the roof and impacted the ground. Adrienne flipped and gasped at the sight. Edith's body, already contorted, had been broken by the collision. Her skin hadn't torn, but the bones inside were jarred to unnatural angles and created sickening tents in the flesh. Her skull was flattened, as though it had broken like an eggshell, and her ribs poked towards the sky. She looked like a jumble of bones held inside a fleshy bag.

A brief spark of hope lit in Adrienne's chest. *Could she actually be dead?* But then Edith shifted, and the hope was drowned in sickening terror.

Edith rose from the yard as though propelled by something other than muscle and cartilage. As she stood, the bones twisted into their correct positions, the rippling and adjusting clearly visible under the skin. A skull plate popped back into place to round out her head as she turned to face the porch.

Adrienne scrambled backwards, trying to crawl inside the house before Edith could collect herself, but the other woman was shockingly quick. She scuttled forward before her body had fully righted itself, her grasping fingers stretching towards Adrienne's face.

They were both through the doorway, sprawled over the thread-bare runner as they grappled. Bony, chilled fingers dug into her skin as Edith tried to crawl towards her throat. Adrienne still held the knife and thrust it forward from instinct more than intention.

It pierced Edith's face, slipping into the space between her nose and her left eye. Momentum forced Edith and the knife together, and the blade crunched through fragile bone as it imbedded itself hilt-deep. Putrid, thick black blood splattered out of the cut, dribbling onto Adrienne's hand and spraying her cheek.

She screamed and kicked at the corpse. The force knocked Edith back through the entryway. Adrienne tried to slam the door, but Edith's arm stretched through the gap, keeping it open, and it twitched as the wood crunched into the fragile forearm bones. Adrienne opened the door an inch and slammed it closed again and again, squashing the limb and sending cracking noises echoing through the hallway with every impact. Edith's long, bony fingers flexed, twitching and twisting like a dying spider, then withdrew through the gap. Adrienne slammed the door so hard that her ears rang.

Please stay down. Please stay dead.

She rose onto her knees and turned the door's lock with shaking hands. Then she huddled there, ear pressed against the wood, as she sucked in panting breaths and listened.

There was the slow, distinct sluicing sound of a knife being pulled out of flesh then a spattering noise as congealed blood fell to the porch. A low, slow hiss of anger was expelled through rotting teeth.

Adrienne didn't stay to listen further but crawled back from the door until she could use a table to pull herself up. Her ankle throbbed, and her limbs were shaking. She'd lost the knife and the makeshift crutch in the yard, but in its place she'd gained two valuable gifts: the torch, and confirmation that Edith wasn't night-bound.

I'm a fool. She staggered down the hallway and into the lounge room that she'd grown to think of as her safe refuge. Wolfgang crouched in the corner, his ears flattened and tail bushed as he stared at the door. Adrienne closed it firmly behind her. *I thought it would be safe. It was only ten paces from the front door, and I thought she'd retreated to the forest. I didn't expect her to be waiting for me on the roof, of all places.*

Adrienne slumped into her chair and gave Wolfgang a bitter smile. "It was so quiet, too. I should have realised that meant she was nearby. Not even a cricket chirping. I was such an idiot."

Lesson learned. Even the safest gamble is still a gamble. And Edith is more cunning than I expected. I've got to give up any hope of walking out of this house. She chewed on her thumb as she stared at the dying embers. *This means my only escape will be if someone comes to check on me and I can get a ride to town in their car. But even that's going to be dangerous for everyone involved; there's nothing to stop Edith from attacking them when they try to get out of their car.*

And that's only if someone comes, which isn't very likely.

A piece of wood collapsed in the fireplace and sent up a little burst of sparks. Adrienne sucked in a breath and leaned forward in her chair. She'd had an idea. It was ridiculous to the point of being laughable, but she thought it might just work.

CHAPTER 34
SPARK

ADRIENNE SHOVED TWO NEW logs onto the fire to build it. She was running low on wood—what she had left wouldn't last through the night—but that wouldn't matter if her plan worked.

She tipped the remaining kindling out of the fireside bucket and looped its handle over her arm then limped through the house, searching for any rubber or small plastic items. In the kitchen, she found three packs of rubber gloves, two drain plugs, and a tin of rubber bands, all of which went into the bucket, followed by the last tea towel.

There were surprisingly few plastic items in Ashburn. At Adrienne's old home, cheap plastic bowls, chopping boards, and watering cans had been common, but Edith seemed to prefer wood, glass, or metal. Adrienne eventually found a thick roll of plastic bin liners in a bottom drawer and a rubber mat in the laundry and dropped them into her bucket.

This'll do.

She hobbled back to the lounge room and knelt in front of the fire. The new wood had caught and was starting to burn nicely. She added a third piece, then all of the kindling, and waited for the flames to build.

The heat coming off it was incredible, and Adrienne had to shed her jacket. Sweat beaded over her forehead, but the heat evaporated it almost as soon as it developed. She took the newspaper off the top of the fireplace and pulled the solid metal fireguard close.

"You might want to keep back for this part, buddy," she told the cat, who was sauntering up to see what she was doing. "It's not going to smell very nice."

Adrienne took the tea towel out of the bucket, tied it around the lower half of her face as a crude mask, then crumpled the last dozen pages of the newspaper and threw them into the inferno. The rubber and plastic went straight on top, then she shoved the fire guard against the fireplace's opening to block it as much as possible.

Tendrils of black smoke began to spill out around the guard almost immediately, and with it came the smell of burning rubber. She'd become very familiar with the stench when her neighbours had decided to start a tire fire in their backyard one autumn morning. She'd never forgotten the gag-inducing scent of burning rubber or the way the smoke, thick and black, had poured across their property and stained the bricks.

This house is visible from town. Everyone could see the light Edith lit every Friday. I'm sure they'll see the smoke too.

She could visualise it, pouring thick and black out of the chimney and billowing high into the sky. From a distance, it would look as if the house was on fire.

That will bring people. And not just a single car that Edith might be able to attack and drive off the road, either; there'll be fire trucks, the police, and possibly even Jayne or a few curious spectators. With enough people, I'll have protection, witnesses, and a way to escape.

Even with the guard, heavy black smoke was pouring into the lounge room. Adrienne gagged and tightened the towel around her face. She'd underestimated how strong it would be; there was no way she could stay in the room. She scooped up Wolfgang, snagged the cat case with her spare hand, and carried them into the cleaner, stylish sitting room at the house's corner.

The smell followed them, but the air was clear enough for Adrienne to take her mask off. She placed her irritable cat onto one of the fancy rose-patterned couches and crossed to the window.

Even with her cheek pressed to the glass and her head angled up, she couldn't see the smoke. She prayed it would be thick enough to draw attention.

It's a twenty-minute drive from town. We'll have a bit to wait.

Wolf was nosing about the new room. He'd need to be inside his carry case before the trucks arrived, but he hated confinement, so Adrienne wanted to let him roam until the last possible moment.

She turned and began pacing. The plan was solid, but there was no accounting for dumb luck. There was the chance that none of the townspeople would look in Ashburn's direction while the rubber was burning. Or that the smoke wouldn't be thick enough. Or that no one would think to call the fire department.

Adrienne quickened her pace and began chewing on the corner of her thumbnail. The wait was excruciating. And there would be no way to be sure that she'd done enough until she heard the sirens.

I need find something to do. She stopped at the window again and peered up, trying to catch a glimpse of smoke billowing across the sky, but the wind was travelling in the wrong direction. *I could pack my bags. It would be difficult to carry both Wolf and a suitcase with my leg like this, but I might be able to manage it. And it can't hurt to be prepared.*

Having a purpose helped reduce some of the nervous tension in Adrienne's stomach. She slipped through the doorway, being careful not to let Wolfgang escape, then crossed to the stairs.

Even though she'd shut the lounge room's door, dark soot leaked through the gaps and made her gag. *If the smoke outside is anywhere near as black as this, it'll be impossible to miss.*

The climb was difficult without a crutch, but Adrienne leaned on the railing, trying to ignore the way it creaked, as she made her way to the second floor. She hadn't brought the lamp, and the gloom of the lightless hallway felt suffocating. She tried to keep her eyes focussed ahead as she shuffled towards the door at the other end of the house, but her attention was pulled towards the paintings coating the walls.

They didn't look like this before.

The subjects had lost their air of placid, haughty indifference. Instead, a sharp terror filled their expressions.

"What the...?" Adrienne limped close to a painting of Mr Ashburn. His pose was the same, but his eyes had widened and his lips tightened. His skin had lost its rosy blush and—a detail so expertly executed that Adrienne felt as though her fingers would get wet if she touched it—perspiration ran over his forehead.

Adrienne squeezed her lips together and stepped away from the picture. She didn't want to see any more but couldn't stop her eyes from skipping to the next portrait.

Mrs Ashburn's expression held none of her husband's restraint. Her mouth was open, and a delicate line of saliva connected a front tooth to the lower lip. Her eyes were glassy with unshed tears, and one hand had come up to clutch at her neckline. Veins bulged in her feminine hand.

No more. I don't want to see any more.

But she couldn't stop herself from turning towards the next painting. Edith.

There was no terror in the child's face, only a flat, cold focus. She stared directly ahead, intense attention squared on the observer, the muscles in her face tight but not from fear.

You're not upset. Of course you're not. Because you murdered them, didn't you, Edith? You were a heartless psychopath even as a girl.

The painted eyes blinked.

Adrienne stumbled backwards. She made a choked yelping noise as her injured ankle twisted, and she clutched at a side table to halt her fall. Her back slammed the wall, sending portraits swaying, their subjects an exhibition of silent dread, as though the likenesses had been captured as they experienced their last moments on earth.

Something moved in the mirror Adrienne had hung in the hallway's midpoint. She had a fleeting glimpse of bulging, bleached-white eyes, then one of the portraits she'd bumped fell off its hook and clattered to the ground.

The twisted fascination broke, and Adrienne hopped as quickly as she could towards the door at the end of the hall. She kept her eyes fixed on the dirty, scuffed carpet the entire way and only looked up when she'd turned the handle and tumbled into her room.

She rested her back against the cool door. Her heart was jumping, and her chest felt tight. It had been easier to live with Edith's presence while she was locked outside and their domains were neatly designated by the house's walls. But the spirit's influence seemed to be seeping inside. It sickened her.

I won't have to endure it for much longer. Soon, I'll hear the sirens as help races up the driveway, then I'll never have to lay eyes on Ashburn again.

She wrenched the wardrobe door open and pulled her travel case out of where she'd tucked it into the corner. She laid it on the bed, flipped the lid open, and began throwing her possessions inside.

It's quiet.

The thought came out of nowhere. Adrienne froze, a pair of jeans half folded, as she listened. It went beyond simple quiet.

The room was muffled, and noises such as her own breath and heartbeat were dampened.

A faint, thin hum cut through the still. It was almost imperceptible but had a jangled, unnatural strain that made it impossible to not hear. Adrienne raised her eyes towards the sound and found herself facing the mirror she'd propped on top of the bureau.

The glass was large enough to capture most of the room. Adrienne could see herself, poised beside the bed, slightly bent as she prepared to put the jeans into the travel case. Her hair was tangled, and her skin had a dirty pallor—testament to the days of stress and fear.

And standing behind her, straight as a ramrod and hands neatly folded over her skirts, was Edith.

Adrienne inhaled and swivelled to face the intruder, hands raised in defence. The space behind her was vacant.

She stared at the empty air, too frightened to even blink, then turned back to the mirror.

The second figure was gone. Now all that remained was Adrienne, ashen and shaking, the crumpled jeans clutched in her fist.

It was tempting to think that she'd been mistaken—that the image had been a result of her imagination or light playing across the glass—but Adrienne knew what she'd seen. The mirror's phantom had been worlds away from the contorted, naked creature outside. The reflection had been tall, proud, and dressed in one of the elegant black silk dresses from Edith's room. The grey hair had been fastened into a sleek bun at the back of her head. Her nails were short and clean, her expression flat and steady, her posture impeccable.

But despite all of the differences, a handful of similarities still ran through: the crepe-like wrinkled skin that bunched up around her eyes, the steel shade of her hair, the sharp bone structure. And her hands, held neatly ahead of herself, stood out sharply against the midnight skirts. The long, bony fingers were impossible to forget.

Two versions of Edith. One was undoubtedly the woman who walked into town every day and terrified the children. The other clings to her old home despite losing her humanity.

Adrienne felt sick. She turned back and forward, checking both the mirror and the room multiple times. The faint ringing had faded, but the muffled sensation persisted. It grew and pressed against her, its weight making her pulse throb and her mouth dry.

She turned back to the suitcase and flinched as her eyes landed on the window. The world outside had disappeared.

CHAPTER 35
FALLING

MOUTH OPEN AND HER outstretched fingers shaking, Adrienne stepped up to the window. She touched the glass, felt how icy-cold it was, and pulled her hand back against her chest.

The trees, the weedy yard, the sky—everything had disappeared as though they'd been erased. All that remained was grey.

It was a dark shade, not quite slate but deeper than a midtone. A hint of light still came through it, but it was dim enough that she felt as though she were submerged in twilight.

Then part of the grey swirled, and Adrienne found she was able to breathe again. *It's smoke, that's all.*

She stepped back from the window, still squinting at the heavy grey fog, as her eyebrows contracted. She shouldn't be able to see the smoke, and certainly not as densely as it appeared then. Ashburn stood on top of a hill. No matter how gentle the breeze, the smoke should still be blowing away.

Adrienne dropped the jeans she'd been holding and hurried to the door. She was loath to return to the hallway of contorted paintings, but she needed to see outside, and the attic had the best view of the house.

The stairs to the third floor were difficult to climb. They were enclosed, and the walls had no fixtures or rails, which left Adrienne with nothing to hold onto. After the first few steps, she turned, sat, and clambered the rest of the way on her backside. It was undignified and streaked dust across her clothes but was faster and easier than trying to walk.

The words cut into the tall black door at the top of the stairs demanded her attention. She reread the familiar phrase as she righted and dusted herself.

LIGHT THE CANDLE

YOUR FAMILY

IS STILL

DEAD

The words were cryptic—possibly put there during a bout of madness—but the reference to Edith's family felt significant. Initially, Adrienne had assumed they were mentioned out of grief. Now, guilt seemed a likelier motivator. *Your family is still dead.* Maybe Edith regretted what she'd done. *Did she try to revive her parents in the same way she managed to resurrect herself?* Adrienne couldn't parse the mystery, so she nudged the door open and stepped through.

The attic, large and airy and filled with crates holding thousands of candles, sent prickles skittering over Adrienne's skin. The wax-coated candle spike and carefully framed photo had taken on an occult subtext, so she gave them a wide berth as she crossed to the uncovered window.

At last she had something to see besides grey. The sky, a dusky blue with thick clouds rolling in from the north, seemed to stretch forever. Below it, Adrienne could see the town, full of tiny houses and tiny people, nestled in the valley.

The woods, thick and tangled, divided her from the town, and between the woods and the house was a heavy blanket of grey.

Adrienne unlocked the glass windowpane and pushed it open. She leaned forward, stretching over the windowsill to see above the roof. There was no plume of black smoke reaching for the heavens; instead, it fell, tumbling over the roof and spilling into the yard like a spectral waterfall.

That makes no sense. Hot air rises; eventually it would cool and the soot would come back down but not this quickly!

Something was moving in the smoke. Adrienne strained to see through the swirling grey, but it was too thick for her to make out any details.

Frustration made her squeeze her lips together, and Adrienne hopped across the attic to reach a window facing the backyard. She pulled the curtain aside and was faced with a nearly identical sight. The dark grey smoke hung heavily between the forest edge and the house, creating an imitation floor that looked almost solid enough to walk on.

Wait, is it dropping lower?

She squinted at the wood's edge and tried to mark how high

the mist rose against the bark of the nearest trees. She'd guessed right; the layer of grey was very slowly, very steadily dropping, like water being absorbed into the ground.

Adrienne hopped back to the first window. The shape that had been stirring the fog grew visible, and Adrienne felt the smart of cold anger as she saw the glint of Edith's bleached eyes.

The woman stood amongst the soot, her withered arms raised and fingers splayed. She was slowly lowering her hands, and the fog obeyed her, sinking closer and closer to the ground and condensing from grey into an angry, dirty black.

I keep underestimating her. She looks like a crazed animal, but she's smart.

The angry, miserable tears wouldn't stay in her eyes this time. Adrienne rubbed them off her cheeks, frustrated with herself for crying, and slammed the window closed.

No fire department. No police. No help. Back to stage one.

She spared the photograph a final glance before turning towards the door. Edith looked so innocently mischievous in the picture, as though she'd been caught playing make-believe in the garden. The contrast with the creature she'd become was striking.

Adrienne refused to let herself sigh as she left the attic, but the defeat was crushing. She'd thrown everything into the plan—including the last of her firewood—and the result was that she would remain trapped in Ashburn for at least one more night. In addition, her comforts were being methodically stripped away. *No lights. No hot shower. Now I also don't have a fire, and the rubber smell in the lounge room will make it impossible to sleep there.*

She reached the base of the stairs and hesitated. The open suitcase waited in her room, but there was no longer any reason to pack it. On her other side stretched the hallway of distorted portraits. Adrienne looked towards them and felt her heart catch. They'd changed again.

She stepped near the closest portrait, and nausea welled inside her. It was an image of Mrs Ashburn. The lady's perfect pose has been disturbed; her head twisted to one side, her eyes pointed away from the viewer, and her delicate brown hair was flung out across the wooden floor.

Her lower jaw had been torn off.

The gore had been rendered fantastically. Even as Adrienne's mind screamed against the image, she felt a small sense of wonder at how perfectly the upper teeth shone amongst the red, how she could see into the lady's throat, and how the withered end of an artery poked free and coiled in the blood like a fat worm.

She turned, but there was no relief from the images. Mr Ashburn's right eye was wide and staring, frozen in shock, but the other eye was missing along with that half of his head. A drop of red blood glistened in his moustache, and more had spread across the floor below him.

The other Mrs Ashburn—Charles's wife and Edith's aunt—had fallen face down. Her hand was extended, palm up, as though she were beckoning to someone, but it had been torn from her body at its wrist. A clump of her impeccably styled hair poked free from her head. It had been cut by the hatchet embedded in her skull.

Adrienne clamped her hands over her mouth. She couldn't avert her eyes from the paintings no matter how much they sickened her. Each image showed the three family members in the same poses but had been painted from different angles to highlight new aspects of the butchery: torn limbs, pools of blood, and a cavity in Mr Ashburn's chest where his heart had been extracted.

Amongst them were scattered portraits of Edith. She alone remained alive. Each painting depicted her in the same position: looking towards the viewer, her face frozen in that calm expression, her eyes hard and unfeeling. A spray of blood had been drawn across her chin and cheeks.

Adrienne reached the stairs. Shock had set in, and she barely felt the prickles of pain as she put weight on her bad ankle. A manic, urgent panic urged her to escape the house and flee to town, where there was comfort and sanity and company. She stumbled towards the front door without realising what she was doing. Turned the handle. Pulled it open. And stopped on the porch.

The smoke rolled across the lawn in thick billows and swirls. It was no longer dark grey but an ethereal, glassy white.

Adrienne stepped back as the mist spilt around her legs and washed into the house. She looked down at where she'd been standing and saw, through the heavy fog, her footprint amongst a layer of black soot that coated the porch.

The bizarre sight shook Adrienne out of her daze. She lifted her eyes towards the forest, where the pale, contorted figure crouched between two trees, and she slammed the door closed.

"Okay." Adrienne squeezed her eyes closed and rested her

forehead on the door as she turned the lock. "Okay. Okay. It's going to be okay. You've just got to try harder, Addy. You can get out of here."

She turned back to the hallway and wrapped her arms around her chest. Shadows draped the entry like ghostly cobwebs. Sometime between enacting her plan and discovering its ruin, day had begun to dip into night.

CHAPTER 36
THE LAST EVENING

ADRIENNE PRESSED HER THUMBS into the corners of her eyes. *Think, Addy. Logic it out. What do you need to do? What do you need to survive tonight?*

The answer came quickly: light. With a woodless fire and no electricity, Adrienne would be blind when the sun set unless she found an alternative. The little plastic torch in her pocket would be ideal, but its battery had been drained the night before. That meant finding new batteries had to be her first priority.

She hopped into the kitchen and began rifling through drawers. They held a wide assortment of implements but no batteries. Adrienne chewed at the inside of her lip as she moved through the other downstairs rooms.

It was hard to imagine Edith living in Ashburn without any batteries. Adrienne had a horrible suspicion that they might be in the upstairs office, hidden inside the desk's drawer or in the cabinet, but she was loath to pass the portraits again; the images had made her regret ever being curious about the Ashburn deaths.

The search inevitably brought her to the lounge room she'd inhabited over the previous few days. She took a deep breath before opening the door, steeling herself against the stench of burning rubber, and was surprised when the room didn't smell.

A black stain spread out from the fireplace, growing fainter the farther it moved into the room. Adrienne approached it, wiped her finger through the grime, and grimaced when she smelt it. Whatever Edith had done to lower the smoke outside had been replicated inside the house. The soot had dropped onto the ground to coat it in a layer of carbon.

Adrienne pulled the grate away from the fire and checked inside. As she'd suspected, not even embers remained. The condensed smoke had choked out the fire and left mostly intact logs and twisted rubber. Adrienne touched the wood, but it was cold, and she didn't have any kindling to revive the blaze.

She left the fire and searched the rest of the room. Despite digging through every drawer and even searching between the bookcase's ornaments, she had to admit there weren't any batteries on the ground floor.

Adrienne wiped her hands on her jeans as she gazed about the room and scrunched her nose. *Looks like we're going upstairs after all. But first…*

Wolfgang was still in the sitting room, so Adrienne went to fetch him and return him to the lounge area, where he had food and water. As she opened the sitting room door, motion flashed through her peripheral vision. She turned towards the mirror she'd hung on the room's back wall. Her own reflection, pale and with a smudge of soot over her cheek, stared back. And in the shadowed hallway just beyond her, tall and straight and impeccably dressed, walked Edith.

The phantom disappeared from sight before Adrienne could even move to look behind her. She pressed her lips together and balled her hands into fists to keep them from shaking.

Wolfgang appeared from behind the chaise lounge and shot past her legs. Adrienne hissed his name and tried to grab the grey streak, but her fingers only brushed his tail as he disappeared into the hallway's gloom.

"Poor buddy." She didn't like the idea of Wolfgang roaming the house but knew nothing would make him return to her before he was ready. She left the lounge room's door propped open so that he could get to his food and water if he wanted then went to the kitchen in search of fabric.

"No mirrors," she said as she returned to the hallway and draped a tablecloth over its mirror. "Looks like you and I agree on one thing, Edith."

A second cloth went over the sitting room's mirror, and the tea towel she'd used as a face mask covered the smaller mirror in the lounge room.

The only other mirror she had any cause to pass was the large gilt-frame affair in the upstairs hallway. *Well, I was going there anyway. Multiple birds, meet my stone.* Adrienne fetched a new knife from the kitchen drawer, checked that she still had the torch in her pocket, threw a tablecloth over her shoulder, and turned towards the dim stairwell.

The sun was already slipping behind the treetops. It wouldn't take more than ten minutes for night to fall, and she didn't want to be on the second floor without the sun.

The lantern waited on the little table, but she moved past it. The weight would make her climb more difficult, and she planned to finish the search quickly. The only upstairs room that had any hope of holding batteries was the study, and its sparse furniture wouldn't take more than a handful of minutes to rifle through.

Adrienne took the stairs as quickly as her leg would allow but stopped on the landing. The second floor, windowless and with only a refraction of natural light coming through two open doors, had always been dark, but with the sun close to setting, walking up there felt like stepping into a tomb. She was grateful she hadn't brought the lamp. It was easier to pass the portraits without light.

She walked along the centre line of the scuffed runner to give herself as much space from the paintings as she could. Her eyes stayed focussed on the end of the hallway, but her peripheral vision caught little glimpses of blood and bone. An aching lump grew in her throat, but she couldn't swallow it. She knew the paintings only contained corpses, but she still couldn't shake the feeling of eyes following her.

The hallway mirror hung at the midway point, reflecting dated wallpaper and broken teeth. Something moved in its depths—wrinkled skin flexing, bulging eyes watching without blinking—but Adrienne threw her cloth over it before the figure could become clear.

She adjusted the fabric to ensure every part of the decadent frame was covered then slipped through the closest door to her left, which opened into the study. The room felt a fraction warmer than the hallway, and its papered walls were a welcome relief from the paintings. The claw-like anxiety in her chest relaxed a fraction.

The last beams of sunlight came between the curtains and lit the wall behind Adrienne. She scanned the furniture quickly. On either side were two bookcases, both holding nothing but books, and a wooden chair and a dark-wood desk rested below the window. The desk had a drawer in its front, which Adrienne hurried to open.

The space was crammed full with knick-knacks. She shifted through a large magnifying glass, boxes of paperclips, envelopes, outdated stamps, spare pens, measuring tape, hole punches, and scissors before finding two packs of batteries held together with a rubber band.

Adrienne exhaled a silent cheer. She pulled the torch out of her pocket, tipped its old battery out, fitted a new one, and tested it. The beam was weak but infinitely better than the alternative. Adrienne took another three spare batteries and tucked them into her back pocket.

When she lifted her gaze back to the window, the sun was no longer visible. The red dusk strained to keep the sky lit, but faint stars were already beginning to appear above the house.

Adrienne pulled the chair out and dropped into it then propped the torch on the table so that its beam would keep the room lit. She knew she would need to go downstairs eventually, but the room felt so safe, and her view of the sunset was so beautiful, that she couldn't resist the temptation to hold onto the moment for as long as it lasted.

How am I going to get out of here?

It was the question that had been living in the back of her mind since she'd escaped Edith. She'd been picking at it, poking and scratching and turning it over, but was no closer to an answer. *If I just knew what she wanted from me, I might be able to find a way to assuage her or use her plan against her. Does she just want me dead, or is there more to it than that?*

Edith had always been an enigma to Adrienne. Even in death, she presented disparate impressions: the contorted, dirtied, naked creature that stalked outside, and the upright, proper, elegantly dressed version in the mirrors. It was almost as though she'd been split on death, and her mind lingered as a memory while her body clung to the earth.

Adrienne knew that couldn't have happened, though. The Edith outside was too clever and calculating to have lost her senses. She'd been shocked by the use of her name and had even told Adrienne to weep for her.

Does she expect me to mourn her after everything she's done? I don't know if I'd be physically capable of it. And even if I did, is there any chance it might help me? This isn't a spirit that needs to feel loved before it can move on. This is a monster that's bent on hurting me.

The day was gone, and night creatures were coming alive in the forest. A very faint clicking reached her through the night air as Edith started to patrol around the house's perimeter.

Adrienne squeezed her eyes closed against the noise. She'd managed to relax while watching the sunset, but the erratic, rough clacking returned the familiar ache of stress to her chest.

Then a new sound rose to drown out the tapping: a deep, drawn-out rumble emanating from the forest to her right. Adrienne's eyes shot open as she recognised the cadence. *A car engine.*

CHAPTER 37
LIGHTS

ADRIENNE BOLTED OUT OF her chair and pressed close to the window. The study was high enough that it could look over the treetops, and she could see the waving glow of headlights moving through the woods.

Her heart kicked into overdrive as her mind scrambled to take in the development. *I need to find Wolf. Has he come out of hiding yet? There's no time to get my luggage, but that doesn't matter. Who is it? I somehow need to warn them not to get out of the car. Will Edith try to chase them off?*

But even as her muscles tensed for running, she realised something was wrong.

The car had been moving along the driveway towards the house but then made an abrupt turn into the trees. Adrienne pressed against the window, bent double over the desk, as she tried to understand what it was doing. Had it gone off the driveway? As far as she knew, there weren't any other roads through the area.

Except...

Peggy had asked if her brother could use a shortcut that ran through Ashburn's land. She'd said the road came off Ashburn's driveway and saved him fifteen minutes if he wanted to go to the next town.

"Hey!" Adrienne beat her fist against the glass. The pane rattled, but she already knew she was too far away for him to hear. "Don't go!"

The car was moving slowly as it picked its way across the land. The path would be overgrown; Edith's driveway had been difficult for the taxi, and the shortcut would be even worse. That meant she had a few minutes until the car moved beyond her vision.

It's less than a hundred metres away. I could almost run to it.

She tried putting some additional weight on her leg and had to grit her teeth against the pain.

No, there's no chance. Even if I somehow got a head start on Edith, I doubt I could reach the road in time. He would have to come here. I've got to find some way to attract his attention.

She grabbed the torch off the table. It was the only light in the powerless building. *If I flashed SOS in Morse code, will he see?*

The headlights had already passed the midway point of her view. The driver would have to look over his shoulder to see Ashburn, and if the road was dangerous enough that he had to crawl along it, she doubted he would be moving his eyes from the path.

Damn, damn, damn.

Adrienne pressed the torch against the windowpane and tried to shine its light in the car's path. The beam was too weak; it didn't even reach past the forest's edge, and the shortcut was more than fifty metres beyond that.

An idea struck her. Adrienne pulled the desk's drawer open so violently that the contents almost spilt out. She scrabbled through it, her heart thundering, to find the magnifying glass she'd seen while looking for batteries.

The car's headlights were growing increasingly distant as the road turned away from Ashburn. The full moon was bright enough to illuminate a gap in the trees. *If I can get my light through there, it should hit that large oak on the edge of the road. That would be unmissable.*

Adrienne shoved the window open and reached the magnifying glass outside. She then pointed the torch at the magnifier so that its beam passed through the glass.

The change in brightness was startling. Normally the torch's beam grew outwards, its light becoming weaker as it was stretched over an increasingly large circle. But by passing the stream through the magnifying glass, it was reflected back in on itself, narrowing instead of widening and strengthening instead of diffusing.

Adrienne let a grin form as the beam became a spotlight. It was a delicate balance. If she held the torch too close to the glass, the stream crossed over itself again and became weaker. She kept adjusting, shifting them closer and farther apart and fixing her angles, until she hit her target: the large oak in the car's path.

The car engine's rumble broke off in a screech of brakes. Adrienne held as still as she could manage, the beam jittering in her shaking hands, as she watched the car. It had stopped only a dozen metres from her spotlight.

He's seen it. Give him a minute—let him figure it out—

Tyres wailed as the car shot forward. From what Adrienne could tell, he'd floored the accelerator. The vehicle passed her spotlight in a cloud of dust. It kept up the insane pace as it crashed along the path, drawing away from Ashburn as quickly as the engine would allow.

Adrienne's smile disappeared. She dropped the magnifying glass and flashlight back onto the desk as she watched the car careen along the road, growing quieter and smaller until it finally disappeared from view. Then, confused and heartbroken, she slumped back into the chair.

You're driving along an abandoned, overgrown road. Somewhere behind you is Ashburn House, a property rumoured to be haunted. You've grown up listening to ghost stories. All of a sudden, a light appears ahead of you. What would your first thought be?

Ghost, of course.

She dropped her head into her hands. The outside world was silent for a moment, then, far below, the clicking resumed. Adrienne swallowed a furious, frustrated scream then took a deep breath and released it slowly.

Will he realise the truth? Probably not. He would have only seen the light for a second before driving away. I'm guessing he'll either continue to believe it was a ghost or convince himself he imagined it. Will he come back later tonight? I'm thinking it's a no for that as well. The shortcut only saves fifteen minutes. He'll use the safer main roads on his return trip.

She slid the magnifying glass back into the drawer then pulled the windowpane back into place and drew the bolt to lock it.

Nice work, Addy. Not only did you chase him off, but you made sure he wouldn't be coming back. Edith should put you on salary.

She snorted in laughter at the idea. She was zero for two as far as escape attempts went. The night outside was darkening, fighting against even its own moon's glow, and hunger itched at Adrienne's stomach. She'd eaten her final cup of instant noodles the night before, and the pantry didn't have many alternatives. Most of her remaining edible food came from Marion's gift basket: two eggs, a jar of jam, and a tin of beans. Everything else she owned—flour, rice, and a bag of dried lentils—needed cooking to be edible.

It was a sad prospect. She could eat the tin of beans and some of the jam for energy that evening. If she hadn't escaped by the following morning, she'd just have to eat the raw eggs and take her chances with salmonella.

Adrienne couldn't bring herself to leave the study. She sat in the chair, hands clasped on the table, as she stared at the expanse of forest filling the window. *I was so close. He saw the flashlight! If he hadn't jumped to conclusions, I could be out of here by now. But instead, I have to go downstairs, eat the world's saddest dinner, and then… what? Sit in the lounge room with just the torch for company while Edith paces around the house?*

275

She sighed and rubbed at her eyes then pushed away from the table. *Enough of the pity party, Addy. You're alive. You still have Wolf. You can escape… if you just figure out how.*

The hallway felt deeply hostile, and Adrienne, her nerves on edge, flicked the torch's light across its length. The portraits were still doused in gore. Half of the doors were open, their dark insides veiled from her light. The door to Edith's bedchamber waited opposite, its ornate bronze handle glittering in the dark. *I never want to step foot in that room again. It felt sour even when I was trying to like Edith. The black clothes, the dark curtains, the words scratched above her bed—*

REMEMBER YOUR SECRETS

Adrienne, halfway to the stairs, froze, and her eyes widened. *Edith wrote the messages to remind herself of things. "No mirrors" anywhere a mirror could have been placed, "Is it Friday light the candle" on the dinner table where she would see it every evening, and "Light the candle your family is still dead" on the door leading to the attic. All of these memorandums were placed strategically. "Remember your secrets" is on her headboard. What if it was put there for a reason?*

She swivelled on the spot to face the bedroom door. Frightened prickles scurried across her skin and made the hairs on her arms rise. She didn't want to return to Edith's room, but understanding the spirit and her motives could be the difference between a safe escape and death.

Adrienne felt in her jacket pocket to ensure the kitchen knife was still there then tightened her sweating hand on the doorknob, turned it, and stepped inside.

The curtains were drawn, but they still let a sliver of moonlight through. It cut across the room in a harsh line, running over the rug and the bed and up the wall. Either side of it, the area was a mess of swimming shadows and obscure shapes. Adrienne raised the torch and panned the light across the room. The light gleamed over the polished wooden wardrobe, the bedposts, and the desk. She was alone as far as she could tell.

Adrienne lifted her chin, inhaled, and closed the door behind her. The room, protected from the sun, felt unpleasantly cold. She could hear her breaths, the subtle crunch of carpet being crushed under her feet, and faint creaks from higher in the building as the wood shifted.

She had to pass the wardrobe to reach the bedside, and she glanced through the open door. The black silk and crepe glistened in the torchlight. Adrienne wondered if she would find the mirror phantom's dress if she searched through the apparel, but she let it alone. She didn't want to touch anything so intimately associated with the dead woman.

The bed remained as she remembered it. Dark curtains hung from the posts, framing the indent where Edith had slept every night. Scored into the headboard, just above the pillow, were the words REMEMBER YOUR SECRETS.

She would have seen it every night before going to bed. Adrienne stretched out a hand to brush the scarred wood. *And it would hang above her while she slept. Remembering this was important to her. But what secrets did she mean?*

As much as she hated disturbing Edith's space, Adrienne

couldn't leave while there was the chance that something in the room could help. She opened the bedside table's drawers and scanned their contents. A historical-fiction book, a pair of reading glasses, and a bible sat in the top drawer. Adrienne squinted at the leather-bound book. *Why would she own a bible after everything she'd done? Scripture and occult resurrections aren't terribly compatible.*

She looked into the second drawer, but it was full of under-garments, so she moved past it quickly. The lowest drawer was empty. Adrienne bit back a sigh as she closed it.

Am I grasping at straws? Maybe Edith didn't leave any additional clues. Maybe the nightly reminder was enough to help her to remember.

On impulse, Adrienne moved closer to the bed, hovered her head above the pillow, and looked towards the ceiling. It was the same position Edith would have taken each night. And there, on top of the canopy, nestled amongst the dusty fabric, was a small wooden box.

Adrienne gasped and reached for the container. It was beauti-fully carved, made of dark wood, and had a little gold clasp on its front. For a second, she was afraid it would be locked, but it wasn't; the lid lifted easily, and the insides were full of Edith's secrets.

CHAPTER 38
MEMORIES

AS ADRIENNE LOWERED HERSELF to sit cross-legged on the floor she scattered the box's contents over the dusty carpet. Edith's clicking joints passed below the window, and Adrienne, feeling as though she were trespassing, held her breath. The tapping rose, prodding and poking across the wall, then faded as the corpse moved on. Adrienne released her breath and raised the torch high as she turned over the items.

The box was full of newspaper clippings. Adrienne flipped through them and counted at least twenty. *The articles Edith cut out of the* Ipson Chronicles. *She kept them after all.*

Underneath was a small, tarnished locket. She opened it and saw a familiar face: Edith's mother, the brown-haired lady who had lost her jaw. Adrienne felt a small prickle of unease at the fact that Edith had kept such a memento after killing her family.

She unfolded the papers and quickly read the top one. After

speaking with Greg from the café and seeing the deformation of the portraits, she didn't find much new information in the newspaper. It described the discovery of the bodies, used phrases such as *horrific carnage* and *inhuman barbarism* without mentioning any gory specifics, and urged townspeople to lock their doors and be vigilant, as the killer was still at large.

Only the final paragraph made Adrienne pause.

As the populace of our fair town well knows, the Ashburns have long been a source of controversy, whether it's from the intrigue of Charles Ashburn's illness and reclusiveness or the censure of their child-raising practices. As the remains of the five bodies are removed from the property, the editor ventures to suggest this is not the end of the Ashburn legend.

Five bodies? Adrienne counted them off on her fingers. There had been Mr and Mrs Ashburn plus Charles Ashburn and his wife. Edith would have made five, but she had lived. *Did the editor make a mistake? Was there a servant or employee living at the house?* She scanned the article again, but no names were given except to note that Edith had been found alive.

She opened the next clipping. It was from the following week and expanded on the first article.

As the only survivor, young Miss Edith Ashburn faces a cold and lonely passage through life. Yesterday, following a third police interview and a doctor's examination, she was released into the care of her grandparents, Mr and Mrs Ellsworth. They arrived in a handsome Ford automobile and are presumed to be removing Miss Ashburn to their home in Bridgeport.

While we are still waiting for an official statement from the constables, we now have some understanding of how Miss Ashburn survived the massacre. A reliable source has come forward to say that Edith Ashburn was found in the basement, in which she had been locked, presumably by one of her family members. Curiously, the Ashburn basement had a second door that opened outside the building, but young Edith did not try to escape, nor did the attacker attempt to break in.

Miss Phillips, a friend of the neighbours, is quoted as saying, "It's really so tragic. I don't blame her, you know, but if little Edith had run for help—that is, if she'd left the basement on the day of the attack rather than waiting to be rescued—perhaps she would not have been the only survivor."

The Ashburn killer remains at large. Police urge any citizens with additional information to come forward.

Adrienne's mouth had gone dry, and her head was starting to throb. *I didn't know Ashburn House had a basement. Is the article right? Does it have a second door leading outside the building?*

She dropped the bundle of clippings and lurched to her feet. The outside world was unpleasantly quiet following Edith's circuit. *She knows about that basement entry, surely. That means the door must be locked. Otherwise, she would have already gotten in.*

Adrienne crossed to the window and twitched the curtain back. A full moon hung in the sky, and it bathed the ground in a heavy, ethereal glow. Adrienne searched for any humanoid shapes crouching amongst the weeds, but she couldn't see her great-aunt.

I locked every window and bolted both the front door and the back door. But I never considered there might be a third door to lock. Panic was steadily growing. No matter how forcefully Adrienne tried to tell herself she was safe—that if Edith had been able to get in through the basement, she already would have—she couldn't assuage the sensation that she was vulnerable. Exposed.

It should be checked at the very least. Best-case scenario, I find it and it's already locked. Worst-case scenario… she's already inside. Adrienne grimaced. *Let's not think about that.*

She left the memorabilia spread over Edith's carpet and hurried to the door. Her ankle began to burn again as she put weight on it, but Adrienne tightened her lips as she followed the hallway to the stairs.

The paintings were openly watching her. She tried not to look at them, but when she glanced towards the wall, she found the dead, glassy eyes fixed on her, rolling slowly in their sockets as she passed them.

She stumbled down the stairs, clattered to a halt in the hallway, and raised her torch to check the surrounding area. It seemed untouched.

Where is the door to the basement? The article didn't say. There are so many doors in this house—would it be near the front or the back?

Adrienne turned in a circle, breathing heavily, as she thought. Most of her time spent in Ashburn had been near the front of the house, so she turned to the lesser-seen rear. She checked the back door. Then, following the right-hand wall, she began opening every door she passed as she cycled through the house. *Cupboard, cupboard, laundry, cupboard, kitchen, pantry, empty room, main door…*

She'd reached the front of the house, so she turned and tried all of the doors on the opposite side of the hallway. She hunted through both the sitting room and lounge room in case she'd missed something inside them, then she looked in the final empty room at the back of the house.

Maybe the newspaper was wrong. Adrienne returned to the hallway and leaned against the bannister so that she could lift her throbbing leg off the ground. *Maybe there is no basement. Greg from the coffee shop said Edith was found inside a cupboard. Maybe there were a lot of rumours circulating at the time, and the newspaper just picked the one it thought was most likely.*

As she turned towards the stairs, her light flashed over something metallic. She bent to one side to see the behind the staircase and found a tiny, square door hidden in the shadows.

You've got to be joking.

It blended into the staircase's wood perfectly. The only suggestion that a door existed there at all was the glint of the small, curved handle and the dark crease that ran around its perimeter.

Adrienne got to her knees to reach for the handle. *It certainly matches the story no matter which version you go with: Mrs Ashburn hiding her daughter, or Edith hiding herself. You wouldn't think to look here unless you knew about it.*

She pulled on the handle. The lower end rose, and a small click told her the door was, indeed, unlocked. The square swung open, and Adrienne held her breath as she bent forward to shine her light inside.

Dust motes swirled in her light like thin, anaemic snow. The space seemed to stretch on forever, but the torch was too weak to bring much of it into relief. Adrienne could see steps leading from the door to a dirt floor. Beyond that were several ancient crates and what she thought was a pile of rotting sacks. She clicked her torch off to allow the darkness to flow around and swallow her. It took a second for her eyes to adjust to the dark, but then she was able to see the blue glow of moonlight far away to the right. The basement had a door leading outside, after all, and it was *open*.

Adrienne's pulse kicked into overdrive. Very carefully, as though moving too quickly would undo the perfect equilibrium she existed in, she nudged the door closed. There was a keyhole below the handle. Adrienne tried to fit the house key inside, but the cut-out was too small.

It needs a different key, then—one that I don't have. That's okay; I can pull something heavy in front to block the opening. I wonder if I can move the grandfather clock.

The huge, chiming monolith was the largest and heaviest piece of furniture in the hallway and only a few feet from the door. She hurried to it, put her shoulder against the wood, and shoved. She had to strain until every muscle in her body screamed and her lungs burnt, but it scraped forward several inches.

She relaxed, leaning her back against the clock and panting. *It's a nightmare to move. Good. There's no way Edith's getting in once this thing is in place.*

Then Adrienne felt her body stiffen. Something tugged at her instincts. It was a vague sense—like a scent that she could barely smell—but she instinctively knew that something was wrong. Adrienne closed her eyes and tried to pinpoint the source of the uneasiness. *There*—it was the same straining, jangling noise she'd heard in her bedroom. Like off-key violins being stressed, but so quiet it was almost possible to convince herself she was imagining it.

Adrienne opened her eyes. Directly ahead and a little to the right hung the hallway mirror. The cloth had fallen off without Adrienne even realising and lay in a pool on the floor. And inside the reflection stood Edith, tall and stately and crowded by the hallway's shadows as their gazes met.

Adrienne sucked in a sharp breath. Her eyes reflexively darted to the space beside the lounge room door where the reflection showed Edith to be standing. It was empty. Adrienne brought her focus back to the mirror.

Edith could have been a photograph for all she moved. She faced Adrienne, her hands folded over the black skirts and back straight as a post. Her face was flat, neither grinning nor contorting like the creature outside, but her eyes were hard and commanding. Even with ninety years separating them, the similarities with the upstairs portraits were eerie.

Does she want to talk? Can she be reasoned with?

Adrienne licked her dry lips and prayed her voice wouldn't crack. "Edith? I-I don't know why you're lingering here after death, but—"

Edith took a step nearer. Her expression remained flat, but her eyes flashed in the reflected moonlight.

Adrienne found it increasingly difficult to breathe as the torch's light jittered in her shaking hand. "I hope you're not angry with me. I… I'd like to leave, please. I can go right now. Walk to town. The house will be all yours—you'll never see me again—"

Edith took a second step forward, bringing her close to the glass. She looked so corporeal that Adrienne half expected the spectre to step through the mirror. Edith's unblinking gaze didn't leave Adrienne's face as she shook her head. *No.*

"Please—" Sweat beaded over Adrienne's body. Her mind, frightened and exhausted, whirled out of control as she tried to think of an argument that might sway the spirit. "Whatever happened here—whatever happened with your old family—I don't want any part in it. Let me leave."

Another shake. This time Edith raised one bony, pale hand, extended the index finger, and pointed down.

Adrienne frowned. *What is she pointing at? Her feet? The floor?* A drawn-out creak echoed from behind her as the little square door drifted open. *Oh no—the basement.*

It was hard to tear her gaze away from Edith, but Adrienne did, turning to the door under the stairs. It had drifted open, smoothly and effortlessly, as though moved by a breeze. Fear about what might come through crashed over Adrienne, and she reached for the knife in her pocket.

But nothing came out of the door. Instead, a small grey shape caught in her shaking torchlight. Wolfgang had approached the opening. He raised his nose to sniff at the wood in the way he did whenever he encountered a new item in his domain, then he turned to the dark hole.

"No!" Adrienne darted towards him, both Edith and stinging ankle forgotten as she raced to pull her cat back from the door. She was too late. As elegant and uncatchable as smoke, Wolfgang slunk forward and disappeared into the basement.

CHAPTER 39
THE BASEMENT

ADRIENNE DROPPED TO HER knees. Her heart felt as if it might thump its way out of her chest as she stared at the black opening, her hand stretched towards it, disbelief and cold horror rising through her.

"Wolf—" The word came out as a squeak. She knelt there, unmoving, praying with every fibre of her body that the cat would reappear in the door. He didn't.

Of course he wouldn't. The house has him now. Swallowed whole, sucked down into its belly, where it can digest him and eventually spit out his bones.

Adrienne tried to force the idea from her mind, to purge the image of the grey tabby wandering sightless in the black for the remainder of his life, but she couldn't.

This is my fault. He escaped from the lounge room because I wasn't careful when I opened the door. He got into the basement because I was too slow to stop him. If he suffers, it will be on my head.

Adrienne bent closer to the basement's entry and passed her light inside. The deepest region of the house seemed to repel illumination; it appeared to thrive on darkness and silence and desolation as ardently as its deceased owner had.

She sat back on her heels and wiped her hand over her mouth. *No, it's not my fault. Not really. I closed the basement door; I remember it making a little click as the latch caught. Edith reopened it. Edith lured Wolf inside.*

"Give me back my cat."

She turned towards the mirror, teeth bared and face scrunched as she prepared to clash with the spirit. But Edith was gone. The mirror showed the hallway, long and cluttered and full of memories, but no dark-clothed woman.

"Give me back my cat!"

The words echoed through Ashburn's empty rooms without answer. Adrienne pressed a hand to her chest, where her heart was burning. She was incapable of stopping the tears that dripped onto the dusty wood floor.

I promised myself I would not take any risks. The risk-free option would be to close the door, push the clock in front of it, and forget Wolfgang ever existed.

She could still remember trying to revive the soaked, bone-thin kitten on her mother's kitchen table. A classical music CD played in the next room, and the operatic songs had washed over them as Adrienne gently massaged the lump of wet fur. Adrienne's mother had thought the kitten was a lost cause; it wouldn't drink the drop of the milk they'd dabbed on his lips or even open his eyes. Then the Mozart composition hit its crescendo, and right on the final beat, the kitten opened its mouth and let out a tiny peep.

Naming him had been a no-brainer after that. Wolfgang Amadeus Mozart. And no matter how big he grew, he was the most precious creature in Adrienne's world.

Her only choice was whether to go into the basement head first or feet first.

"Bloody cat." She spoke to give herself courage, but the words came out as stutters. "Always getting into trouble."

Her feet went in first. The doorway was small—just a little larger than her torso—so Adrienne had to contort her body into an awkward angle to squeeze through. Her feet touched one of the stone steps, and she began wiggling the top half of herself after them.

She couldn't see while her body was blocking the doorway, so she had to worm into the basement blind. It was a horrifying sensation to imagine that something might be lurking just past her toes, waiting for her to shift another inch into their domain.

Adrienne had to raise her hands above her head to fit her shoulders through. She was carrying most of her weight on her one good foot, and her thigh muscles were shaking.

"He probably won't even appreciate what I'm doing for him. The ungrateful lump."

Her throat was tightening, and the bravado-infused words came out as a squeak. As her head slid through the doorway, she gasped. The basement's air was like ice.

All that was left was to slip her arms through the door, then she was crouched on the second step, head bent to avoid scraping the rough-wood ceiling, with little plumes of condensation rising with every exhalation.

She turned her torch over the basement. The beam caught a jumble of objects, not all of them identifiable. She thought the space must have been used either for storage or as a workshop. Clusters of equipment, from spindles to ploughs to furniture, were pressed against the walls. They looked as though they had broken well before being placed in the basement to attract a blanket of dust and cobwebs.

To her right, thirty paces away, a rectangle of pale-blue light streamed through the open trapdoor. Adrienne hadn't seen the entry when circling the house, which meant it was likely surrounded by tall weeds. The hole wasn't much bigger than the space she'd just crawled through, but it still threatened danger, either from things getting *in* or from Wolfgang getting *out*. If she lost the cat in the woods surrounding Ashburn, she held very little hope of getting him back.

"Wolf?" Adrienne cautiously moved off the stairs and onto the dirt floor. She kept her voice light, knowing that her cat would hear even a whisper. "Wolf, food! Come and get some food!"

He would have normally come running at that word, but the only moving shapes she could see were the clouds of dust her feet had disturbed. Adrienne swallowed, turning slowly, her beam playing over the clusters of shapes and shadows as she tried to pick out any signs of life. "Food, buddy! Food!"

A flash of something pale caught in her light. She swung

towards it, but it wasn't the cat. Instead, a small white rectangle lay on the floor.

That struck Adrienne as odd. Everything else in the basement, including the ground, was coated in a century of dust. But the flat shape was perfectly white and clean, as though it had been placed there the week before.

Did Edith put it here? She took a step nearer and craned her neck as she strained to see more clearly. She thought it was a piece of paper.

"Wolf?" she said a final time, turning in a full circle as the word created a plume of vapour in front of her face. She couldn't see anything, human or feline. She tightened her muscles against the shivers running through her and turned back to the paper.

As she neared it, she saw it was an envelope and not perfectly fresh as she'd thought. Small flecks of dust had developed on the surface, suggesting it had been there for several months. She bent and picked it up. A single word was written on the front: *Adrienne.*

Prickles of uneasiness writhed over her skin. She held still a moment, listening and waiting for the telltale clicking that accompanied Edith's movements, but the space remained quiet.

The letter was unsealed. She couldn't help herself; she turned it over and took the sheets out. The careful, immaculate penmanship was familiar. It had been on the small note in her bedroom, too. *Edith wrote this.* Adrienne frowned. *What's it doing down here? Did she really expect me to find it... or... no, surely not...*

She pointed the torch towards the ceiling. The basement's rough wooden boards were nearly an arm's length above her.

They had gaps in them—not large, but a hundred years of aging and carrying feet had gradually widened them. She traced one of the slits. *This would be under the lounge room, wouldn't it? I remember noticing how the boards had spaces between them on my first night here.*

Adrienne pictured how it might have played out: the note would have been left on the little table beside the fireside chair, waiting for her eventual arrival. But some disturbance—possibly a gust of wind from an open window, a draft from the doorway, or even a bump from Edith's elbow—had sent it plunging towards the floor. The envelope was flat. It could have slipped between the floorboards with the grace of a tumbling leaf, its absence never noticed.

It's improbable but not impossible. I remember thinking how odd it was that the bedroom note was the only missive Edith left.

Adrienne shook the paper open with trembling fingers. The words were small and daintily formed, and she had to hold the paper close to her face to read it in the torch's light.

CHAPTER 40
MISSIVE

My dear Adrienne,

I suspect I am a stranger to you, though I have had a keen interest in you since you were young. You did, in fact, visit me once when you were a small child. I regret that the meeting was not long; your mother did not approve of me or my intentions, I fear.

There is a very particular reason why I left you my home. As my only remaining relative, I believe you will be both willing and well-suited to perform a particular task that accompanies ownership of this house. What I ask is no small feat; I pray you will one day forgive me for passing this burden on to you.

To explain this task, I must first tell you about our family. My parents were honest, kind people. When I was very young, our home saw the addition of my uncle and his wife.

She was a sweet woman; my uncle, a well-regarded painter, was not fully sound of mind, though he was attempting to rehabilitate himself through solitude and work. Together, we were happy more often than not and fortunate enough to be respected by our neighbours.

But there is one more member of my family, the architect of every painful moment in my life: my twin sister, Eleanor.

Eleanor and I were identical in appearance only. I believe doctors in modern times call her condition sociopathy. She had a wilful disregard for the health and happiness of others. From as young as four, she was killing the chicks in our garden and pricking me with pins. There are very few people I consider heartless, but she is one of them.

Eleanor had another disturbing trait in addition to her callousness. It is something that I fear you will find difficult to believe. My dear Adrienne, as hard as it is for you to consider what I am about to tell you, I pray you will read the full measure of my story before passing judgement.

My sister Eleanor had a supernatural aptitude. It manifested as small talents when she was young but grew as she aged. She was so guarded with her secrets that I never fully understood her limits or how her ability worked, but a lifetime of research has caused me to believe she holds the reincarnated soul of a magic user. This soul is reborn again and again, in different bodies and with different minds but always with the same talent. She may have passed through many eons as a biblical seer, an Egyptian priestess, a Salem witch—and finally, that talent found itself born into Eleanor Ashburn.

From my experience with her, it seems that her abilities were based largely on what she believed. If she convinced herself something was the truth—no matter how unnatural—her body would obey that rule. For example, she held the Victorian-era superstition that a person's soul could be trapped inside a photograph. And because she believed it, it held true for her. She never allowed us to photograph her and never gave Uncle Charles permission to create her portrait, though he obsessively painted the rest of the family.

These are some of the gifts and weaknesses that I witnessed manifest in my sister:

She is strengthened by moonlight

She is debilitated by candlelight

She does not sleep

A part of her soul can be trapped in photographs

If she kills another human using her hands, her lifespan is extended by the number of years they had remaining

Her body ages like that of a mortal

You may have noticed that each gift is balanced by a curse. She abhorred unbalance or inequality in all things and was rigid regarding those rules. At night she would stand by her open window and allow moonlight to bathe her but would scream and fight if you brought a candle or lamp too close to her skin.

As I'm sure you can imagine, those gifts were toxic when

combined with her callousness. I don't know how much you have heard about our family, but my parents, aunt, and uncle were murdered when I was eight. The deaths were never officially solved. I alone knew the truth, and it has been a weight around my neck for my entire life.

Eleanor killed them.

When she was six years old, my father happened upon her attempting to drown one of the neighbour's children in a water trough. From that day forward he kept her locked in the house. As she had never ventured far from home before, and because she and I looked alike, her existence became something of a legend; people in town would debate whether she was real or not and whether she was still alive.

It was not so bad during the day, but because she did not sleep, we were vulnerable at night. My parents would lock her bedroom door every evening an hour before bedtime and unlock it in the morning for breakfast. This system kept us safe for years until one night, when my sister and I were eight, my mother forgot to lock the door.

My family was slaughtered. I will not distress you with the details, but the crimes were so violent that I, the only survivor, was cleared on account of my young age. No one could believe a child was capable of such atrocities.

I was supposed to be my sister's final victim that night. Instead, I managed to kill her. That day is my single greatest regret. Had I been more prepared—had I not underestimated her powers—I might have saved my family. Still, it is what it is. We must accept our failings, my dear, and respect ourselves in spite of them.

The remainder of my teenage years were spent living with my grandparents. When I became old enough to inherit Ashburn, I decided to renovate the building and sell it. I moved in to oversee the improvements, but as you must know, what was supposed to be a few weeks turned into a lifetime of occupancy.

I had thought my sister conquered and vanquished. I was wrong; by killing our family, she had gained an unnatural lifespan that transcended even death. She dug her way out of her grave within a fortnight of my moving into Ashburn. She came to kill me, to take my remaining years and replace me in the home. We looked similar enough that I expect she could have worn my clothes and adopted my identity.

Once more, I was able to defeat her, though this fight was nearly my undoing. I buried her in a little grave within the woods. That was when I realised my stay at Ashburn would need to be one of permanent occupancy and vigilance lest Eleanor rise once again. I did not expect to survive a third encounter with her. She had grown cautious, and her patience could outlast mine.

But through vigilance, I have succeeded in keeping her dead for these last eighty years. Do you remember the rules above? She believes candlelight will weaken her, and she believes a part of her can be trapped in a photo. When we were children, I took a single picture of her. For my whole life, I have been using it to keep her locked in her grave.

Once a week I light a candle so that the glow falls across her photo for an hour or two. It is enough that, with no moonlight to strengthen her again, she has been incapable of escaping her tomb.

This is what I ask of you, Adrienne. As little as you may believe my story, and as insane as this letter must sound, I pray you will do this for me—if nothing more than as an old lady's final request. Please live in this home. Please enjoy it. And once a week, please light a candle in the attic so that my sister cannot hurt you.

"Ooh." There was a second page, but Adrienne felt too sick to read it. Her fingers, numb from the cold, shook as she tucked the papers into her pocket. Everything made sense. Everything was explained.

The photograph in the attic wasn't of Edith, as Adrienne had first assumed. Instead, it was of the camera-reticent sister. Adrienne pictured the child's face, eyes slightly widened and lips quirked as the flash surprised her, and could very easily imagine the cherubic expression morphing into anger as she realised what had happened.

She had grown into the deformed, furious creature that had dug its way out of its grave and stalked her back to Ashburn. Even after a hundred years of being contorted by a too-small grave, she had the same strong cheekbones and sharp eyes as her twin.

Then Adrienne remembered how, during the scuffle on the lawn, the corpse had loosened its hold on Adrienne's leg at the sound of Edith's name. At the time, Adrienne had thought it was the shock of being addressed, but now she realised it was conditioned caution. Eleanor had learned to fear her sister. And the phrase whispered into her ear, *Weep for Edith*, had not been a request but a taunt. *Weep for Edith, for she is dead.*

Adrienne tried to remember every time she'd encountered the corpse, both before and after she'd realised what it was. Initially, when she'd thought children were pranking her, she'd used the lamp to explore outside the house. If Eleanor truly feared fire, that little flame might have been the only thing that kept her alive. Both times Eleanor had attacked and hurt her, Adrienne had been using the torch instead of the lamp.

She thought of the shadowed figure that appeared in the mirrors, and fresh unease washed over her. The corpse and the reflection weren't one and the same, as she'd thought; both sisters—the animalistic, contorted corpse and the impeccably tidy spectre—had lingered past their deaths.

Adrienne's mind was racing with questions and ramifications, but she was also conscious that she'd spent a dangerous amount of time in the basement while she read the first half of the note. Knowing that her stalker was Eleanor rather than Edith would make little difference if the cadaver tore Adrienne's heart out.

"Wolf!" Adrienne twisted to flick her beam around the icy room. A cold sweat had broken out across her skin, and it stuck her shirt to her back. She glanced towards the open trapdoor again and prayed her cat hadn't slipped through it.

The basement seemed to dampen sound. Every breath,

footstep, and heartbeat came out muffled. *It's the dust,* Adrienne thought as she bumped a broken chair and sent a small shower of the musty grey powder pouring to the floor. *It's so thick.*

She bent to look inside a crumpled metal barrel then froze as a low, quiet rumble became audible. *Is it an earthquake? No, surely not; I'd feel the ground move.* She strained to make out the sound and inhaled as the pitch, though distorted and muffled, resolved itself into a motor. Adrienne shot upright and turned towards the trapdoor, where the rumble floated in on the cool night air. *A car. Peggy's brother? Doesn't matter. It's rescue.*

"Hey, Wolf!" she hissed, becoming reckless in her urgency as she dug through the detritus. "Get over here! We've got to go!"

A sharp bang made her startle. She twisted towards the source of the noise. The trapdoor, which had been open, was firmly closed.

Adrienne licked at dry and fear-numbed lips as she moved the torchlight over the room. The beam jittered across cloth sacks, rusted wash basins, and a cobwebbed armchair missing its seat, sending distorted shadows racing over the walls.

Maybe it was the wind.

Her heart ached from the rising stress. She held her breath, listening to the basement's oppressive silence and the distant car engine, hunting for any hint that she might not be alone.

Then a sound broke through the quiet: a single click. Adrienne's heart lurched unpleasantly, and she took a step back. Silence resumed for a beat, then the clicking came again, louder and repeating, becoming a cruel tempo that matched her throbbing pulse.

She's here.

CHAPTER 41
RESCUE

ADRIENNE DREW THE KNIFE out of her jacket pocket. She moved slowly, careful not to rustle her clothing or cause any noise that might attract the dead woman, as she backed towards the door leading into Ashburn.

The basement's acoustics made it impossible to tell the direction or distance of the clicking. Adrienne raised the knife ahead of her and continued to turn, shuffling in a circle and passing the torch's small beam over the myriad of shapes surrounding her. The temperature, already frigid, was dropping with every passing second, and the cold was drawing into her core and making her feel as though she would never be warm again.

Edith's letter said her sister couldn't be reasoned with. But perhaps, after all this time… "Eleanor?"

The clicking stopped. Adrienne took a quick breath and continued as clearly as her shaking voice would allow. "I don't want to be your enemy, Eleanor. I can't imagine how… horrific… these last eighty years must have been. I'd like to help you, if you'll let me."

There was no answer. After a second, the clicking resumed. Adrienne kept swivelling and squinting through the dust for signs of life as she backed towards the doorway. The sound of bones bumping together steadily grew louder, but as far as she could see, she was still alone.

A sudden, awful, crawling premonition came over Adrienne. She raised her light towards the ceiling. There wasn't much space between her and the wooden boards—two feet, at most—but that was plenty of room for Eleanor.

The first things she saw were the bony, twisted feet jammed between two supports; the toes had been splayed against the wood to keep her body wedged in place. Adrienne felt a heavy, horror-filled nausea rise as she traced the form, her light dancing over the thighs, buttocks, and the dirt-creased back, before the beam finally illuminated the two globe-like white eyes poised inches above her head.

She didn't even have time to part her lips for a scream before the corpse released its grip and dropped onto her. They collided with a horrible crunching sound as the desiccated woman's bones knocked against Adrienne and jarred the wind from her. The world became a blur of motion as they crumpled to the ground, tangled together in a flurry of kicking, clawing limbs. Adrienne tried to stab the knife into the corpse, but Eleanor was pressed too near for her to put enough force into the slashes.

Teeth fixed around the tender skin of her lower throat. Adrienne threw her head back to avoid the bite, and lights flashed through her vision as her head cracked against the basement floor. Bony fingers dug into her cheeks, her jaw, and her neck as Eleanor strained to find purchase for her teeth.

Then the pressure was abruptly released, and the dead woman jerked back. A screeching, hysterical yowl filled the basement. Adrienne tried to crawl backwards, and her hand bumped the torch she'd dropped. It spiralled away and came to rest against a crate, its light diffusing over the corpse.

Wolfgang clung to the back of Eleanor's head. His fur had fluffed out, making him look twice as large as normal as he clawed Eleanor's face and darted sharp bites into it.

Putrid, congealed blood squirted from the cuts as Eleanor stretched her grasping fingers towards her assailant. She snagged a handful of Wolfgang's fur and threw him away. Adrienne shrieked as the grey cat flew out of the light's circle.

Eleanor dropped into a crouch. The torch illuminated her torso and face, and Adrienne smothered a moan. Wolf's claws had shredded the fragile skin. One eye had burst, and a clear liquid dribbled over the scraps of her cheek, which billowed in and out with every rasping breath.

"Wolf?" Adrienne squeaked.

Eleanor took a step forward, her lips peeling back from the rotting gums and teeth, then howled. A streak of grey shot up to her then darted away before she could turn on it. Spots of blood welled on her leg where Wolfgang had bitten her.

I've got to help him. I lost my knife—I lost my torch—but—

Adrienne didn't risk hesitating any longer. She turned and scrambled towards the small door leading back into the house. Eleanor made to follow, but again, Wolf darted out of the shadows to plant a bite and then frisked away with a throaty hiss. Eleanor, prepared this time, swiped at him. Her fingernails barely brushed his tail.

Please be careful, Wolf. Don't get too close. Don't let her catch you.

The doorway's outline was visible from the thin blue moonlight that flowed down the hall through the front windows. Adrienne had no time to wiggle through the gap carefully; she pointed her hands ahead of her body and launched herself at the opening like a gymnast diving through a hoop. Her shoulder bones scraped the wooden frame, making her hiss from the sting, but her head and torso went through. She pressed her hands onto the carpet runner to drag her legs out behind her.

A hand fastened over her injured ankle and pulled. Adrienne screamed as the cuts were reopened, and she pushed her hands to the wall to keep herself from being dragged back into the basement. There was another yowl followed by a guttural, enraged shriek from Eleanor, and the grip loosened enough for Adrienne to slip through and tumble fully into the hallway.

A crash echoed from the basement. Adrienne prayed that the projectile, whatever it had been, had missed its target. She rolled towards the staircase's landing, grabbed the lamp that rested on the table beside it, and scrambled to remove the glass cover. She splashed oil into the reservoir then shoved the metal bottle into her jacket's pocket in case the lamp needed refilling.

Something moved behind her, and Adrienne swivelled to face it. Although the moon was full, very little of its light extended into the hallway, but she could still recognise Edith's tall, ethereal form in the mirror. The black-clad lady pressed close to the glass, gesturing towards Adrienne while mouthing mute instructions.

"I know, it's okay!" Adrienne struggled to open the matchbox. Her fingers were numb and shaking. Matches spilt over the floor, but she managed to catch one. "I've got the lamp!"

She struck the match and watched the flame bloom. She could see Edith's gestures in her peripheral vision, but her focus was on lighting the wick. As the lamp caught, the golden glow spread out around her, growing larger and brighter and creating a little circle of safety.

"This will work, right? You said candlelight will hurt her." She turned back to Edith and felt a spasm of unease. The older woman's face was hard and deeply creased with worry. She pointed a finger towards Adrienne, mouthing the same phrase over and over again. Adrienne squinted as she tried to lip-read the words.

"Look… behind… you…"

She turned. A figure stood by the open basement door. The pressing darkness and numbing fear had prevented Adrienne from seeing it when she'd scrambled through the portal, but the flickering lamp light now played across a familiar face.

"Marion?"

The woman didn't reply. Her blank, shadowed eyes stared sightlessly out of a sallow face as she swayed from side to side. Sweat beaded over her skin, and a knife—the same knife Adrienne had used to defend herself the day before and that had dropped on Ashburn's lawn—gleamed in her hand.

Adrienne had left the basement door open, having planned to climb back through it once she'd lit the lamp. And while the golden light brought Marion and the staircase into relief, it was incapable of reaching into the heavy black beyond the doorway.

A voice whispered out of the darkness. The words were slow and sickening and in a language Adrienne didn't recognise. They felt so weighty and corporeal that Adrienne half expected them to take physical shape as they slithered out of the basement and writhed along the floor.

Marion inhaled, and purpose flowed back into her face. Her large brown eyes fixed on Adrienne, who crouched on the floor, hobbled and weaponless save for the lamp. A muscle above Marion's eye twitched. Then the knife arced through the air, aimed at Adrienne's hand.

The attack was frighteningly quick, but Adrienne's nerves were keyed to breaking point, and she twisted aside a fraction of a second before the knife began to move. If Marion had targeted any other body part, she likely would have hit her mark, but the blade made a low whistle as it passed Adrienne's side and embedded itself in the floor.

"I'm sorry!" Adrienne cried as she kicked at Marion's closest leg. The woman toppled, turned, and grabbed the lamp as she fell.

She wants the light; that's why she attacked my hand rather than my face.

A crunching noise rose from the glass as Marion's hands

tightened around it. Adrienne, knowing how vital the flame was to her safety, tried to prise the lamp away without upending and extinguishing it. Marion's face contorted into a grimace that almost perfectly mimicked Eleanor's as her fingers tightened to crush the glass.

It wasn't a fair fight. Adrienne's muscles were already taxed to exhaustion, and Marion had a height advantage. The lamp was forced against the floor, smashing the panes and bending the metal holder.

"No!" Glass cut into Adrienne's hands as she scrambled to save the flame, but it had already gone out. Inky shadows poured around her, clustering close and almost thick enough to taste.

She knew what would happen next. Marion, her job done, would step back and let the blank expression fall over her face once again. And Eleanor would crawl out of the basement, inch by inch, her terrible form twisting through the hole and her one remaining eye flashing in the moonlight as she prepared to sink her teeth into warm flesh.

Adrienne squirmed to look behind her. One of the rectangular windows at the end of the hallway had been smashed, and the door stood open; Marion must have broken the glass to get inside the house. Her car would be in the driveway. The keys might even be in the ignition.

But that would mean both abandoning Wolfgang and trying to outrun the corpse—and that hadn't worked too well last time she'd tried it.

There's got to be another source of fire. Edith lived her whole life in preparation for this day; she must have owned backup lamps, surely?

If she had, Adrienne didn't know where to find them. The fireplace was choked with soot and had no kindling. The only other source of fire in the house was…

The attic's candles.

CHAPTER 42
BEST-LAID PLANS

SHE HAD JUST SECONDS until Eleanor emerged. Marion stood close by, her outline visible in the thin moonlight, poised to throw Adrienne back to the floor if she tried to run. Adrienne reached for the lamp, grasped the twisted metal handle, and launched herself forward.

As Marion reached out to drive her back into the ground, Adrienne smashed the lamp across her head. Marion exhaled the beginning of a strangled cry then crumpled.

"Sorry again!" Adrienne scrambled towards the table beside the stairs. Marion wouldn't stay down for long, and clicking noises were already echoing from the basement door. Adrienne grabbed the matchbox she'd dropped when trying to light the lamp. It was nearly empty, but she shook one of the matches out, struck it, and held it towards the black doorway.

Eleanor's head and torso poked through like some grotesque

insect crawling out of the ground. Her one good eye widened as the match's light touched her, and she sucked herself back into the basement with a cracked wail.

The match went out almost as soon as Eleanor disappeared. Adrienne began scrambling up the stairs as quickly as her torn leg would allow and struck a second match as she passed the fourth step. She held it over the bannister, aware that the light was faint but would still reach the base of the stairs, then dropped it when the flame came close to burning her fingertips.

She repeated this with her remaining two matches, knowing that with each step she drew farther away from the door and her tiny flame would have less influence over the shadows clustered there and be less of a threat for the vengeful spirit.

The top of the stairs was in sight when she threw her final match away, so Adrienne dropped the box. She stumbled on the last step but regained her feet and staggered down the hallway towards the dark attic stairwell.

Moonlight came through two open doors. It let her see her path but also illuminated the paintings. They were no longer static, but the subjects moved, twisting and struggling as teeth and knives and claw-like fingernails tore their limbs from them and poured their blood across the floor. The images repeated, playing in an appalling loop, a visceral memory of the Ashburns' bloody demise. Only Edith's paintings stayed static.

As she passed the gilt-frame mirror she'd hung at the hallway's midpoint, Adrienne caught a glimpse of dark motion. Edith's ghost ran alongside her, invisible save for the spectre in the mirror. She made eye contact with Adrienne as they passed and gave a small nod.

The encouragement warmed Adrienne and carried her to the end of the hallway. She collapsed against the end wall, drawing in ragged, painful breaths and scrunching her face up against the ache that radiated out of her leg.

Don't stop. Don't let her catch you.

She fumbled up the stairs, using her hands as much as her legs. The attic door glided open with a low creak as she neared it, and Adrienne brushed her fingers over the words cut into its stained wood.

LIGHT THE CANDLE
YOUR FAMILY
IS STILL
DEAD

Eleanor is still dead. At least, she was when this message was written. That was its purpose. A reminder for why the candle had to be lit: so that her sister would not rise again.

Adrienne crossed to the nearest crate. She shoved its lid off and tore one of the candles out then hobbled to the table at the centre of the room.

How much time do I have? Eleanor's fast. Once she starts moving, she could reach here in just a few seconds. But how long will she stay afraid of the matches' light?

The black-and-white photo waited in the table's centre, and the nymph-like child stared at her in curious wonder. Adrienne tried not to meet the eyes that now seemed eerily aware; she reached for the box of matches Edith had left beside the photo. She counted the seconds in the back of her mind as she shook one out. Edith's letter had said her sister had grown cautious. But she wouldn't wait in the darkness for long, Adrienne knew. She wanted to have Ashburn for herself and would not suffer opposition.

The match-head flared. She touched it to the wick and held it there until it caught. Then she shook the match to extinguish it, unzipped her jacket, and held one lapel around the flame as she crept back to the room's entrance.

She slipped behind the attic's half-open door to make herself invisible to anyone climbing the stairwell. Her jacket blocked most of the candle's glow, and she twisted to keep the light from shining over the ceiling. If Eleanor suspected her plan, the corpse wouldn't enter the attic—and Adrienne would remain trapped there until she collapsed from exhaustion.

Being careful to keep the candle hidden as well as she could, Adrienne tugged the bottle of lighter fluid out of her jacket's pocket and used her teeth to unscrew the lid. Then she pressed close to the wall, forced her breathing to be shallow and quiet, and waited.

It took a moment, but the quiet clicking reached her. As she'd expected, Eleanor was being careful; her movements were slow and patient, and the clicking paused repeatedly before resuming. Adrienne readjusted the jacket shield, hoping there wasn't enough light to give her away, and held her breath as the clicking drew closer.

It's strange; it doesn't sound like it's coming up the stairs. Are the acoustics playing tricks?

She'd half closed the door to make the gap too narrow for a person to fit through. Even in the near-darkness, it would be impossible for Eleanor to enter without making the door shift.

The clicking was growing nearer. It was close enough to be inside the room, but the door remained still. Hot wax trickled down the candle and seared Adrienne's thumb, but she clenched her jaw against it and kept her position. She was certain her thundering heart was loud enough to be audible to the corpse. Her lungs burnt with the held breath, and the candle's flame licked at the jacket's fabric. She couldn't keep still much longer.

The sound was so close that she felt as though she could reach out and touch the corpse. But the stairwell remained undisturbed—

Something fell together in her mind. Earlier that afternoon, she'd come into the attic to see why the smoke was falling and had unlocked and opened a window to lean through.

I closed the pane when I was done... but I don't remember locking it.

She turned just in time for the knife to skim her cheek and hit the wall. Eleanor's face, contorted with hatred, stopped just inches away from her own. She could smell the rotting flesh as the corpse exhaled and hear the wet smacking of its shredded cheek flapping open.

The knife had cut Adrienne just below her eye, and hot blood poured down the side of her face. It hurt, but not enough to incapacitate her. She twisted to one side to avoid Eleanor's grasping, bony hand but was a fraction of a second too late to stop it from fastening around her throat.

Eleanor's jaw stretched open, exposing gums that had sunk away from the yellowed teeth, and leaned forward to bite into her victim's neck.

Adrienne moved on instinct. She thrust the candle towards Eleanor, shoving the flaming tip into the dead woman's chest, and threw the bottle of oil after it.

Eleanor's one remaining eye bulged as the candle came into view. She leapt out of reach but not before the flame grazed her wrinkled skin. The flesh turned an ugly sooty black, but the contact hadn't been enough for it to catch.

The corpse clutched at her scorched flesh and released a violent bellow. The sound shook the building, rattling the wooden slats and windows as though they were props. Adrienne dropped the candle and clasped her hands over her ears to block out the noise. Her own scream was almost inaudible compared to Eleanor's fury.

Cold, bony fingers grasped her wrists. Adrienne had no time to realise what was happening; Eleanor threw her to the ground, and she skidded across the dusty floor until she hit the candle-holder. The impact fractured the metal holder's wax crust, and the stand tumbled over with a low thud.

She couldn't breathe. Her light was gone, her ears rang from the after-effects of Eleanor's scream, and her whole being hurt. But she could feel something cold and waxy under her fingers, and she fastened her grip on it reflexively.

Eleanor was scrambling towards her, reckless in her anger, and Adrienne heaved the candle stand at the corpse. It was heavier than she'd expected and missed the target, cracking against the floor instead. In the pale-blue moonlight, Adrienne saw that the thousands of coats of dried wax had split and were shedding free from the long metal pole.

She didn't hesitate but brought her weapon around and thrust it forward. It connected with Eleanor's skull as the monster scuttled close to land a killing bite. The stand's metal spike—designed to keep the candles in place—pierced through Eleanor's remaining good eye, digging deep into her cranium and shattering her skull. Eleanor bucked away, her jaw flexing open to release another bellow as she fought to free herself from the barb.

A small, pale shape rolled towards Adrienne. Panic and adrenaline clouded her mind so badly that she didn't see it until it wobbled to a standstill beside her hand. It was her candle, its wax still warm from the short-lived flame. As Adrienne stared at it, the wick caught, flaring back into life as though it had never been extinguished in the first place.

"Edith…" Adrienne whispered. She picked up the candle and held it close with shaking hands.

The metal stand hit the floor with a loud clunk. Eleanor stood before her, swaying, her bony fingers twitching. Her second eye was gone, leaving her blind, but her nostrils flared as she hunted for her prey's scent. The skeletal head turned to face Adrienne, and her blackened tongue dipped out to moisten her lips as she scuttled forward.

Instead of backing away from the contorted, twitching monstrosity, Adrienne threw herself forward, candle extended, and forced it into the corpse's already-blackened chest.

Eleanor seemed to feel the flame's heat a second before it touched her, and she sucked in a rattling breath but was too late to twitch away from it. The fire caught, first as just a small smoulder at the base of her ribs but rising and growing into licking flames as it spread across her breasts, shoulders, and neck.

The screams were unlike anything Adrienne had heard before—high, filled with wrath and pure hatred, and with bellowing undertones that cracked and failed as her lungs were consumed. Eleanor twisted and writhed as she tried to escape the flames, but they continued to spread, drawing down over her hips, thighs, and calves and finally coating her feet. For several long minutes, the woman was nothing but a pillar of fire spewing toxic black smoke as the flame consumed congealed blood, crumbling bones, and dead organs.

Then the flames shortened, dimmed, and eventually went out as their fuel disappeared.

Dense smoke swirled about the room, clouding the moonlight and sticking in Adrienne's throat. She leaned against the wall, coughing and clutching a hand to her bruised ribs as embers floated over her. The black cloud gradually thinned, eventually clearing enough for her to see the clump of soot, quietly smouldering, that was all that remained of Miss Eleanor Ashburn.

It took Adrienne a long time to go downstairs, but eventually, the bitter-tasting smoke became repulsive enough to override her exhaustion. She took the attic's stairs carefully, wincing with every jarring step, and entered the second-floor hallway.

The portraits had returned to their original, complacent poses. She still felt their eyes follow her as she passed them, but this time, the secretive little smiles held no malice.

She was dreading the climb down to ground floor, but just as she reached the top of the stairs, a faint whining buzzed through the house, and the downstairs lights turned on.

The light was both welcoming and comforting and made the climb easier. As she turned the staircase's corner, she caught sight of the woman standing in the hallway.

Marion was turning in slow circles, her gaze switching from the smashed lamp to the open basement door to the broken front window. She startled and turned as Adrienne's footfalls drew close.

"Oh, there you are, Addy." An uncertain, frightened smile twitched at her mouth. "Um, is your cat okay? He looks like he ate something rotten…"

"Wolf!" Adrienne staggered forward. Wolfgang waited in front of the lounge-room door, his back straight and proud and his face coated in the disgusting congealed blood he'd bitten out of Eleanor. Adrienne tried to kneel to hug him, but pain shot through her leg and ribs, so she settled for scratching behind his ears. He shook his frame, looking pleased with himself, and sauntered towards the kitchen with his tail held up like a flag.

Thank goodness he's okay. I owe him every tin of tuna that convenience store will sell me.

"Um, Addy?" Marion hovered behind her, hands twisting together, as confusion and fear threatened to submerge the tight smile. "I... I don't know what's happening. Or, um, how I got here. A-Are you okay? You're bleeding..."

Adrienne felt a rush of pity. Marion seemed to have no memory of the evening. The damaged front door, the blood running down Adrienne's cheek, and the bump on her own head had to be equal measures of frightening and confusing.

"Everything's okay now." Adrienne managed a smile as she patted Marion's shoulder. "But I'm going to need a lift to the hospital, okay?"

"O-Oh, yeah, sure. My car's outside." She coughed. "I think."

Adrienne leaned on her friend's shoulder as they shuffled towards the door. As they passed the hallway mirror, Adrienne caught a glimpse of Edith. The tall, immaculate woman stood in the shadowed corner beside the grandfather clock, her hands folded neatly over her skirts. She was smiling.

CHAPTER 43
ANSWERS

From the Second Page of Edith's Letter

As long as you light the candle every week, Eleanor will not be able to reach you. But you must be dutiful about it.

You may have already noticed some messages scratched around Ashburn. I am no longer a young lady, dear Adrienne; my memory fails me increasingly each day. One week I forgot to light the candle, and my sister's face appeared to me in the mirror I keep in my drawer.

It frightened me so badly that I created permanent testaments so that I could never again forget my purpose.

Every morning, I walk to town and purchase, along with my groceries, a newspaper. The paper sits on the mantel above the fireplace and is burned when I start that night's fire. Every evening, as I eat my dinner, I see a message on the table reminding me to check if it's Friday. If I cannot remember, I go to the newspaper and read the date; six nights a week the paper can be burnt to make room for a new paper the next morning. But on Friday, I go to the attic and light my candle.

I have a little box on top of my bed that is full of newspaper clippings in case I ever doubt that my past truly happened. You are welcome to read through them if you like.

Finally, I wrote no mirrors about my house. One of my sister's tricks is to appear in the reflection, especially as her power begins to return. If you ever see her there, divert your eyes immediately. She can take control over your body if you stare at her for too long. This is one of the reasons I never welcomed guests to Ashburn. Even though I cleared the mirrors out of my home—save for that little frame in my room—a visitor might bring one of their own or look into their cars' rear-view mirrors and fall under Eleanor's spell.

There is a final thing I must tell you, dear Adrienne, and I hope it is something you can forgive me for. Shortly following your father's death, I invited your mother to visit me. We had never met before, but I was growing old and wished to find a successor to keep my sister contained.

I had hoped to offer her Ashburn and request that she continue my practice of lighting a candle once a week. However, she was resistant to my story and did not wish to take occupancy here. I do not blame her. She was young and had a small child to care for; tales of ghouls and curses must have been as unnerving as they were unbelievable.

You, a child of four, wandered off while we were speaking, and our discussion was so heated that neither of us noticed for several minutes. When we did, we searched for you. I found you first; you had somehow made your way up to the attic, as though drawn there by a force beyond yourself, and were looking at the photo of my sister.

I sensed, in that moment, that you were destined to be my replacement.

Now comes the part that I must beg your forgiveness for. You see, while my sister held the raw talent and power that comes from an ancient soul, I had picked up a few of her tricks while growing up alongside her. I used this knowledge to bind our souls together.

The ritual involved a cut on both of our hands to exchange blood. Your mother, when she found us, was understandably hysterical. She took you away immediately and never replied to any of my future correspondence. I am deeply sorry for upsetting her so.

Please know that this binding is not something that will harm you; I made sure all of the risk would be on my side. The magic simply tied me to you so that, once I die, my soul will linger in Ashburn for as long as you remain alive. I did this to ensure I could watch over and protect you if possible. I do not know how much power I will have in that form—probably very little—but I will always be there if you need my help.

If you wish to see me, hang a mirror somewhere in the house, and I will try to appear in it. Just be careful that my sister's face does not materialise instead. You shouldn't have trouble telling us apart; a life underground had disfigured her and stripped away her sanity.

And finally, if the worst should happen and my sister rises from the dead, remember that fire is your sanctuary. Eleanor burns quite nicely.

> *Regards and love from the great-aunt who wishes she had the joy of knowing you more,*
> *Edith*

CHAPTER 44
THREADS

"OH, I ALMOST FORGOT; here's your mail." Jayne dug a small stack of letters out of her bag and passed them to Adrienne. "It must be an abominable walk to the end of the driveway, so I thought I'd collect them for you."

Beth, who had one scone in her mouth and another in her hand, spoke around the food. "Ask the mailman to hold them at his office. It'll be a shorter walk."

"I'll introduce you when you're feeling well enough to come into town," Sarah added.

"That would be amazing." Adrienne nodded at her leg, which was swathed in bandages. "I should have these off in a couple of days."

"And if you don't, just give me a call," Jayne said. "We'll bring some extra food and whatever else you need."

"You guys are amazing. Thank you." Adrienne glanced at

Marion as she spoke. The other woman kept her eyes fixed on her feet. She hadn't spoken a word since she'd arrived.

"Have another scone," Adrienne said, nudging the plate towards Marion. "The jam's incredible. I don't think you could make a bad batch if you tried."

Marion snorted and kept her eyes averted, but Adrienne saw a grin flit onto her face.

When the doctors had asked what caused Adrienne's injuries, she'd told them she'd been attacked by a wild dog. It had been a weak excuse; human teeth and canine teeth made very different imprints, and the doctors' sceptical looks confirmed they didn't buy her story. But in her defence, she'd been high on painkillers and so tired that she would have sold several of her organs in exchange for an uninterrupted sleep.

Adrienne had no easy way of confirming her suspicions, but she thought Marion blamed herself for what had happened that night. The vet student didn't seem to remember anything after seeing Eleanor in her rear-view mirror on the night she'd crashed. Her family must have told her she'd spent days in a fugue, and then she'd woken up to the scene of a break-in with a knife in her hand and Adrienne covered in blood.

To her frustration, Adrienne didn't have any way to explain her friend's innocence without bringing up ghosts, curses, and a whole host of stories that would sound thoroughly made up. The best she could do was studiously avoid mentioning that night and make Marion feel as welcome as possible.

Something positive had come out of the whole mess, though;

she was certain Marion was to thank for the visit. The last time she'd seen Jayne, she'd been certain the four friends wouldn't be returning to Ashburn. But just four days after she'd been discharged from hospital, they sat on the rose-pattern chairs in the sitting room, a basket heaped full of fresh food next to Adrienne. She guessed Marion had wanted to visit to make amends but hadn't wanted to come alone.

Adrienne couldn't have asked for a better day for the visit, either. The sun was warm and bright as it streamed through the freshly cleaned windows. The light transformed Ashburn; what had once felt cold and aged was now comforting and homely.

Peggy's brother had fixed the laptop in exchange for access to the road that used part of her driveway. What Adrienne hadn't expected, though, was that other townspeople were willing to trade for the same privilege. Despite Adrienne repeatedly telling them they could use the road for free, she'd had her windows washed, the lawn mown, and the fireplace cleaned. As the news that Adrienne welcomed visitors spread, more visits and offers came in each day.

The interest in the old house was so strong that Beth had asked permission to start a ghost-tour business. She intended to lead people around the house and share the history, rumours, and ghost stories with them and had offered to split the profits with Adrienne.

"Oh!" Beth clapped her hands together. "I almost forgot—people are telling me the light appeared in Ashburn's attic last night. What's that all that about? Ghosts aren't causing you problems, are they?"

Adrienne laughed. She'd rehearsed her excuse a dozen times. "The Friday light seems really popular in Ipson. Since Edith maintained it for eighty years, I thought I might as well continue the tradition and give the kids some muse for their ghost stories."

Following Adrienne's discharge from the hospital, the first thing she'd done on her return to Ashburn was visit the attic. Eleanor's ashes had lain where she'd left them, scattered over the wooden boards, so she'd swept them into a bucket.

Edith's letter hadn't been explicit, but it seemed reasonable to conclude that she'd defeated her sister—both as a child and then again as a young adult—by burning her. But because Eleanor had stolen the rest of her family's years, simply turning her to ash had not been enough to kill her. She'd slowly regenerated over several years until she'd been whole enough to dig her way out of her grave.

Adrienne had taken the ashes to the little cemetery in the forest and buried them in the open grave. She'd then placed one of the fat, heavy candles onto the attic's spike and lit it so that it shone over the photograph.

Edith had been able to contain her sister with one candle per week over eighty years. Adrienne would continue the system. She was also keeping the mirrors hung about the house. If Eleanor ever began to strengthen, glimpsing her in the reflections would give Adrienne ample warning. The sunset phenomenon—when Eleanor's burgeoning power terrified the birds out of their trees—would be a final caution.

Adrienne had done the math. Eleanor had killed four of

her family members, all of them in their mid to late thirties. Assuming they'd had between twenty-five and forty years left, and minus the time she'd spent in the grave, Eleanor could be expected to live for another twenty to eighty years. That meant there was a good chance Adrienne could keep her trapped until the living corpse's hours ran out.

It was less of a chore than she would have expected. She felt welcomed into the town, had four new friends, and her laptop had been returned to her fully functional. There was still a lot to do before she could consider her life back to normal, but she felt that the worst was over.

Before leaving, Jayne casually mentioned that she hoped Adrienne would join in the club's activities the following month. "Pilates," she said as she slung her bag over her shoulder. "We can improve both our bodies and our minds with just a few thrice-weekly sessions—"

Her three companions all groaned, and Beth shoved her out of the door. "C'mon, Marion's gonna run late for her shift if we dawdle any longer. Let me know about the ghost-tours gig, okay, Addy?"

As they piled into their car, Marion glanced back at the house. Adrienne raised her hand in farewell, and Marion returned the gesture, a hesitant smile filling her face.

Adrienne kept waving until the car disappeared into the forest then stepped back inside and leaned her back against the door. She closed her eyes and inhaled, savouring the peace that came with an empty house. Wolfgang emerged from the kitchen, stretched, and sauntered towards her. Adrienne bent to give his head a quick scratch. "Do you want your lunch, my fearsome corpse conqueror?"

He exhaled a purring mewl, and Adrienne laughed as she led him into their lounge room. As promised, she'd bought him a small stack of tinned tuna on her first day back from the hospital, and she added a portion of it to his meal.

As she put the food away, a black-clothed woman drifted into the large mirror over the fireplace. She paused near the glass and smiled at Adrienne.

"Ready?" Adrienne asked.

The reflection dipped her head in a graceful nod. Adrienne moved to the fire, placed a new log on the blaze, and picked up the novel propped on the little side table. Edith moved through the reflection to sit in the chair beside Adrienne's.

She wouldn't have noticed it if she hadn't been listening, but Adrienne caught the faint creak of shifting wood and saw the empty chair beside her shift a fraction of an inch. The woman in the mirror folded her hands tidily in her lap and smiled as Adrienne opened the novel and began to read aloud.

ABOUT THE AUTHOR

Darcy Coates is the *USA Today* bestselling author of *Hunted*, *The Haunting of Ashburn House*, *Craven Manor*, and more than a dozen horror and suspense titles.

She lives on the Central Coast of Australia with her family, cats, and a garden full of herbs and vegetables.

Darcy loves forests, especially old-growth forests where the trees dwarf anyone who steps between them. Wherever she lives, she tries to have a mountain range close by.